MW00713339

Hobo

Justice

Larry Benson

CyPress Publications

Tallahassee, Florida

Copyright © 2011 by Larry Benson

Cover art copyright © 2011 by Ann Kozeliski

All rights reserved. No part of this book may be reproduced in any form or by any means, electronic or mechanical, including photocopying, recording, or by any information storage and retrieval system, without written permission in writing from the publisher, except for brief quotations contained in critical articles and reviews.

All characters and events in this novel are fictitious and any resemblance to actual persons, living or dead, or to events, is purely coincidental.

Inquiries should be addressed to:
CyPress Publications
P.O. Box 2636
Tallahassee, Florida 32316-2636
http://cypresspublications.com
lraymond@nettally.com

Library of Congress Control Number: 2011932504

ISBN: 978-1-935083-35-1

First Edition

HOBO
Justice

To Erica and Ron —
All the Best!

Larry
08-16-2011

Dedication

To Members of the Big Bend Model Railroad Association

Tallahassee, Florida

I shall pass through
this world but once.
Any good therefore that I can do
or any kindness that I can show
to any human being
let me do it now.
Let me not defer or neglect it
for I shall not pass this way again.

—Stephen Grellett

1

THE BODY HUNG UPSIDE DOWN, suspended on rope thrown over a stout limb of an ancient oak and snubbed off at the base of its huge trunk. A full head of kinky, blond hair cascaded down, mingling with clusters of Spanish moss clinging to the giant tree.

Just before daybreak on a spring morning, barking dogs aroused hobo Benjamin Reed, who peeked out of his sleeping bag and smelled wood smoke from someone's chimney. Dew clinging to the Spanish moss reflected minuscule droplets of light, glinting like millions of tiny pearls. It promised to be another typical day in South Georgia, ideal for hopping trains and enjoying the outdoors.

Ben spotted the body above his head the minute he awoke that Monday. At first, he refused to believe what he saw. He scrambled out of his sleeping bag and tugged on his brogans without bothering to lace them up. He walked slowly in a circle below the body, staring up at the gruesome sight. The purple face, although swollen, looked to be that of a teenage boy. His ankles were tied by a thick rope. He dangled, twirling slightly in the breeze. Ben had seen death all too often while working as a cop in Florida. This young kid, cruelly hanged, brought back visions he had hoped to forget. Why would anyone hang a mere child? What awful crime could the boy have committed at such an early age that warranted being murdered? And why was he hanged upside down? These questions haunted Ben as his trained eyes took in the details at a glance.

The barking dogs were getting closer. He needed to grab his stuff and move out.

Ben noted the boy was gagged and his arms bound to his sides. The rope by which he was hanging had been thrown high up over a limb. The kid

1

was fully dressed in bib overalls with a long-sleeved blue shirt showing out the top. He wore white socks and tennis shoes.

Before turning in just after midnight, Ben Reed had jumped down from a boxcar at Flint City junction. Flint City was the county seat of Nagel County, Georgia, with a population of approximately 3,753 souls. The town was laid out in typical South Georgia style, with a square in the middle that was dominated by a Nineteenth Century, three-story red brick county courthouse with entrances facing the four points of the compass. Tall arched windows with white marble eyebrows testified to its late 1800s vintage. Adjacent to the courthouse were the morgue and small county jail that housed the sheriff's office. Locally owned shops, two insurance agencies, a barber shop, hotel, movie theater, and drugstore surrounded the square.

The boxcar Ben Reed had abandoned was coupled in northbound Flint River Railroad freight number 41 headed for Atlanta. Trains passing through Flint City changed crews and occasionally cut out cars, which they left on sidings in the yard for later pick-up by freights going to Waycross and Jacksonville then south down Florida's east coast. Ben was headed northeast toward Jessup and Savannah, so he decided to bed down until he could catch a freight later in the morning that was headed in that direction.

Reed hadn't slept much on the swaying boxcar the night before. He was tired and needed to sleep. The crump-crump sound of freight cars banging and slamming as the switchmen jostled them into position for pick-up wouldn't keep him awake because he was accustomed to the noise.

Ben had walked back down the tracks along the edge of the rail yard, picking his way carefully in the dark. On an earlier trip along this stretch of track he had spotted a grove of enormous live oaks near the yard, which he imagined would provide ideal shelter from the dew that was sure to set in before morning. He found the massive oaks about fifty paces south of the tracks.

He crawled into his sleeping bag fully clothed as he always did when he slept outdoors. Even though spring had begun to sneak into South Georgia, the brilliant sun warmed up the days but abandoned nights to the chill. He was wearing black jeans, a long-sleeved wool plaid shirt, warm quilted jacket, military-style brogans he found ideal for walking, thick socks, and a stocking cap he exchanged for a baseball cap as the day warmed up. Reed's wardrobe wasn't that of a typical shabby hobo drifter.

Ben had stuffed extra clothes in his backpack before leaving Titusville near Port Canaveral. He inherited a substantial fortune when his father died, so money wasn't a problem. He carried a small amount of cash, his checkbook, and a letter of credit from his home bank guaranteeing checks he cashed. He was able to purchase new outfits along the way as his originals wore out. In addition to extra duds, his backpack cradled a camera, gun, film, toiletries, cigarettes, which he was trying to give up, a thermos of water, and snacks.

His fully loaded 9 millimeter Beretta was a comforting companion when riding the rails and frequenting hobo camps, especially in the late 1950s. His gun was kept handy in his jacket pocket by day and in his sleeping bag at night. Every few days, when he checked into a motel to shower, shave, and do laundry, his automatic was kept within reach. In his mid-fifties, Reed carried no fat on his six-foot frame. His body was firm and athletic, kept fit by constantly walking, exercising, and lugging his heavy backpack and bedroll.

He looked like the outdoors type, tanned and rugged. His nose, slightly bent to one side, acquired playing football as a youngster, was set perched below pale gray eyes. A scar under his chin was an award he received during a bar fight with another hobo Ben pummeled into submission. Inquisitive his entire life, he was blessed with an above average memory, but he also kept good notes during any investigation.

Before his wife was killed, Reed spent thirty years as a cop and police detective. He had also been a railroad "bull," chasing down criminals, assorted miscreants, and hobos who tried to hitch free rides on freight trains. Now he was one of the hobos he had pursued. For nearly two years he had been drifting around the country, avoiding those same railroad "dicks." He hopped freights from town to town, sleeping on the edge of hobo camps most nights unless a storm threatened.

When the dogs' ruckus woke him up and he spotted the hanging body, Ben knew intuitively the kid had been hung up to die. Whether he was dead before he was strung up, or he died from being hanged upside down all night, Reed couldn't tell. There was no doubt about what the local constabulary would do if he stayed around until the body was discovered and cut down. They would pin the killing on him.

Reed knew a hobo riding the rails, no matter how respectable he might appear, who was found anywhere near a crime scene would become the prime suspect. That's the way it had always been and would be with him. He had tracked down and arrested hundreds of criminals, tramps, and vagrants while working on the Titusville police force and for the Gulf and Eastern and Florida East Coast Railroads. He was well versed in crime scene investigations and knew that authorities begin by rounding up suspects then releasing those who had solid alibis.

Ben didn't have a good alibi. In fact, he didn't have an alibi at all. No hobo did.

2

FOUR HOURS BEFORE BEN REED arrived in Flint City, kinky-haired teenager Jeremy Martin was cutting through the Flint City railroad yard on his way home when parking lights on a rusty blue pickup truck winked on. Startled, he squatted down behind a railroad switch signal and froze.

Milo Scroggins sat hunched behind the truck's steering wheel. Scroggins was not much above five feet tall and almost as round. He was blubbery. For a fat man, he was quick enough on his feet, although he wheezed like a puffing railroad locomotive if he ran any distance at all. His round, sagging jowls were unshaven, he always smelled sweaty, and his breath was so rancid it wilted flowers. Townspeople said Scroggins had a black personality to go with the black clothes he usually wore. Others claimed he wore black underwear so you couldn't tell if he had changed recently. Nobody was curious enough or courageous enough to try to find out. It was enough fun just to laugh behind his back and contemplate if their suspicions were true.

Scroggins and his kin operated on the dull edge of the law. More than once, he got out of close scrapes around Nagle County because his family went back to the early days when the State of Georgia was first settled by Europeans. Nobody was brave enough to stand up to the Scroggins clan, at least not for long or they wouldn't be up-standing much longer. Rumor was he had done time in the federal pen in Leavenworth, Kansas, but the rumor was just that and never proven.

Next to him slumped sleepy-eyed, yawning Sherman Getts. He was a certified do-nothing in Flint City with a dull mind, but who was clever enough to live off other people's good graces and sympathy. Some town folk felt sorry for Getts, and he knew it, too, so he took full advantage of opportunities to prey on their kindnesses and generosity. He was six feet tall, a gangly string bean, stooped over with a hollow chest, with exceptionally long legs and arms. He had a red nose, and his piercing eyes bugged out from behind glasses as thick as the bottoms of whisky bottles. And Getts was personally acquainted with his share of whiskey bottles.

A couple of local ne'er-do-wells, they had been hired to find a boxcar with numbers matching those on the back of a stained envelope Getts grasped in his grimy hand. Their objective sat in a string of boxcars that a northbound freight had set off on a siding before midnight on Sunday.

The yardmaster and his assistant had helped the train crew spot the cars, locking them down for the night. Afterward, he and the switchman went home and were not due back until later when an eastbound freight headed for Waycross would pick up the waiting cars. So Scroggins and his partner Getts needed to work fast to remove certain objects from the train. They had just enough time if things went as planned. A moonless night was on their side.

Scroggins cranked up his truck, shifted it into gear, and eased quietly toward the boxcars. He drove slowly without headlights along the side away from Flint City so the train blocked the view of anyone who might glance in their direction. No need to alert the curious about moving vehicles in the yard.

"Sherm, you got the number we're supposed to be lookin' for?" Scroggins asked, concentrating his attention on the string of boxcars.

"Got it right here, Milo."

"Well, don't just set there like a dummy, what is it?"

"I'll haveta turn on my flashlight to read it."

"Then do it, man. Do I have to tell you ever' move to make?" Scroggins' question was rhetorical. Getts was a slow thinker who rarely did anything on his own. Scroggins was always the job boss, and Getts did what he was told. Getts turned on his flashlight, aimed it at the wrinkled envelope, and read 83247—on an L&N marked car. "We ain't seen no L&N boxes yet, so guess we ain't passed it already," Scroggins said. He didn't want to have to turn around and go back down the line. One pass was plenty. No need to press their luck.

About halfway down the string of parked boxcars, Getts shouted, "There it is!" ringing Scroggins' ears.

"Damnation, Sherm, you don't have to yell. I ain't deaf."

"Shit, Milo, I thought you wanted ta know when I spotted the car."

"Okay, okay, just shut the hell up." Scroggins stopped his truck as close beside the boxcar as he dared. He ordered Getts to open the toolbox in the back and fetch his tin snips and a crowbar. Scroggins shone Getts' flashlight on the railroad seal and padlock hanging from the door latch.

"Sherm, you did remember to bring the other seal your cousin up in St. Augustine got for us, didn't ya?"

"It's right here, in my pocket."

"Must be somethin' mighty special in this here car to have a seal and a special lock on the door," Scroggins said. "Wonder what's in them crates we're supposed to lift?"

Getts snipped the seal and wedged the crowbar between the door handle and lock, prying it open with a loud crack. Just like The Man said, piece of cake. Together they slid the heavy door open. Scroggins was too fat to climb into the boxcar, so the gangly Getts clambered up on the side of the truck bed. He figured it would be best to snake his way inside the boxcar on his belly.

"I'm in, Milo."

"I see that, you dummy. No need to tell me what I already know. Are them wooden crates we're after in there? Here's the light," Scroggins grumbled, becoming impatient, his nerves as tight as the lid on an unopened jar of pickles. Sweat beaded on his forehead.

"Yup, they're here, just as The Man said they'd be," Getts confirmed. "On one side there's two large wood boxes near 'bouts the length of the car, one stacked atop the other. Across from them two is the two smaller wooden crates I guess we's after," he said.

The two smaller crates had been anchored to the wall of the boxcar with metal straps so they wouldn't shift in transit. Getts soon snapped the restraints with the crowbar, loading them one at a time on their handcart Scroggins had handed up to him. On one side of each crate, stenciled in black capital letters, were the words "Operation Old Reliable." Printed underneath, in red ink, it said, "This Side Up—Handle With Care."

"Here's the first one, Milo." Getts rolled the crate down to the doorway then slid it into the back of their pickup. He and Scroggins manhandled the heavy box toward the cab of the pickup. Getts returned a second time and wheeled the other small crate to the door, then climbed down into the truck to help Scroggins position the second box.

"Okay, now we gotta shut this here door and reseal it so no one will spot it until the car is opened somewhere in Florida," Scroggins ordered. "Let's hope the dummies who open it can't read the numbers on the seal. I worked 'em over real good with a hammer."

They slid the door shut, closing it enough to go unnoticed until someone down the line unlocked it. They threw the damaged lock onto the front seat of the pickup, covered their haul with a tarp, threw their tools in back, and cranked up the motor.

Scroggins turned on the headlights. The truck's beams lighted up what Scroggins and Getts first thought was an animal of some kind. Then they saw what looked like a young boy hunkered down on his knees, trying to hide behind the switch stand.

"Catch that damn kid," Scroggins growled at Getts, as the truck lurched toward the shadowy figure, back wheels spitting ballast rock like sparks from an arc welder. The sudden approach of the pickup terrorized Jeremy, and it spelled danger. He had barely time to scramble to his feet before the truck slid to a stop, belching the two burglars who ran toward him.

"Stop, kid! We is the law!" Scroggins yelled, thinking his warning might give them a chance to catch the boy. They needed a clever ruse if they hoped to collar the kid before he disappeared into the darkness. Jeremy would have escaped except he tripped over a discarded railroad tie, sprawling face down on the gravel. He was so scared, he pissed his pants.

"Here, you little shit," Getts hissed as he pinned the boy's arms behind his back. "I gotcha now, so quit squirmin' or I'll bash your head in right good," he threatened.

"Let me go!" the boy pleaded. "I ain't done nothin' wrong. Just let me be!"

"Well, I'll be damned, if it ain't Jeremy Martin, Carol's son," Scroggins panted, mouth agape. "You remember Carol, the sexy gal who works down at the carpet mill runnin' looms." After a bit Getts remembered her, recalled her slim waist, outstanding tits, kissable lips, shiny black hair and long, shapely legs. He also remembered trying to get in her pants and was eager to take revenge on her son because she had spurned him. Called him a bastard, she did. True, Getts didn't know who his real daddy was, but his birth was nobody's business 'ceptin' his own.

"Whatcha doin' out here, boy? Tryin' to steal somethin' from the railroad, I betcha. Have you been watchin' us all along?" Scroggins accused.

"No, I ain't stealin' or watchin'. I was goin' home from Billy Kleggin's house and takin' a shortcut through the switchin' yard." He hoped the men wouldn't know he really had been watching them break into the boxcar and load crates into their truck. He thought they might turn him loose once they knew he was Carol's boy. The trouble was, they knew him and Jeremy recognized both of them. He knew they weren't the law, they were law-breakers.

Scroggins held Jeremy down beside the tracks, pressing a knee in his back, the right side of the boy's face hard against the gravel, while they discussed what to do with him.

"He knows us," Scroggins said, panting.

"Well, of course he does. He's knowed us for years, ever since he was born." Dim-witted Getts nodded, grinning stupidly.

"Yup, and he'll tell the sheriff and the whole county he saw us out here tonight. It'd be just like him to do it, 'cause he's probably a snitch," Scroggins mumbled.

"Can we let him do that, Milo?"

"No, you idiot! We better make sure he don't tell on us."

"Please, let me go! I won't tell anybody I saw you two."

Scroggins pushed his head down even harder on the gravel, making his cheek hurt inside and out. Then he pulled the boy's hair, lifting his head up and threatening to cut Jeremy's throat with his switchblade. "Brat, are you a gonna tell on us?" Scroggins demanded with a growl.

Already scared silly, shivers ran down Jeremy's back clear to the soles of his white sneakers. "No, no, I ain't," the boy whispered through his bloody mouth and throat twisted like a pretzel. "I promise, if you'll just let me go."

Scroggins whispered to Getts to go to the truck and bring him something to knock the boy *slightly* unconscious. "Once he's out, we'll clear outa here and take our time decidin' what to do with him."

Scroggins was bossing this job, so the skinny man knew he better do what he was told.

"Be quick about it."

Getts returned, carrying a heavy crescent wrench, which he tried to hand to Scroggins.

"Don't give it to me, you dumb ass! It's your job, not mine, so get with it. Slam him right above his ear and he'll blink out like a light."

Getts grasped the wrench by the handle and cracked Jeremy just above his left ear. He hit the teenager hard enough to knock him out, but not with enough force to kill him. Hopefully. The boy moaned, went limp, and quit struggling. His breathing became shallower, but the two burglars didn't notice.

"We ain't just gonna leave him here, are we, Milo?"

"No. We'll carry him 'round to the back of the truck, tie him up good and gag his tattletale mouth, then slide him under the tarp. There oughta be plenty room to hide him next to them crates."

With Getts grasping his feet and Scroggins cradling his arms, the two hijackers carried Jeremy to their truck, dumped him in, and covered him over with the tarpaulin. The truck's motor was idling, so Scroggins shifted into gear and drove slowly through the switching yard toward town, hoping they hadn't attracted attention.

3

AT SIX O'CLOCK IN THE MORNING, the telephone rang in Nagle County Sheriff William C. "Sandy" Bates' home. Out of habit, he answered, "Sheriff Bates."

"Sandy, there's a body all tied up hanging in one of those old oak trees down by the rail yard. You know, it's where the old Krieger's house used to sit before it burned to the ground and was scraped away. And, Sheriff, I think it's Carol Martin's son, Jeremy."

"Now, Emma, what are you telling me?" Just what the sheriff needed first thing on a Monday morning. A nosey old lady who was a busybody to boot. "Calm down. You expect me to believe someone has hanged that boy down by the railroad tracks? You sure you ain't seeing things? It's barely daylight."

"Look here, Sandy, I know what I saw!" Emma Lake said, her anger growing. "I went out to get my morning paper just a bit ago, and them damn hounds of Deland's was barking their heads off. I went down the block a piece to see if they had something treed, and they did! I'll lay you two to one it's Jeremy Martin. Him with all that long curly blond hair and all."

"Okay, okay, don't get all wrought up about it, Emma." Then with a sigh he added, "I'll go right down there and take a look. You say he's in a tree in that grove of old oaks right south of the yard?" the sheriff asked, repeating what Emma had told him to see if she would change her story.

"Yep, that's right."

"Appreciate you calling." The sheriff was a small man, barely taller and heavier than a jockey, with red-tinged hair that earned him the nickname "Sandy." He had served Nagle County as High Sheriff for eight years, and nobody would challenge him in an election. He was astute and skilled at

11

keeping the peace. He believed in preventing crime if he could, but if that failed, he wasn't afraid to wade into a brawl even down at Shakey's Pool Hall. Bates would tackle and cuff a drunk lightning quick if one needed to be subdued. He knew how to fight because in his youth Bates was the Georgia lightweight boxing champ three years running. While fighting he was dubbed "Windmill William," and people said he could pug a person's nose, raise a whelp on his eye, and cauliflower an ear with just one lightning punch and all at the same time.

His sandy hair was kinked, and he kept it close-cut. With his oversized .38 caliber revolver strapped around his waist, he looked like a small boy playing cops and robbers. He was a tough cookie, though. Few saw him as a comic figure. Those who did and called him a shrimp or munchkin, whether to his face or behind his back, lived to regret it. He was in his mid-fifties, married over thirty years, and he and his wife had two teenage children.

Bates was awake and out of bed when Emma called. He dressed hurriedly, telling his wife he had an emergency. He drove out to the edge of town to investigate the hanging Emma reported. He sped toward the grove without turning on his flashing lights or siren. It would be a shame to wake up the whole town, especially if old Emma was imagining things. What a laugh that would be if word got around town he had been chasing Emma's hallucinations.

As the sheriff neared the oak grove, he heard the dogs barking and howling. "Sure sounds like they've got something treed," he said. He parked his car on the side of the road nearest the trees and yelled at the dogs. "Stop your damn barking! What in the hell are you three causing all this ruckus for?" he asked, as if the dogs could understand him and answer. They kept up their howling and jumping up on the trunk of the biggest tree in the middle of the grove. Bates walked through the dry knee-high grass and looked up in the tree.

"Well, I'll be damned," he said as he took off his hat to get a better look at Jeremy's body dangling upside down and slowly rotating. The boy had rope wound tightly around his ankles that was wrapped all the way down his torso to his neck. His face was purple. "Poor kid. Someone really did a number on you, that's for sure." He strode as quickly as his short legs could carry him back to his patrol car, leaned in through the window, punched in his deputy's code, and keyed the microphone on his radio.

"Mel, this is Sandy. Looks like the Martin kid's got himself hanged. Get your lazy butt down here to the grove near the railroad switch yard, and do it on the double, you hear me?"

Bates knew his deputy, Melvin Phipps, would have his monitor turned on and tuned in at his garage apartment on the other side of town. At least he better have!

Deputy Phipps wasn't the ideal law enforcement officer, but he was the only male in town who would work long hours every day for low pay. His uniform was usually wrinkled like he had been sleeping in it, which he probably had, but if it didn't get to looking too wrinkled, Bates would cut him some slack. Phipps was single, and taking clothes to the cleaners on a weekly basis cost more money than he wanted to part with. He was always a bit disheveled, with his shirt collar unbuttoned behind his wrinkled, misaligned tie. His six-foot frame was stuffed into scuffed size thirteen double-E shoes. His hair was jet black, combed straight back over his head. He was overweight, with a beer belly protruding beyond his chest and hanging down over his belt buckle. He was cunning, sometimes surprisingly so, and suspicious of everybody, including old Emma who was still spry at ninety. But he appeared to be loyal to the sheriff, which made up for some shortcomings.

Deputy Phipps answered his radio. "I hear ya, boss. Gimme a minute to get my gun on, and I'll be right down there." Phipps strapped on his gun, also a huge .38 caliber revolver, which looked small dangling from his bulging waist. He locked his apartment and hurried down the steps to his patrol car, his huge belly bouncing at every footfall. He cranked the engine and headed for the oak grove.

The sheriff realized he needed more help than just his deputy to get the Martin kid down out of the tree. But he didn't have to radio for more help. Bates knew that the two full-time firemen on duty down at the station monitored all radio calls between him and his deputy. The firehouse crew would respond once they were alerted about what was afoot and they would call in volunteer reinforcements if more help was required. Bates was leaning on his car still cussing the yelping dogs when his radio cracked into life:

"Sheriff Bates, this is Gabe down at the fire station. Do you need me and some guys down there with our ladders to help cut the kid down out of that tree?"

"Sure do, Gabe, and thanks for the holler. I sorely need you, like yesterday. And by all means, if you happen to see Carol Martin on the way, don't say anything to her about the deceased being her son. That's my job, and I'll be doing it just as soon as we can get the boy down and transported to the county morgue."

While waiting for the firemen and his deputy to arrive, Bates paced off the crime scene, sketching it on paper attached to a clipboard and making pertinent notes in the margin of his drawing. He had just begun to string yellow crime scene tape around the area when Deputy Phipps and the Medical Examiner, Cletus Poole, arrived. They parked their vehicles on the street behind the sheriff's.

Bates greeted the ME. "Hey, Cletus, you must have heard me call Mel, too."

"Yep, I always monitor your radio signals. What we got here?" Poole asked as he and Phipps walked to the tree where the Martin boy's body was hanging, being careful not to destroy what might be evidence.

"Well, Cletus, we've got ourselves a hanging, it seems," Bates said with a grimace. Then he ordered Phipps to chase the hounds off and to go tell the Delands to pen them up or he was damn well going to shoot them one by one. The deputy did his best to run the dogs off by kicking and yelling at them to shut up, but they kept yelping. Giving up, he got in his patrol car to go tell Deland to come call off his dogs. He wouldn't think of walking even a block whenever he could drive.

"Those damn dogs are something, and they're in the way," Bates said. "I just hope Mel can get Deland to come after them before Gabe's crew gets here to cut the boy down. They're about to wake up the whole town, too, and it's barely seven o'clock."

Phipps, with old man Deland slumped beside him in the patrol car, and the firemen arrived at the same time. Deland squinted up at the hanging corpse. "Is that Carol's boy, Jeremy? What's he doing hung up like that?"

"Now listen here, Deland. It's the Martin kid all right," Bates said. "But don't you go blabbing it around town until I have time to tell Carol or I'll bust your head wide open. You hear me?"

Deland grumbled as he collared his dogs, dragging them down the street away from the crime scene. As soon as the dogs were out of the way, the deputy completed running yellow crime scene tape around several of the oak trees encircling the one where Jeremy was hanging. He was not too careful about where he walked in the tall grass.

Fire Chief Gabe Furnace and two other firemen carried an extension ladder to the tree, ducking under the yellow tape, and leaned it up against the trunk. The ladder wasn't needed after all. The rope suspending the kid's body was wrapped around the trunk of the oak and tied within reach of the men standing on the ground.

"This is terrible," one fireman said. "I ain't had to deal with anything like this during my entire lifetime." The second fireman agreed through tight lips as he tried to choke down the feeling of an imminent eruption in his stomach.

Furnace glanced toward Bates, then Poole. He asked if it was all right to cut the boy down, keeping in mind the legal and ethical questions involved when there was a killing.

"Sure, go ahead, but let me get some pictures first," Poole answered, nodding. Bates stood by silently watching while the ME took photographs of Jeremy's hanging body. Poole knew he should inspect the body before it was moved, but he couldn't very well do that with Jeremy swinging twelve or fifteen feet above the ground.

With the boy's weight on the rope, the knot was too tight to untie. Furnace offered his large pocketknife to Poole and asked if he wanted to do the cutting. Poole said he didn't need to. He warned Furnace and his firemen to be careful about lowering the boy when the rope was cut. "Slow and easy like, Gabe, so there isn't any more damage than is already been done to him."

The firemen grasped the rope just above the knot to relieve the weight of Jeremy's corpse as Furnace began to slice through it with his knife. The rope was cut and the firemen, true to instructions, let Jeremy down ever so slowly until his head was just above the ground. Bates and Poole, one on each side of the body, gently lowered him the rest of the way down on his back.

Poole observed, "Jeremy is missing one of his tennis shoes. I wonder if it could be somewhere in the tall grass?" Poole kneeled down on one knee beside the boy's body to take more photos from different angles. "Hanging isn't a pretty way to die, and it's not quick. Strangling is silent because the victim can't talk when his throat is constricted. Anyway, he was gagged, I see. He couldn't have uttered a sound or cried out for help muzzled and with rope tied around his neck that way. An autopsy will tell us the cause of death." The ME continued to examine the boy's body.

Poole soon found the bruise above Jeremy's left ear. "He's been hit on the head. Possibly knocked unconscious before he was strung up, 'cause the resulting bruise has bled some. At this point, I can't tell for sure whether the blow fractured his skull and he died instantly, or the hanging did him in. I mean to find out soon enough. I'll report back to you, Sandy, as soon as I have something."

"That'll be fine, Cletus, you do that. Mel and I will just have a good look around after we've loaded the kid into your van. We'll see if we can find any clues about what took place here." Then the sheriff asked Poole, "Have any idea when the boy cashed in?"

"Well, I'll have to make sure, mind you. With a hanging, it's hard to tell. He's stiff with rigor mortis. I'd say no more than twelve or less than six hours."

With the firemen's help, Jeremy's body was lifted onto a gurney. They wheeled him to the waiting van, which also served as the town hearse. Bates thanked Poole, who drove away toward the county morgue located next door to the courthouse. After Bates thanked Chief Furnace and his men for their help, they headed back to the fire station.

Bates and Phipps couldn't find the missing shoe. Nor did they find any clues except for a cigarette butt lying in an area where the grass was tromped down. They could see where someone had recently walked into the grove from the direction of the railroad yard. Whoever it was, if it was the same person, headed west, angling back toward the tracks. Phipps had noticed the matted grass when he wound the yellow tape around the trees. He said nothing but took care not to walk anywhere near the area. If there was a clue in the grass, the deputy wanted the sheriff to find it.

"Mel, go get my camera out of the trunk of my car. I want to get some pictures of this trampled-down spot where we haven't walked yet." Phipps ambled to the sheriff's car, got his camera and returned, handing it to the sheriff. Bates took several photographs of the matted grass from different angles.

Deputy Phipps stood and watched, his head drooped above his fat gut. He was quiet. Had he shouted, Bates would not have heard a word above the screaming whistles of two steam locomotives coupled together that rumbled into the yard with a string of boxcars bound for Waycross and down Florida's east coast.

When the whistles stopped blaring, Bates said, "Now we gotta go over this whole area with a fine-tooth comb." Their search turned up two rusty tin cans hobos had left behind long before the hanging, a few bricks from the Kriegers' old house, but no missing sneaker or other evidence. Whoever hanged the teenager was careful not to leave any clues behind.

"Okay, that does it. Now I got to find Carol down at the mill and tell her that her boy has been murdered." The two officers returned to their cars. Phipps turned toward their office in the jail. Bates headed for the carpet mill.

As he drove, he thought about how Carol had raised Jeremy all by herself following her divorce ten years ago. She had done a good job, too. The boy had been in trouble a time or two for minor skirmishes at school, but that was about all. She kept herself and Jeremy tidy, her house clean, clothes washed and ironed. Bates knew her to be a solid citizen, volunteering on several community causes each year. Working at the mill, taking care of Jeremy, and volunteering helped partially to fill up her lonely days.

The sheriff parked his patrol car in a guest slot in the mill parking lot. He fetched his hat, opened the door of his car, and crunched slowly up the gravel walkway toward the mill office. The sound of looms cranking and sighing assaulted his ears. Inside, where the din was more or less subdued, he was greeted by a secretary.

"Good morning, Sheriff. What can I do for you?"

"Good morning to you. I need to talk to Carol Martin. I got something to tell her that's private like. Suppose that can be arranged?"

"Sure. First, I'll double-check with the boss to see if it's okay to call Carol off the floor." The secretary disappeared into an adjacent office then returned after a few moments. "The mill manager said it would be all right to send for Carol. What's this all about, anyway?"

"Never you mind. It's between Mrs. Martin and me, what I have to tell her."

The secretary pressed a button on her desk. A young man stuck his head around a door. "Go tell Carol to come up to the front office. There's someone here wants to see her."

In a few minutes, the door to the loom room opened again. Carol came in. Her face darkened when she saw Sheriff Bates wearing a hangdog expression. He was leaning against one wall, hat in hand.

"Sandy, what's happened? I just know something has, or you wouldn't be calling me off the floor otherwise. Is it Jeremy? He stayed at Billy Kleggin's last night." She began to cry. "Has something happened to my son?" She stared into his eyes.

"Let's go outside to my car where we can talk in private." Bates put his arm around Carol's quivering shoulders.

As they walked toward the sheriff's patrol car, Carol began to shake uncontrollably. Between sobs, she kept mumbling, "Oh God, I just know Jeremy's in some kind of trouble! What'd he do, Sandy, that's so bad you had to come down here to tell me to my face? He stayed at Billy's house last night."

Bates leaned against the front fender of his car and looked into her eyes. "Carol, I hate awful having to tell you this. There's just no way to soften what I've got to say. Jeremy didn't stay at Billy's last night as you thought. And he won't be coming home tonight, either."

"You locked him up for somethin' he did?"

"No, worse than that, Carol. Jeremy's been killed."

"Killed! How? Like in a car wreck? He doesn't drive and neither does Billy. Was . . ." Her voice trailed off as she teetered on the verge of hysterics.

"At this point, we just aren't sure what happened."

But before he could go on, Carol blurted out, "You're not sure! You don't know what happened! My boy's dead and you don't know what happened or nothing? Why, tell me, *why*!" Tears were streaming down her face into the corners of her quivering lips, dripping off her chin.

He offered her his handkerchief. She wiped her eyes and dabbed at her nose. Bates took her hand in his then began to explain quietly and factually how Deland's dogs riled old Emma up just about daylight that morning. How she had telephoned Bates and how he had gone down to the grove where he found Jeremy hanged.

Carol stared at him. He told her Gabe Furnace and Cletus Poole came to help take Jeremy down. Cletus had Jeremy with him now, trying to find out when her son died and the cause of death. By the time the sheriff had finished explaining what had happened, Carol was a basket case.

Now Carol faced even more loneliness. Her life changed suddenly and forever when she heard those dreadful words all mothers fear—*your son is dead.*

4

B Y THE TIME JEREMY MARTIN's body was placed on a slab in the morgue, Benjamin Reed was five miles down the track. His pace was steady along the path bordering the tracks. Trash of one sort or another littered both sides of the right-of-way, from beer cans and paper plates to railroad spikes and rotting ties. It was always a mystery to him how much garbage accumulated along the tracks. Windows on passenger trains were sealed, so certainly travelers couldn't have thrown trash out. It never seemed to be picked up, either.

He was in sound physical shape from miles of walking and chasing trains all over North America. He was breathing normally as he hurried west away from Flint City, back the way he had come. As he walked, thoughts kept coursing through his brain like the windswept trash cluttering the railway.

Reed wondered if the barking dogs woke him up because they had smelled death. Were they coming to see what was in the tree, or did their noses tell them a stranger had invaded their territory? Was the local county sheriff running his dogs, or just some innocent local person out early walking his pets? In either case, he had not waited. Prudently, he had gathered his belongings and skedaddled. Fast.

From Reed's experiences over the years investigating crimes, he knew law enforcement officers take the most logical action first. They follow in the direction where they think the killer, or killers, might have gone. Would they assume the perpetrators hopped another freight going east to Florida or the one headed north to Atlanta? Ben felt relatively safe heading west back toward the town of Button. He knew from the timetables he carried that no other trains were due going west between midnight and mid-morning. When the authorities checked with the yardmaster they would find out a

Flint River freight headed north to Atlanta had stopped at the yard in Flint City and dropped off cars sometime before midnight on Sunday.

Advantage to Ben. He thought his best chance of avoiding detection was to head back west in the direction he had come from. He would be on foot, at least until he reached Button, where he could stop to eat and get off the streets. Later, he would slip aboard a train going in any direction except back east toward Flint City and the hanged teenager. He considered renting a car but decided against that. Too easy to trace him because he would have to show his driver's license at the rental office, and the cops would certainly "make" him. Catching a bus was another option. But he would have to be careful about who saw him waiting around too long in the bus station, too.

Ben hitched his backpack, canteen, and bedroll higher on his shoulders. It wasn't all that heavy, but he normally did not carry them more than a few blocks at a time. Even with the extra weight, he lengthened his stride.

The county sheriff would probably assume that more than one killer was involved in the kid's murder. That was a safe assumption because Ben figured it would take at least two big, strong men to hoist the boy's body up into the tree after tying him up, even if he wasn't struggling—or already dead. Then too, the grass was already tromped down under the trees where Reed had walked during the night looking for a spot to unroll his sleeping bag. He had also mashed down enough grass for a dozen men. The sheriff would be convinced he was looking for more than one killer. Again, the advantage was Ben's. He was traveling alone, and as far as he knew no one had seen him in Flint City that morning before his hasty departure.

As he walked, Reed thought about what he had seen of the youngster hanging in the tree. He had studied the body from different angles in the short time he had before bugging out. The boy's face was smooth, no wrinkles, his cheeks rounded and purple now from hanging upside down. There were neither whiskers nor sign of a beard. The boy was obviously too young to shave. He was probably in his teens. Ben's sorrow deepened as he pictured the young boy so cruelly hanged. A shame. No, worse than that, a tragedy.

Just like that day when he was still a cop in Titusville. He had been summoned to the scene of a terrible traffic accident at a major intersection downtown. Reed remembered, when the call came in to the dispatcher he was the only officer available. The operator keyed Reed on the radio and dispatched him to investigate the wreck. One of the vehicles involved had been broadsided on the driver's door and was so mangled the make of the automobile was unrecognizable at first glance.

Only after Reed looked into the front seat did he realize it was his wife Mary's car. He couldn't believe it. He stood for several seconds staring into her face, watching as her life slowly trickled away through an open gash in her left temple. Blood was splashed over the dashboard and front seat; shards of broken glass were scattered everywhere, reflecting the sun. The steering wheel was bent down on both sides of the column from the force of Mary's arms and chest impacting against it.

"Mary. Oh, Mary. Don't leave me!"

The driver's side door was so caved in and twisted Ben could not hope to open it. He ran around to the other side and somehow managed with all of his considerable strength to pry the jammed passenger-side door open. He kneeled on the front seat beside her lifeless form and held her hand, stroking it tenderly. Ben could tell that her pulse was fading along with his world. He felt helpless and hopeless.

"Mary, can you hear me?" No response. "Mary . . . Mary, I love you." His throat closed and his voice failed. He stood aside frozen as the Brevard County coroner who had just arrived examined Mary and pronounced her dead at the scene. Ben began to tremble. His world—his reason for living—had just winked out.

Reed watched helplessly as his fellow police officers prepared to lift her body out of the wreckage. As they worked slowly and carefully, his sorrow turned to rage. Once the passenger door was off and Mary could be lifted out, Ben turned on his colleagues in a rage and barked, "Don't touch her! Leave her to me!" He gathered Mary gently in his arms and carried her to a waiting ambulance, which also served the county as a hearse. Reed rode beside her to the morgue, holding her hand and sobbing. He removed the simple gold wedding band he had placed on her finger when they were married thirty years before and slipped it into his pocket. Later, he strung Mary's ring on a gold chain he wore around his neck for months to come.

Reed's decision to quit being a railroad bull to join the Titusville police force was the first thing they had disagreed about after their marriage. "But, Ben," Mary had said, "being a city policeman is a dangerous job, more dangerous than being a railroad detective. Chasing down criminals, some of whom may be murderers or who knows what, and dragging them into jail isn't child's play," she had said.

"That's different, and you know it," he replied in self-defense. "And just how is arresting wanted men, some running from the law, any different from what I've been doing with the railroad?"

Tears began to well up in the corners of her eyes. "For one thing, most of those men you caught trying to hitch a ride on a train didn't carry guns. They weren't out to shoot you!" Mary argued. "I'll worry every minute you're out of my sight."

Ben hugged her close, nibbling at her earlobe. Taking her by the hand, he led her into their bedroom where, after a while, he convinced her he'd be fine. At the time, Mary wasn't concerned about her own safety.

After Mary's funeral, Reed resigned from the Titusville police force. He thought seriously about resigning from life and spent the next several weeks in a deep depression. He drank too much, smoked too much, and ate too little. His daughter, Lynn, finally convinced Ben to accept Mary's death. Lynn loved her mother deeply, but Mary was gone and she worried about her dad. Lynn tried to convince him to give up the bottle, to exercise more, and to cut down on smoking. It took his eighteen-year-old daughter to return him slowly to reality and begin to accept the fact he would never again see Mary. At least, in this world.

Reed trudged along the path beside the tracks, occasionally kicking some litter out of his way. No matter what thoughts crowded his mind, they all returned to Mary. *Am I running away from another tragedy? Am I doing the right thing by ignoring that kid's early and tragic death? Should I be doing something about it?*

Ben's thoughts about the boy were still puzzling him. *What was it—other than the fact the kid was cruelly tied and strung up by his heels? Was it his young age? Yes, that was part of it. Was he killed before he was hanged, or did he die from being hanged upside down for hours?* It was impossible for Reed to know without a coroner's examination. He sure couldn't get an autopsy report while he was on the run. Or could he?

As he walked he was careful about passing houses alongside of the tracks, particularly if people were outside in the yard. He spied an old rusty bucket in the edge of the trees near the right-of-way. He climbed the embankment, turned the bucket bottom side up, and sat down for a brief rest. He sipped water from his canteen and lit up only his second smoke of the day and tore open a Baby Ruth candy bar.

As he munched and smoked, Reed recalled what he had seen of the body. Not much to go on. In his mind's eye he could see the boy with his hair hanging down, all trussed up head to toe with rope, tied by his ankles, and hanged. How was he dressed? In bib overalls and a blue shirt. The scene was like a photograph, except—except for the boy's white socks. What was it about those socks? Then he recalled what had been nagging him since daylight. The boy wasn't wearing white socks on both feet! No. He had on one white sock, but on the other foot his white sock was showing above the top of his shoe. *That was it—his left sneaker was missing! Why? How did he lose it? And more importantly, where was it now?*

Reed wondered if he had missed seeing the kid's other shoe in the tall grass. *Could I possibly have missed a clue?* Not likely. He hadn't missed many during his long career. He finally decided the other shoe probably wasn't under the oak tree or he would have seen it. Perhaps the killer, or killers, saw the shoe drop while stringing the boy up and took it with them. Not very likely. The shoe would be damaging evidence if they were caught with it in their possession.

Reed hung his canteen back on the side of his backpack, carefully snuffed out his smoke and put the filter tip in his pocket. He kicked the bucket back into the tall grass under the trees, stepped carefully down the embankment, and after looking down the tracks behind him, regained the footpath alongside of the tracks.

The missing white tennis shoe, or sneaker as folks were now calling them, still bothered Reed as he continued to ponder. After exploring several scenarios, he came to the most logical explanation. The boy was knocked out or killed, then tied up somewhere else before he was carried to the tree and hanged. More than likely the killing happened that way, Ben reasoned. He hoped the local authorities would be clever enough to come to the same conclusion. Would they launch an extensive search for the missing shoe? It could prove to be a vital clue that would help solve the murder, for murder it surely was.

Not long after Reed started to walk again, he heard the oncoming whistle of steam locomotives approaching from the west. The sound had to be from two steam engines. Newly introduced diesel locomotives had horns not whistles. Ben knew one other thing—he couldn't let the engineer or firemen see him. An investigation of the boy's death would surely spread to the Flint River Railroad within hours because the hanging took place next to their tracks. The two engines were coming on hard, smoking, panting, and rumbling along. They were approaching in a rush and would not slow down until they entered the Flint City switching yard. Reed's only chance to avoid being seen was to take cover in the trees and thickets bordering the tracks.

Reed barely had time to crouch down before the monstrous black locomotives pulling freight cars roared past, shaking the ground and blowing up dust. If the Flint City sheriff had already discovered the body, they probably wouldn't be looking for suspects on a train coming in from the west. Nobody in his right mind, especially if he was a murderer, would think of hitching a ride on a train headed back to the scene of the killing.

Resuming his retreat, Ben tried to avoid a pack of howling dogs that were running around a lakeside fishing camp, chasing each other and barking at boat trailers towed behind pickup trucks. He gave the camp and its dogs a wide berth. Detouring around farmhouses, settlements, and hiding while the long freight passed by took time, which Reed didn't have. He glanced at his watch. It was approaching noon. The day was half gone and it was getting hot. He exchanged his wool stocking cap for a cooler baseball cap with mesh in the top.

Much later, as daylight faded, he unrolled his sleeping bag under a railroad trestle. Supper was another candy bar and water, followed by a smoke. During the night, Reed dreamed about the boy. In one vivid, mixed-up dream, Mary was standing under the oak tree, staring up at the hanging body. She seemed to be telling Ben something, but he could not quite make out her words. The confusing images of Mary and the teenager haunted him all night.

By daybreak, he realized what Mary had been trying to tell him in his dream.

5

T HE SLEEPLESS NIGHT, FULL OF CRAZY, haunting dreams of Mary and the boy, convinced him of what he should do—what he *must* do. The right thing, the only thing Reed could do, was to return to Flint City and to offer to help the local sheriff with his investigation. Going back was risky. But a risk he must take. He might be arrested on suspicion of murder, but he had an idea how to reduce the odds of that happening.

Ben Reed planned to leave the tracks at the next grade crossing. He hoped to hitch a ride with someone going to Flint City. He would have to ride the highway instead of the rails. He had hitchhiked before when he was ready to move on and no freights were headed in the direction he wanted to travel.

By mid-morning he arrived at a crossing just outside the town of Button, Georgia. Before long, Reed flagged down a pickup truck.

"Howdy. Where 'bouts ya headed?"

"Flint City," Ben replied.

"Me, too. Hop in."

He thanked the driver, threw his belongings in the back, and crawled into the cab next to an old man. While riding with the old guy, who turned out to be a farmer, Reed was silent. Thinking. *He couldn't run away from the boy's murder. He had tried to forget Mary's death by running away, but it hadn't worked. Over and over he had tried to hold onto Mary's memory while trying to forget the way she died.*

He focused on what he had to do. First, rent a car if he could locate an agency. Then find a place to stay. Just before noon, the farmer's rusty pickup approached the outskirts of Flint City.

"Where da ya want down?"

"Do you know where the closest car rental office is?"

The farmer looked askance at Reed. A day's car rental cost more than his pickup was worth. "Yep. It's a block yonder. You want out there?"

"That'll be fine." Luckily, the office lights were on and there were cars for rent in the parking lot. "Looks like they're open."

The farmer braked to a stop at the curb. Ben thanked him, retrieved his sleeping bag and backpack, and entered the rental office. He presented his driver's license and paid for a week in advance. The attendant handed him a receipt and the keys, and Ben walked to the lot, hunting the car he was assigned.

After loading his belongings into the trunk, he began to look for the motel he and the farmer had passed on the road into town. He soon found it. Hard to miss a garish blue neon sign reading "IdaHO Motel." The motel was vintage 1930s stucco painted blue with fading red trim. All ten rooms faced the gravel parking lot. Ben pulled in and parked in front of a room marked OFFICE.

He cut the engine and entered the lobby. To the left, between the door and counter, two worn wicker chairs flanked a low table strewn with rumpled magazines. A ceramic lamp shaped like a pelican and topped with a ragged shade hovered crookedly over the magazines. Behind a high counter almost hidden from view sat an obese woman. Her shoulders and neck supported a head crowned with flaming orange hair. Her sagging jaws and wildly painted red lips gripped a smoking cigarette. She was reading that morning's newspaper and ignoring Reed. The front page headline read, "LOCAL BOY HANGED NEAR FLINT RIVER TRACKS—SHERIFF SEARCHES FOR KILLERS."

Behind her on what passed for a desk sat a telephone, peeking out from under the remaining sections of the morning's paper along with pencil stubs and a broken file tray and other litter. An ashtray overflowing with stale cigarette butts was surrounded by a yellow-colored sleeping cat oblivious to the world. Someone's amateur attempt to fabricate a wooden key box hung on the wall. To Ben it looked like all of the keys except for the one to Room 3 were hanging in the box, which probably meant only one of the motel's ten rooms was rented. That prospect suited him fine.

"Lookin' for a room?" the enormous fat woman finally asked, smoke rising from her dangling cigarette. She reminded Reed of a Japanese Sumo wrestler in drag. He wondered how long she would sit there before getting up to check him in. The thought crossed his mind that she might be too fat to get up. To keep from laughing, he smiled.

"Yep. You got any vacancies?" She didn't catch his sarcasm. If she did, she didn't let on. Or smile.

Smelling business, she finally struggled to her feet, pulling herself up by holding onto the corner of the counter. "How many nights?" she asked with a straight face, like every room was booked up for the whole week and beyond.

"Not sure. I'll probably be here a few days, maybe even a week or longer. Just not sure right now," he repeated, fanning smoke away from his face.

"Just passin' though, then." More of a statement than a question.

"Right. Do you have a room around back that's quiet at night? One away from the noise of all those big rigs I've seen?"

"Nope. Got no rooms 'round back. They all face up front. What you see is what you get." Still no smile. She slid a registration card across the counter for Reed to fill out.

"Okay. If I can have the room down on the end? I'll take it for the rest of this week. What's your rate?" Instinctively, Reed didn't trust her. It would be just like her to demand an exorbitant amount later.

"It's twenty-two dollars a night plus tax. Our governor's got to have his cut," she said with an unexpected laugh, ending in a cough spurting spit mixed with cigarette smoke across the counter. "With tax it comes to twenty-two forty-four per night. You can have Number 10. It's the one on the far end."

"Good enough." He took one hundred forty dollars out of his wallet and handed it to the woman. "Take it out of this for the next six nights. I'll want a receipt."

"No problem." She dropped rather than sat back down at her desk, did the math, and slowly printed a receipt on a sheet of wrinkled motel letterhead stationery. She scribbled her signature at the bottom then, struggling back to her feet, handed the makeshift receipt across the counter to Reed along with his change dug out of her skirt pocket. Pointing at the receipt,

"That okay? We don't have any non-smoking rooms, either, like them fancy places. We're not very formal around here."

"That's fine; I smoke." He folded the receipt carefully and made sure she was watching when he stuffed it into his shirt pocket.

"By the way, in case it makes any difference, my name's Ida—Ida Wainright—or had you guessed?" Then without being prompted she went on to explain, "Me and my husband Bert, actually his name is Bertram but everybody hereabouts calls him Pug, moved down here from Pocatello fifteen years back to escape the damn cold weather. Bought this place and we've been runnin' it ever since. I take care of the business end, and Pug does the housekeeping, laundry, and fixin' up when something breaks—that sort of thing. We hunted around for a name, then a cousin of mine who helped us move down suggested IdaHO—a combination of my first name and where we hail from, you see?" Ben already guessed where the name came from before Ida finished her story. Almost too cute!

"Right. And I'm Benjamin Reed from Florida. Here's my registration card all filled out." She handed him the key to Room 10.

As he turned to leave, an elf-like bald-headed man limped through the doorway. Ben knew without being told this tiny gnome of a person was none other than Ida's husband. Pug had pointy ears set too low on his oversized head. His squinty eyes were the color of lily pads and almost the same size. Pug and Ida looked like a comic set of salt and pepper shakers. Ben wondered how they made love, being so physically mismatched.

Reed returned to his rental car, backed out, and drove along the front of the motel lot, parking in front of the door marked 10. He expected to find a dark, grungy, and smelly room. To his surprise, the room was clean, smelling a little like stale smoke, but not unbearable. He checked the small bathroom to see if there was mold around the tub or along the wall behind the stool. There wasn't. A sanitary band crossed the commode.

Ben thought, *No wonder Ida was able to keep the rooms clean, but without the diminutive Pug to do the work she would never pass county health inspections.*

He stowed most of his belongings in dresser drawers. The rest he left in his backpack in the closet. His Beretta stayed in his jacket pocket. He sat on the edge of the bed and dialed his daughter Lynn in Titusville. She wasn't happy when he ran away after Mary's death, and earlier telephone calls hadn't patched things up much.

"Hello."

"Hi, Lynn. It's Dad." Silence.

"Oh." More silence.

"Lynn, are you there?" He could hear her breathe.

"Where are you?" Not *how* are you, he noticed.

"I'm in a small town in South Georgia. I'm okay, no problems. How are you?"

"I'm fine. Nothing much changes around here, you know that."

She began to warm up to their conversation. Her voice sounded more like the Lynn he knew and loved.

They talked for several minutes about Titusville, the Cape, and her friends who were dating or engaged to be married. He told her about some of the humorous adventures he'd had since they last talked on the phone a month or so earlier.

"You sound very grown up of late, Lynn. Your voice is a lot more mature—more sure of yourself."

"Well, Daddy, I'm twenty. That's pretty grown up."

His next sentence was a long time in squeezing around the lump in his throat. "You've grown up while I've been acting like a runaway child these past two years. I'm sorry, but I'll be making it up to you real soon. I've grown up too, and I'm planning to give up life as a hobo as soon as I can clear up a situation here."

"Does that mean you're coming home before long? Grandma keeps asking."

He noticed Lynn didn't want to know, but his mother did. He told her about seeing the tragic hanging of a local youth and how he was through running away from tragedies.

"This afternoon I'm going to offer the sheriff my help. As soon as this murder is solved, or if they reject my help, either way, I'll be heading home. It shouldn't take more than a week or so to figure this killing out."

"You've made me happy saying you'll be home before too long. I miss you terribly, Daddy."

"I miss you and love you, too. Always remember that."

"I love you, too, Daddy."

"If this thing takes any longer, I'll call you again soon."

Relieved, Reed wiped a tear off his cheek. He took a shower, shaved, and changed into clean clothes. Time to explore the town. The square downtown was a mere six blocks from the IdaHO Motel so he decided to walk. He strode up Bond Street, which was the main artery into downtown and served as a secondary state highway. The county library, post office, and a pool hall faced Bond. Halfway to the square, Reed crossed double tracks of the Flint River Railroad. One of the tracks diverged into a siding that ran parallel to the depot's loading platform. Passenger trains were no longer visitors to Flint City, and the depot sat abandoned.

After he decided to return to Flint City, his former hearty appetite also returned. He was hungry and looked for a restaurant. Sal's Café, too small to be called a restaurant, was in one of the red brick buildings along Bond Street and the only eatery in view. He glanced at his wristwatch. It showed twelve o'clock. The noon rush of hungry locals was about to begin. He had noticed that, in the rural South, folks tend to eat by the clock rather than by how hungry they felt.

Only one faded pickup truck with a gun rack in the back window, its color almost hidden by splashed mud, was parked in front of the café. Several cars were scattered up and down the block on both sides of Bond. Nobody was on the sidewalks, which convinced Ben there probably weren't many customers in the café. Reed figured a local type or two might be eating lunch while flirting with the waitresses, especially if they were young and pretty.

Reed walked past slowly, glancing in through the front window. He was wrong about the number of customers but right about the local yokel. A man wearing blue jeans and a white shirt straddled a bar stool, hunched over the counter with his back to the window. A waitress was refilling his coffee mug. After standing for a few moments at the end of the block watching the street, Reed retraced his steps and entered the café.

The man sitting at the counter took only casual notice of Reed when he came in. The raunchy-looking character, wearing a three-day beard and with long dirty hair hanging out from under his greasy cap worn backwards, was too busy trying to make time with a waitress to notice much else. The man's eyes never left the waitress's narrow, swiveling hips as she walked up and down behind the counter.

Reed's practiced eyes quickly surveyed the café's interior. He decided the decor wouldn't make a professional decorator envious. Five booths ran along one wall, and four tables sat crosswise on black-and-white checkered linoleum down the middle of the room. Booths and tables with red Formica tops were set with upside-down coffee mugs, utensils wrapped in paper napkins, and menus supported between salt and pepper shakers. Each table and booth was decorated with a vase holding plastic flowers. Bare light bulbs hung down on electric wires from the high ceiling of white sculptured tin.

Although an old establishment, the café smelled and looked clean. Satisfied, Reed headed for the back booth. He passed by a young couple who were snuggling together on the same side in a booth, each with a straw sipping out of the same soda and seemingly oblivious to the world. An elderly couple, sitting at one of the tables and finishing their desert, was holding an animated conversation. As he sat down facing the door, Reed couldn't help but hear what they were saying.

"Poor Carol. Everyone's concerned about Jeremy, but they ain't worried about her. Not much anyone can do for him, but she needs help. Consoling and such. The church took food in to her yesterday afternoon and will again this evening. She's been through a lot, you know, with her divorce and all."

The waitress brought a coffeepot and a smile to Reed's booth. She was young, with long, flowing blonde hair obviously out of a bottle, which she needed to apply again soon.

"Want some coffee now?"

"Sure, why not?" He looked up at her, smiled, and turned his coffee mug right-side up, sliding it toward the edge of the table.

"My name's Penny, short for Penelope, which I hate," she offered without being asked and in a deep Southern drawl. "My grandmother insisted on calling me Penelope Sue, and she still does even today."

"I'm Ben. Ben Reed."

"What else can I getcha?"

"Am I in time for lunch—say chicken fried steak with mashed potatoes and white gravy?" He knew chicken fried steak was a specialty in almost every Southern café.

"Not 'tall."

"Good. That's what I'll have. You can keep the coffee coming, too." Ben looked up, giving her his best smile.

"Gotcha." She headed for the kitchen to turn in his order.

"How old you reckon Jeremy was, anyway?" the old man at the nearby table asked.

"I ain't sure, but seems to me like he was in his teens. Maybe fifteen or sixteen. Somethin' around that."

"I hear the sheriff's out lookin' hard for the killers. He's been down there in that old grove of oaks by the railroad, pokin' around and takin' lots of pi'tures."

Ben sipped his coffee. He thought, *They're talking about that kid I saw yesterday morning. Big headline in Ida's morning paper. Funny neither she nor Pug said a word about the hanging. Curious.* He lit only his third cigarette since smoking nearly half a pack while camped under the railroad trestle.

The café door opened. The sheriff and his deputy entered. Conversation stopped. The sheriff wore khaki pants and shirt with a broad-brimmed straw hat turned up on the sides cowboy style. His deputy was dressed the same way, except his uniform was wrinkled and looked like he had worn it a week. They both appeared harried. Murder investigations make a person look drawn. Reed had had his share of senseless murders, so he knew the look.

The two officers smiled and nodded cordially to the old couple as they walked toward the back of the café. The seniors hailed the sheriff as he approached their table. Reed listened.

"Sandy, you found them killers, yet?" the old guy inquired.

"Now, Bailey, you know we haven't. Hardly had time to gather evidence, let alone set out after anybody special. We're doin' all we can, though, I promise you that."

"You sayin' you don't have any suspects?"

"You know damn good and well I wouldn't tell you if we did. But to ease your mind, we don't."

"Well, I heard tell Emma called you to report Deland's old hounds had somethin' up in one of those oak trees. Down by the railroad, it was. And what they had was the Martin boy all trussed up and hanged by his heels. Now who'd do a trick like that?"

"A couple of real mean killers. Anyway, that's who we're lookin' for, a couple of bad ones."

So, I was right, Reed surmised correctly. *The sheriff thinks there were at least two killers. In that case, maybe he won't bother with a lone stranger in town. I'll just finish my meal and catch him in his office later this afternoon.*

"You'll have to excuse us, Bailey. Mel and I are fixin' to have some lunch then get back to work. It's been a tiresome, hard day already, and we haven't eaten since breakfast."

The sheriff turned away from the elderly couple. He glanced casually at Reed as he and the deputy sat down in the next booth, taking off their hats as they did so.

The deputy sat with his back to Reed. The sheriff sat across from his deputy facing Reed. Ben felt his nerves began to knot. He avoided looking directly at the two officers. By shifting his seat slightly, he was hidden behind the bulky deputy and out of the sheriff's line of sight.

So far so good, Reed thought. *They seem to be intent on looking at the menus and ordering lunch. Mine will be here before long and I can eat and go.* He pulled his baseball cap down further over his eyes and looked away. Penny brought the officers iced tea instead of coffee and took their orders.

Reed was still edgy but tried not to show it. He had to be careful about letting them know how uneasy he really was or how his heart was in overdrive. *They must be curious about who I am and what I'm doing in Flint City. Surprised they're not talking about me already. But they will. Count on it.*

Minutes later, a skinny cook with white hair revealing her age walked out of the kitchen with Reed's order. "More coffee?"

"Yes, please." He tried to hear what the officers were saying, but they talked in muffled tones. Once or twice he heard mention of the boy, killers, and the word "investigation." Beyond that, he was at a loss to hear anything.

The cook fetched the coffeepot and poured him another mug full. Ben forced himself to eat slowly, although he wanted to wolf his meal down and leave the café. He didn't want to confront the sheriff now or do so in a public place. He ate leaning on his left elbow with his hand partially screening his face.

Confrontations could wait until after he had a chance to get his act together. He was still tired from lack of sleep the night before and the long warm sunny day on foot. Tomorrow morning would be time enough to tell the sheriff who he was, why he was in Flint City, and how he'd been at the scene of the kid's hanging. Soon enough to offer his help finding the boy's killers.

Ben thought, *If they're wondering about me, they haven't let on except to glance briefly in my direction. First thing they'll ask me is why I was in the vicinity of the hanging and how come I waited a whole day to report to them. They'll want to know why I didn't come to their office as soon as I returned to Flint City. Will they understand and accept my answers?* he wondered.

Reed finished his coffee and steak and glanced at his lunch ticket. He left some bills on the table along with extra change as a tip for the hapless Penny. Without looking at the officers who were busy eating or at the old couple who had renewed their conversation, Reed got up to leave. As he passed by the sheriff's booth, the big deputy reached out and grabbed Reed by his jacket sleeve, stopping him in his tracks.

The deputy challenged Ben in a loud voice heard by everybody in the café: "You ain't from around here, are ya?"

6

REED WAS FURIOUS. TOO ANGRY TO answer the deputy directly. Instead, he glared at the sheriff whose name badge said "SHERIFF WILLIAM BATES" in capital letters.

"If your deputy doesn't let go of my jacket, his fried chicken will be garnished with knuckles." Reed's expression left little doubt he could and would back up what he said. The sheriff saw determination boiling up in Reed's threatening eyes.

"Melvin, let him go." The deputy seemed reluctant as he turned loose of Ben's sleeve. He glanced at the sheriff then back at Reed, his expression one of hatred.

Once more all conversations stopped. Heads turned in their direction. The elderly Baileys were unsure whether to sit still or dive under their table. They froze and gawked, wide-eyed.

Reed growled, "Now, I'll answer your question. No. I'm not from around here. My home is on the east coast of Florida near Port Canaveral. My travels brought me to Flint City earlier. I'm back now to tidy up some unfinished business." *Damn, I've just given myself away. I'm out of practice with this sort of thing. He's going to ask me next what unfinished business I have in Flint City. Maybe I should lie. No, he'd see through me for sure.* In an attempt to hide his blunder and regain his composure, Ben softened his eyes and widened his grin into a bigger smile.

He was relieved when the sheriff asked instead, "What's your name?"

"I'm Reed, Ben Reed."

"You got any kind of ID?" Sensing that Reed was about to boil over again, the sheriff said quietly, "Routine. Usual routine, you understand."

Reed hadn't forgotten the routine—don't take anyone's word for anything. Check 'em out. Reaching for his wallet, he said, "Here's my Florida driver's license. Also, you might care to look at this." He handed his license and another wallet card to the sheriff.

Bates studied the driver's license and checked the renewal date and seemed to be satisfied. Turning the wallet card over he read only loud enough for Deputy Phipps to hear: "*CITATION: This Certifies that Benjamin A. Reed Has Been Named an Honorary Lifetime Investigator by the State of Florida in Recognition for Meritorious Service and Having Successfully Solved Over 300 Crimes During His Outstanding Career.*" The citation was signed by the governor and the head of Florida's crime detection center.

"Wow-e-e! Looky here, Mel, we got ourselves a celebrity." He held up the card for the deputy to see but didn't hand it to him.

"You must've done some mighty fine investigating to earn this honor. So I reckon you're who you say you are." He gave Reed's citation back to him but held onto his driver's license. "Is it safe to assume you'll be staying in town for a couple of days?"

"I expect to be here a few days. I planned all along to check in with you this afternoon or first thing tomorrow morning."

The sheriff thought a minute about what Reed said. "Glad to hear it. Let's make it this afternoon, shall we?" Reed knew it wasn't a question but rather a command. "And in the meantime, where you stayin'?"

"I'm checked in at the IdaHO Motel."

"So you've met Ida, huh? She's a case. Old dwarf Pug ain't much above."

"I've just met them, but I'd say they're sure mismatched, all right."

"Well, Mel and I will be going back to our office after we eat our lunch. You look like a man who can be trusted, and this café isn't any place to be holding an interrogation. Tell ya what, why don't you drop by my office behind the courthouse, say about three, three-thirty, and you and I will have a little chat. What say?"

"I'll be there, Sheriff."

"Don't go disappointing me, Mr. Reed. I'd hate to have to put out an APB on you." The sheriff started to hand Reed's driver's license back to him. "On second thought, the IdaHO Motel is within walking distance down the street. Since it's so close, you won't be needin' to drive there so I'll just hold onto your license until this afternoon, what say? You don't have a problem with that, do you?"

"I walked here from the motel, and I can walk back. I can walk to the courthouse just as easy. I've walked a lot these past two years." The sheriff slid Reed's license into his shirt pocket and patted his chest to make sure it was there.

As Reed turned to leave, the sheriff shot one more question at him. "By the way, what business brings you back to Flint City, anyway?"

"Like you said, this isn't a place to be interrogating someone. I plan to share all that with you at three-thirty, assuming that's soon enough?"

"We can wait, I expect, since we know who you are and where you are. I'll wager you're not likely to leave out of here in the meantime without your license." Reed could easily have caught another freight going anywhere and requested a duplicate Florida driver's license, claiming he had lost the original one. But the sheriff did not know at the time how Ben managed to travel about the country. He would find out at their three-thirty conference.

Reed read the sheriff's name on his badge. "Thanks, Sheriff Bates." He shook hands with the sheriff, intentionally ignoring the deputy.

Reed headed for the door. As he neared the front counter, Sally Simpson, owner of Sal's Café, nodded to him. "What was taking place back there between you and the sheriff—if you don't mind me asking?" Sal looked like the typical proprietress of many small cafés in backwashes across the country. She was on the heavy side, although she carried her weight well, looked to be middle-age, with thinning but attractively styled white hair. Her pale blue eyes were hidden behind saucer-sized horn-rimmed glasses. Her joviality was reflected in a broad infectious smile. She was aware of everything that happened in Flint City. Even the local barbers depended on her to keep them informed.

Reed returned her smile. "I don't mind telling you. Sheriff Bates and his overzealous deputy wanted to find out who I am and what I'm doing in Flint City. It's all cleared up now."

"I'll be seeing more of you, then?"

"Sure. If all your meals are as good as today's chicken fried steak, I'll be here again tonight for supper. That's a promise."

Reed stood on the sidewalk outside the café and breathed a sigh of relief. He hadn't been around so many people all at one time, not counting hobos along the way, for quite a while, and having to make conversation when he would rather not made him a little nervous. He walked back to the IdaHO and unlocked the door to Room 10. He bolted the door behind him, sat down on the bed, took his pistol out of his jacket pocket, and with it in hand pulled the curtain aside just a crack and peeked discreetly out the room's front window. He started to let the curtain drop back into place but then hesitated. Parked down the block but not far enough to be totally out of sight was a Nagel County Sheriff's patrol car. Reed couldn't tell whether the man in the driver's seat was Bates or his deputy. *It has to be one or the other of them,* he reasoned. *I doubt a town the size of Flint City has more than a couple of full-time paid county officers.* After watching for a few minutes, he decided it must be the deputy because Bates would have had sense enough to at least park out of sight. He closed the curtain.

So, the sheriff isn't taking any chances I might run. Or perhaps the deputy has staked me out on his own and Bates doesn't know he's on watch. Reed sensed that the deputy wasn't a threat to his safety. Just in case, he checked his automatic to make sure it was loaded. It was.

Reed sat on the side of his bed thinking about why the patrol car was there and about how best to approach the sheriff when they met. Just before leaving for the sheriff's office, he peeked out the curtain again to see if the patrol car was still parked outside. It was gone. It did not matter one way or the other, except it might give him something to use to his advantage at the right time.

He tucked his gun under his jacket, went outside, and locked the door behind him. Reed decided to hide his Beretta in the trunk of his rental car in case Ida or Pug became too inquisitive about him or his belongings. Not having a driver's license didn't deter him from starting the rental and backing out of the parking lot. He glanced at the office as he passed. Ida from Pocatello was watching through the front window. Reed gave her a big wave. He wanted her to know he saw her.

He drove toward downtown and parked across the street from the courthouse. On his approach, he noticed that only one patrol car was parked by the courthouse in the two spaces reserved for sheriffs. He had an idea where the other one was. That's why, before leaving his motel room, he had attached a black thread to the flap on the back of his backpack. If Pug or anyone else got curious and searched his closet, he would know.

It was just about three-thirty when Ben reached to open the door to the sheriff's office, but Bates had been watching for him and opened it.

"Benjamin Reed, I do believe. Come in, come on in. You're right on time. I like a man who's punctual." The sheriff dripped Southern hospitality, which Reed figured was partially an act. At least Bates was making an effort to be friendly. "Have a mug of battery acid. It's hot and fresh-brewed."

"You said to come around three-thirty. So I'm here."

"There's a cup." Bates pointed at a small table behind his desk.

"No, thanks. I don't drink coffee in the afternoon."

"I make mighty good coffee, some say best in South Georgia."

"Look, Sheriff, I'm sure it is, but I didn't come here to debate the taste of your coffee." Reed smiled broadly as he sat down in a rickety folding chair beside the sheriff's desk. He hoped his widest smile would show that he knew how to return Southern hospitality.

The office was furnished with four scarred-up chairs and two desks, one of which had Deputy Melvin Phipps' nameplate on it. Georgia and United States flags hung from poles behind the sheriff's desk, a water cooler without paper cups, two beat-up four-drawer wooden file cabinets, and a small table with a coffeepot and mismatched mugs along with an open tin of coffee and a half-used roll of paper towels completed the decor. The floor was painted-gray concrete with bare spots worn by shoes shuffling across high traffic areas. Behind the sheriff's desk, a door with iron bars led to two jail cells, one on each side of a center hallway. At the end was a small iron-barred window opening to the outside. The best that could be said is that the office was functional if Spartan.

"Tell me more about yourself," Bates said, sipping his fresh-brewed mud. "And while you're at it, do you have a permit to carry a concealed weapon? I could tell you had it in your jacket pocket at Sal's. Didn't want to cause a ruckus in the café at lunch, especially in front of other people."

Ben assured him he had a permit for his Beretta. "Like I said before, my name is Benjamin Reed—middle name Alford—same as my dad's first name. I'm from Florida, Titusville to be exact. I've been traveling around the country for the past two years or so, riding the rails, following where the tracks lead me." He continued, telling the sheriff how he could afford to be a hobo, if that is what people wanted to call him. "I am the only son of the late Alford Brandon Reed and I inherited considerable wealth stemming from patents my father received for his many spin-off inventions and wise investments."

Ben went on, "Before he died, my father provided in his will for a large mortgage-free house, along with a generous monthly income for the remainder of my mother's life. I have one daughter, Lynn. My parents lived in Orlando, but they moved to Titusville when my dad accepted a lucrative position at Port Canaveral." He paused to ask, "Am I boring you with this?"

"Not at all. It's fascinating," Bates lied.

"I was a typical hard-tale kid and dated several frizzy-headed, giggly girls while in Titusville High School and later at the University of Florida in Gainesville. Many of the girls tried to finagle me into marrying them, but I always backed away until that day on the Florida campus when I first glimpsed my one and only true love Mary Kirkham, who became my wife. I was a detective with the Gulf and Eastern and the Florida East Coast Railroads, but then hired on with the Titusville Police Department."

He told briefly about Mary's death in the car wreck but skipped over the gory details. "That's why I've been riding the rails and how my wandering brought me to Flint City night before last.

"I spent Sunday night, actually it was early Monday morning, bedded down in the grove of trees down by the switching yard." He stood up and paced the room, while keeping his eyes on Bates. Ben thought: *Watch his facial expressions. See what he's thinking.*

"So, it was you who tromped around in the grass and mashed it down?"

"Yes, I'm one of the people, I guess. There may have been more before or after I arrived and left." Reed continued, "At daylight, I saw something that startled me and still haunts me even now. That's why I'm here."

"Do you want to tell me what you saw that's got into your brain?" Bates asked, not waiting for Reed to go on with his story.

"I saw a kid hanging upside down in a gigantic old tree." He watched as the sheriff frowned and his eyes narrowed. *Suspicion, or is he trying to listen hard to what I'm saying? In either case, I've captured his full attention,* Ben thought.

"Tell me what you were doin' down by the tracks. And, by the way, how come you saw the boy?"

"I'm coming to that."

Reed explained that he arrived in Flint City after midnight on Monday morning on a northbound freight headed to Atlanta. He had hopped the train in Montgomery. He knew the train was to be broken up at Flint City junction, with the string of boxcars he was riding in scheduled to be set aside for later pick-up by a freight headed to Waycross and down Florida's east coast. Ben said he didn't want to go north but northeast to Savannah. In fact, he was toying with the idea of going home to Titusville in another week or so. He continued telling Bates about bedding down in the tall grass under the canopy of trees near the switching yard. He reminded the sheriff the night was dark and he didn't look around or witness anything unusual. When a pack of howling dogs woke him up in the morning, the first thing he saw was the body hanging upside down in the tree. "I looked around some and saw that the deceased was a young kid. Then I decided it was best if I didn't waste any more time being curious. I wanted to get the hell away before I was blamed for the boy's death."

"So you took off? Which way did you go?"

"West, down the tracks back toward the town of Button where I had come from on Sunday. I walked down the tracks until I was about halfway there then changed my mind about leaving, so I hitched a ride with a farmer back here. I've run away from tragedy before, but I can't continue to run. I've returned in the hope I might be able to help you solve the hanging of that youngster." Reed returned to his chair and mopped his brow with a handkerchief. He thought, *Even though I'm not guilty of anything except running away, confessions are never pleasant whether you're making them or hearing them.*

Bates sat in stony silence for what to Ben seemed like an eternity. Then he said, "*You* help solve the crime? *You,* who may be a suspect yourself; *you* who may be booked; *you* help me find out who hanged the kid? Don't make me laugh."

"Sheriff, I assure you I'm no comedian."

"I'm sure you've heard of the 'm.o.m.' factor—means, opportunity, and motive. So, let's see what we've got here: If you had rope, you had the means. You admitted you spent the night in the trees where we found the boy hanged and that gives you the opportunity. I'll admit we don't have a motive yet, but we're working on one right now. You get the picture?"

Reed bolted out of his chair. He put both hands on the sheriff's desk, leaning over until their noses were almost touching. Rage boiled up in Ben like steam in the boiler of a coal-burning locomotive. "Hell, Sheriff! If you believe I had anything to do with that boy's murder, you're completely out of your mind!"

"Well, that may be! And it also may be you big-city boys think we're all a bunch of dumb country bumpkins around here, but if I lock you up for a spell in one of my cells back here, maybe you won't think me quite as dumb as I may seem," Bates shot back in a tone of voice that sounded to Ben mighty like a threat.

Ben recoiled at the sheriff's outburst and began pacing again. "I didn't say or mean to imply you're dumb or stupid. I didn't get this crooked nose from calling a police officer, or anyone else for that matter, dumb or crazy. For some reason you're still not convinced about my background. Come to think of it, I probably wouldn't be either if the situation were reversed." He rested his hands on the back of the chair and smiled as his anger began to ebb.

Bates smiled back, a little forced, but a smile nonetheless. "Quit pacing, will ya. You're wearin' the paint off my floor." The sheriff's eyes softened a little above a wider unforced grin, and his demeanor became friendlier.

Reed sat down, took a cigarette from his pack, and lit it. His first of the day. Exhaling, he said, "Before making a big mistake, one you might regret, telephone the Florida Crime Center, the governor, the Chief of Police in Titusville, call my immediate supervisor when I worked for the Florida East Coast Railroad. They'll confirm that I'm no criminal. They'll tell you I'm what I say I am and who I say I am. I'll pay for the calls even now during the day when the rates are higher." Reed leaned back, drawing on his smoke. Calmer now and resigned. He had done all he could. Now it was up to the sheriff to lock him up, believe him, or make some long distance calls.

"I may make those calls. What are the phone numbers of the crime center, the Titusville Police Department, and your former supervisor on the FEC Railroad? We'll forget the governor for now." Without hesitating, Reed pulled a small card out of his wallet and read off the three phone numbers as the sheriff wrote them down on a notepad.

With a genuine smile this time, Bates handed Reed's driver's license back to him. "I'm a good mind to trust you, Benjamin Alford Reed," he said. "And I see you drove to my office without this. If you insist on driving, then you better have your license. I wouldn't want to have to give you a ticket for operating a vehicle on our streets without having a valid license on your person."

"Thanks, Sheriff. You're all heart."

They had reached an impasse—a truce of sorts. At least their expressions were less grim and their conversation less hostile. The tension had eased noticeably as they quit sparring. Being professionals, they recognized the importance of being cooperative instead of combative.

It was Reed's turn to ask questions. "Tell me, how come there isn't a police department in Flint City?"

"There's only one incorporated town in Nagel County. The good citizens of Flint City voted not long ago to put all of our public services together, at least until our tax base grew large enough to support two law enforcement operations. So far, that hasn't happened. During consolidation, my office and the police department became one under a sheriff. County offices were determined to take precedence, so we took over the police functions. Simple as that."

"I see," Ben said. "Now let's turn to the hanging. Who's the boy? Local kid, I presume."

"Yes, he's Carol Martin's son. His name is—was—Jeremy, a local high school kid. He's been in a scrape or two at school in the past. Nothing serious. Beating up on a couple of classmates, keeping some girls out beyond their curfew, that sort of thing. For a small town, we got much worse than him in Flint City."

"And his mama, this Carol—uh—Martin, is it?"

"Right. Everyone who knows her likes Carol. She's not too well off financially. Word is she's struggling to make ends meet. Lives in a 1930s period house back of the IdaHO Motel. Since her divorce, she's been working mighty hard down at the carpet mill to raise Jeremy, clothe him, and give him a good education and a decent start in life. Carol works so her son can—could—devote full time to his studies. Damn shame, him being murdered and so young to boot."

"How's she doing?"

"Holding up mighty good under the circumstances. The time or two when Jeremy got into trouble we kinda smoothed things over to save Carol and her son any embarrassment. No need to make matters worse. We weren't going to prosecute him for some minor teenage infraction anyway."

"What's the cause of death?"

"Not in yet. Our medical examiner, Cletus Poole, is doing an autopsy. Not much we could tell at the scene, except that he had been dead between six and twelve hours. He was hit on the head, and the blow may or may not have been the cause of death. The coroner and I took some photographs then loaded him into the medical examiner's van and transported the remains to the morgue. That's where he is now."

"I suppose you're the one who told Carol the tragic news after you found her son hanging in the tree?"

"I did. Right after we took Jeremy down and looked him over, I went down to the mill and told Carol. She took it real hard. Thought for a while she was going to faint on me on the spot. She certainly had cause to, if you ask me."

"May I see the autopsy report when it's ready?" Reed figured two days should be enough time for Poole to complete the autopsy and write up his findings.

"If he's done with his report, he hasn't brought it to me yet." Bates ignored Reed's question.

"I guess the rest of my questions can wait until we get the autopsy." Reed thought for a minute. "One more thing though, when is the funeral?"

"Wednesday afternoon at four. I expect nearly the whole town will turn out."

Reed suggested they visit the morgue, ask Poole for his report if it was done, and look at Jeremy's body. "Since the funeral is tomorrow afternoon, this may be our best time to see Jeremy's remains. The funeral home will need the rest of the time to prepare him for the service."

As they started to leave, Deputy Phipps barged into the office, slamming the door back against the jam. His expression of triumph quickly turned to dismay when he saw Reed with the sheriff—a fact which Ben noted. The deputy was panting like a 5K runner. Ignoring Reed, he blurted out, "Sandy, I need to talk to you right now!"

Sheriff Bates turned to Reed. "Wait outside for me, please. I'll be with you in a jiffy." Reed went out and leaned against one of the sheriff's patrol cars.

As soon as the door shut behind Reed, Bates turned on his deputy, scowling with his eyes shooting fire. "What in hell is so damned all-fire important, Mel, that it can't wait until Reed and I finished our conversation?" He glared at his deputy. "And while I'm at it, you look like you slept in your uniform!"

"I did but that's another story. What I want to report is that after lunch I staked out the IdaHO where Reed is stayin'. I parked down the street across from the motel and watched a while to see what he's up to."

"Well, what is he up to?"

"Nothin'. He didn't move at all so when he left again to come here, me and Pug went into his room and had a look-see." Phipps puffed up with pride, with a goofy grin spread across his face.

"You did what!"

"Wait till I tell ya, Sheriff. We found a pair of army boots in his closet. He's got a military-style backpack full of winter clothes and a rolled up sleepin' bag. What's more, we found packages of trail mix and a canteen of water in one of his dresser drawers and summer clothes stashed in another. Me and Pug think this here Reed is nothin' more than a drifter, a hobo, a sure nuff bum."

Bates turned red in the face. He was about to explode and splatter all over his deputy.

Grinning like a catfish eating worms, Phipps spouted the final clincher. "Sandy, he ain't nothin' but a low-down mangy bum, a sure nuff bindle stiff. What's more, I betcha he had somethin' ta do with the Martin kid's hangin'!"

7

WHEN DEPUTY PHIPPS FINALLY ended his tirade to take a breath, Bates was able to shout, "You're standing there telling me you made illegal entry into that man's room! And you plainly had a look-see? You bottom-feeding baboon! He's already told me he's a former railroad bull and a police investigator from Florida, with a citation to prove it. He's here to help us find out who killed the Martin kid. He hasn't done a thing wrong we know of."

Phipps sputtered, "But—but I thought . . ."

"That's your problem, Mel, you don't think! He claims he's on our side. Can you understand that, you nitwit?" Bates roared, his anger almost overwhelming his better judgment.

In his defense, Phipps offered a lame excuse about Pug being in Reed's room anyway to clean up, so he saw no harm in snooping around to find out about him and what he's doing in Flint City. All this he offered to the cement floor, rather than to the sheriff's face.

Calmed down somewhat, Bates continued, "Well, let's just hope for both our sakes he doesn't find out about it. I have an idea he could make a lot of trouble if he had a mind to, and we don't need any more trouble right now, what with this killing on our hands." Bates dismissed Phipps, ordering him to go outside and tell Reed he had received an important phone call and that he would be right along. "Think you can do that, Mel? You think you can get it right?" As soon as Phipps shut the door, Bates picked up the phone and dialed one of the numbers Reed had given him.

"Titusville Police Department."

"This is Nagel County Sheriff William Bates in Flint City, Georgia. Let me talk to your police chief."

After a pause, "Chief Timmons here. What can I do for you, Sheriff?"

"Won't take a minute of your time, Chief. Tell you why I'm calling. We got a guy up here by the name of Benjamin Alford Reed, says he was an investigator down there with your department."

"That's right. You got a problem about him?"

"No, no problem. Did you think there might be cause?"

"No, but he could be sick or dead or something."

"He's okay, rest assured. He's said he was with your force down there. He showed me a citation for meritorious service. I'm just checking up that it's genuine, not a forgery or just made up, something like that."

"It's genuine, I assure you. He was one of the best investigators we ever had. Solved over three hundred crimes during his career. He was a top cop. Wish he was on our roster now."

"That's good to hear, Chief. Says he was a dick with Gulf and Eastern and Florida East Coast for a while too, that right?"

"Yes, and I'm told he was one of their best railroad detectives, and they were sorry when he resigned to come on board with us."

"We got ourselves a strange type of killing up here. Reed is offering to help me solve it. If he's as good as you say, likely as not he will."

"You can count on it, Sheriff. He knows his business."

"Reed seems to be a contradiction though. He dresses good, drives a rental car, and is stayin' in a motel but says he's been a hobo riding the rails for about two years. What can you tell me about him?"

"His dad was one of the top engineers here at Canaveral. Dabbled around with some successful inventions on the side and amassed a small fortune. When he died, Reed and his mom inherited some big bucks. I'd say he's well-heeled. Doesn't have to steal and won't go hungry, if that's what you mean."

"You've certainly cleared up how hobo Reed can dress well, drive a rental, and stay at a motel rather than living under a bridge or off in the woods in a lean-to."

"Reed almost cashed it in when his wife was killed in a car wreck. He took off right afterward, and we haven't seen or heard from him since. I'm glad to know where he is. Be sure to tell him hello for me," Timmons urged.

"I will. Thanks, Chief, and if I can ever return the favor, just give me a call." Bates cradled the phone. His anger, built up during his run-in with Phipps, dissipated some when he learned Reed had checked out.

He grabbed his hat, went out the door where Phipps was standing by his patrol car just feet from where Reed was leaning against the front fender of the sheriff's car. They were looking past each other without saying a word. Bates ordered his deputy to stay around the office while he and Reed went to the morgue to talk to Cletus Poole and view Jeremy's body.

As they walked, Bates said, "Oh, by the way, Chief Timmons says to tell you hello for him."

"So, you checked me out after all?"

"Yep, and he says you're who you say you are, in spades."

Then he changed the subject. "In case you're wondering, I talked at length to Emma, the old lady who reported Martin's hanging. She didn't have much to add to what she told me yesterday morning when she called. She said she saw what it was that stirred up Deland's dogs and who it was. She claimed she scurried back home and called me immediately."

"Did you ask her if she saw anybody on her way to or from the oak grove?"

"Sure. Said she didn't see a soul. In her state of fright she probably would not have seen a bright yellow bulldozer if one was hanging upside down on a light pole.

"Something else I need to tell you now that you're on my team. Early this morning I got a call from an FBI agent from Jacksonville, I think that's where he said he was. He told me a high-priority boxcar with classified cargo arrived during the night at the Cape and that it had been broken into. Some of the contents belonging to the federal government are missing. He also said the bill of lading shows the boxcar spent some time Sunday night in the switching yard here in Flint City. He said he and another guy from Florida East Coast Railroad are coming here to investigate. I'll let you know when they plan to be here." Ben listened without comment but wondered if he knew the FEC guy.

They walked around back of the courthouse to the county morgue.

"Poole is a good man and a top pathologist. He's been doing medical examinations for over twenty-five years and sometimes even helps MEs in other counties with their autopsies."

They entered the morgue, passing through an unattended outer office leading into the examining room. The smell of chemicals almost choked the two of them. Poole was leaning over an examining table, dressed in a white smock. His eyes and horn-rimmed glasses peered out between his face mask and surgeon's cap. He was examining a body that had a white sheet covering it from head to toe. Poole nodded toward the two arrivals, unperturbed by the interruption.

Peeling off his surgical gloves, Poole shook hands with Bates and looked inquisitively at Reed.

Ben extended his hand and smiled before the sheriff could introduce him. "Dr. Poole, I'm Ben Reed, a retired policeman from Florida. I'm hoping to assist Sheriff Bates in his investigation of Jeremy Martin's murder."

"My pleasure, Mr. Reed. You can call me Cletus. I have a notion we're going to need all the help we can get on this one." Poole pulled off his cap and wiped his brow with the back of his hand. "Martin is in a drawer over here waiting for the funeral home to come get him prepared for the services tomorrow afternoon. It's a good thing you came when you did because I'm expecting the funeral director here any minute." Poole crossed the room and pulled out one of the storage drawers. "Look all you like until they come for him."

Reed and Bates stood beside Poole, looking down at Jeremy Martin's shrouded body lying on the cold metal slab. Poole pulled back the white sheet and began to recite what he had found during his autopsy. He pointed out several visible marks: a contusion over his left ear where he had been hit with something, skinned knees and elbows, rope burns around his neck, ankles, and wrists. "As you can see, his mouth is bruised in the corners from what I think was a gag tied mighty tight. He has tiny pockmark-looking holes on his right cheek. I also noted abnormal swelling in his face along with general discoloration. He had been dead about twelve hours when I began my examination."

"What could have caused these little red pits on his cheek, Cletus?" Reed asked.

"That's where I extracted some tiny particles of grit. Under the microscope they show a reddish tint. They may be slivers of granite or some other hard stone. I'm not sure yet what they are, so I sent them to Atlanta for analysis in our state crime lab."

"Can you hazard a guess now?" Reed asked, hoping Poole might have seen something similar during a prior autopsy because the clues to the boy's hanging were growing older by the minute. It was the second day since Martin was found hanged.

"Tell you what—Reed is it?"

"Yes. But call me Ben."

"Tell you what, Ben, if I had to venture a guess, I'd say the little chunks—small, mind you—are like tiny chips of dirt from a roadside or maybe the type of gravel you find in ballast along railroad tracks. That's only a guess for now, though. We'll have to wait another day or two to see what the Georgia Bureau of Investigation in Atlanta says. They do quick and thorough examinations of evidence sent to their office."

"How did Martin die?" Sheriff Bates asked.

Poole took a deep breath and referred to his notebook. "According to what I found out so far—and this is preliminary, keep in mind—he died from two causes almost simultaneously. I sort of suspected as much when we took him down out of the tree. Being hanged upside down exacerbated the situation. One cause was asphyxiation, which is to say he drowned in his own body fluids. He was tied up hand-and-foot and gagged. After he was hanged, he couldn't wiggle or catch his breath, so his lungs filled up and he drowned. Horrible way to die."

"You said there were two causes. What was the other one?" Reed asked.

"My preliminary exam indicated he suffered from a brain aneurysm. One vessel wall was weak, possibly from birth. When it burst, he bled to death inside his brain. While Martin might have survived the blow to his head, he would have died when that weakened vessel ruptured from the pressure caused by an excess of blood rushing to his head while hanging upside down."

"So, are you reporting cause of death as drowning, an internal brain hemorrhage, or what?" Bates asked.

"No, Sandy, it's a hanging right enough. First hanging in these parts for years, I'd venture. A damned curious one, too, hanging a fellow upside down like that. The fact he wasn't hanged by the neck doesn't make it any less of a hanging. My official report will show he was hanged and that's what caused his death. He might have survived otherwise."

"Thanks, Cletus," Bates said. He and Reed shook hands with Dr. Poole after he slid the drawer shut. As they were leaving the examining room, Bates glanced back over his shoulder. "You'll be sending a copy of your official written autopsy report around to my office ASAP?"

"It'll be there just as soon as I recheck my findings and my assistant types it up."

The coroner's black hearse was backing up to the door to pick up Martin's body as Sandy and Ben walked back around the courthouse to the sheriff's office. It was nearly quitting time, so Reed suggested they take a break and meet again the next morning at the sheriff's before going to the oak grove. Reed wanted a closer look at the scene of the crime in full daylight. Bates agreed, then returned to his office.

Reed headed back in the direction of his car with the intention to return to the IdaHO Motel. As he walked to his car, a woman emerged from the funeral home. His curiosity was aroused. Her big blue eyes were red from crying, and she was holding tissue to her nose. She appeared to be in her early forties, but possibly younger, with a model's figure. She startled Ben because she looked enough like his wife Mary to be her sister.

Reed hesitated and then moved quickly to where she was standing. "Excuse me, please. I hope my timing isn't bad, but are you by any chance Mrs. Martin?"

She looked at him, wrinkling her forehead. Ben had also startled her. Caught off guard, she replied, "Yes. Yes, I am." Tears etched footpaths down her cheeks. "Do I know you?"

"No. I doubt it." Seeing she was still hesitant, he offered his widest, most reassuring smile. A gesture of friendship. He aimed his pale gray eyes directly into hers. Pointing at a nearby bench, he asked, "Shall we sit down? I want to chat a moment if you have time."

She said nothing but cautiously walked over to the bench and sat down. He could see she was hesitant, but who wouldn't be? He joined her on the bench, sitting at the other end. From behind a smile he explained who he was and why he was in Flint City. As she seemed to relax some, he told her he was helping Sheriff Bates find out about her son Jeremy.

All the while, Carol looked at the sidewalk while she dabbed at her nose with a tissue. She listened quietly and intently. Reed talked in the soothing, practiced way that had worked wonders in the past. It did again. When he paused, she looked into his reassuring eyes and said, "I only hope you can catch those people who did that to my son."

"You can count on it, Mrs. Martin." He wanted to get to know this lady much better. "I was headed to Sal's for coffee," Ben said, changing his mind about going back to the motel. "If I'm not being too bold, would you care to join me?"

She hesitated still. Then, "I think that would be very nice." Rising from the bench, she smiled for the first time since the sheriff came to the carpet mill the day before to tell her about Jeremy's death.

8

CAROL WAS SO MUCH LIKE MARY. Graceful walk, great figure, quiet voice, and natural charm. Bates had said everyone in Flint City who knew Carol liked her. He could add Benjamin Alford Reed to the growing list. What was not to like?

While they slowly sipped their coffees, Reed explained the details of his chance passing through town earlier in the week. He told her how he hated injustice in any form.

"I feel sure the circumstances surrounding Jeremy's loss will be cleared up soon." For obvious reasons, he didn't mention the funeral, but an idea was forming in his mind.

Carol touched upon her divorce but omitted the gory details—an omission he respected and admired. "After my divorce, I had to take a job down at the carpet mill. I hate the work, but they were hiring at the time and I didn't want to end up a waitress at Sal's. The pay barely supported Jeremy and me. My home came to me free and clear in the divorce settlement, so without house payments and by watching our spending, we managed— managed somehow."

"Raising children without one or the other parent as a role model is difficult at best." Reed had learned that from experience. He had run away from his responsibility to Lynn.

Tears began to swim in Carol's eyes, prompting him to reach across the table to place his hand on top of hers. She didn't pull away. They finished coffee, content to exchange small talk about Flint City and the weather. Jeremy's death would be conversation for a later time, when Reed had something solid to tell her about her son's hanging.

"May I drop you off somewhere? My car is down the street across from the courthouse."

"Thank you, no. My car is parked behind the funeral home."

He paid for their coffee. As they touched hands again on the sidewalk, she held on a little longer than seemed necessary to Reed. He was pleased and thrilled at the same time.

He seems to be a nice, gentle man who is courteous and thoughtful, Carol thought. Even in her grief, she looked again into his kind gray eyes that framed his bent nose.

"I don't want to be pushy, but may I see you again?" *Perhaps I can find love again,* Ben thought. *She certainly is something. So like my Mary.*

"If you'd like to. That would be nice, Mr. Reed. And you're not being pushy at all. I live in the second house around the corner behind the IdaHO Motel. Think you can find it?"

"I'm sure I can. I'm staying at the IdaHO. And please call me Ben."

She turned and walked away in the direction of the funeral home parking lot. He noticed the parlor was still open. Reed watched her for several moments, then reentered Sal's. An idea involving Carol and Jeremy that had occurred to him had grown while they drank their coffee and was now clear. He ordered another cup of java and sipped slowly to give Carol time to drive away from the funeral home. He walked back to the funeral parlor and entered.

An assistant funeral director greeted Ben at the door and ushered him into one of the cubicles. "Are you here to make final arrangements for a dearly departed?" he asked.

"In a way, yes. Can you tell me if Jeremy Martin's funeral expenses have been paid?"

"May I ask who you are, sir?"

"I'm Ben Reed. I'm here as a friend of the family," Ben said, slightly stretching the truth.

"As to your question, I am not certain, sir, what financial arrangements have been made." He didn't elaborate.

"Would it be possible for me to talk with someone who might know?"

"Certainly, sir. Right this way." He led the way down a hall to the business office, knocked politely, and opened the door for Reed to enter.

"Mr. Granger, this is Mr. Reed. He's here about Mr. Martin's service."

Granger stood and they shook hands. "Please sit down, Mr. Reed. How may I help you?"

"Mr. Granger, to come right to the point, I'd like to know if all the funeral expenses for the Martin boy have been taken care of. I want to make sure he gets a decent funeral, a nice casket, flowers, the works. I'll pay for everything up front. But I'm doing this anonymously, and I don't want his mother to *ever* find out."

"I see." Granger gazed steadily at Reed. "Some of the information is kept confidential except for family members. I don't believe I know you. Are you family?"

"I'm a retired police officer from Florida." Without going into great detail, Ben told the funeral director he was assisting Sheriff Bates in his investigation of the boy's tragic death. He showed Granger the citation on his wallet card. "You can call the sheriff if you need verification. He should be in his office."

"That won't be necessary, Mr. Reed." Granger fussed around on his desk, then held up the Martin folder. "Ah, here it is." Opening the file, he adjusted his glasses as he looked through the papers. He handed one across the desk to Reed. "Here are the expenses. Your offer to pay for everything is awfully generous, Mr. Reed. I assure you, your generosity will be kept strictly confidential." Granger remained silent as Reed studied the list of expenses.

"These all appear justified and reasonable, Mr. Granger. Will a personal check be acceptable? I have a bank letter of credit to back it up if that's necessary."

"Your check will not only be sufficient, sir, but as I said earlier, most generous. Mrs. Martin told me the expenses are concerning her, so I know she will be relieved when she learns everything has been taken care of by a friend of the family."

Reed wrote out a check and marked it "Paid in Full." They shook hands again. As Reed turned to leave, Granger said, "I presume you'll be at the services on Wednesday at four in the afternoon."

"Yes, I'll be there." Reed headed back to Sheriff Bates' office.

Before daybreak Tuesday on the other side of town, Clyde Krebs sat at his kitchen window, smoking a cigarette and sipping coffee. He expected Sherman Getts to show up any minute. Getts owed Krebs money for a Chevy pickup Krebs had sold him, and payment was long overdue. Each time Krebs confronted him, Getts told him to wait a little longer. He expected to hit the *big one* soon. Krebs was in a flap! He began to pace back and forth, glancing out the kitchen window each time a vehicle passed by.

Still no Getts.

Krebs' patience was finally exhausted, and he gave up waiting any longer. He decided to drive to Getts' house. He drove into the yard and parked his truck around back of the house. Getts' pickup truck, the same one he was buying from Krebs, was also there, parked out in the back lot near a shed. Its owner was nowhere to be seen. As he stepped out of his truck, Krebs yelled, "Sherm! Hey, Sherm, where in hell are you? I've come for my money. Don't be hidin'! Answer me, you no-good welchin' bastard."

No Getts and no answer.

Krebs banged on what was left of a screen door on the back porch. "Sherm, damn it! You in there? Answer me!"

Still no answer.

Krebs stepped inside the porch, wondering why the door into the main part of the house was ajar. He knew the man he was looking for never left his back door standing wide except on the hottest part of the summer, and it was a cool spring morning. Krebs hollered again, this time rousing a scrawny yellow cat, which circled around, rubbing up against his ankles. The cat's loud mewing was the only sound in the house. Krebs boldly walked through the kitchen.

No Getts.

He checked the living room.

No Getts.

He looked in the bedroom.

And found Getts.

Getts was lying on a sagging bed on his left side. One pillow was under his head. Another covered it. Krebs assumed he was asleep.

"Now I gotcha, Sherm! You're a lazy sumbitch. You're laying in bed mighty late this morning." He shook Getts.

No response.

Krebs shook him again. Then he lifted the pillow.

"Crimeinitley!" he exclaimed in the vernacular.

He dropped the pillow and recoiled in horror. He knew now why Getts hadn't showed up to settle up. Someone had stuck a gun in his right ear and pulled the trigger. The bottom pillow and bed were a sticky, smelly, red swamp. Krebs could see Getts was deader than yesterday's newspaper.

Krebs swiped the back of his hand across his forehead, now beaded with sweat. Stumbling back in revulsion, he asked the corpse, "What have they done to you, Sherm?" The silent bedroom walls, roaches, and circling cat peered at him but were unable to tell who had pulled the trigger. Almost overwhelmed, Krebs staggered back into the living room, where he collapsed next to the phone, which was sitting on top of the directory. With trembling hands, he began flipping pages. The number he wanted was in the front, but his mind was a jumble and his eyes would not focus. Krebs finally found the sheriff's number and dialed.

9

THE PHONE WAS RINGING WHEN Reed walked into the sheriff's office. "Sheriff Bates." His eyebrows wrinkled into a frown. He held up his hand palm out and shouted into the receiver.

"Dead? Are you absolutely sure, Krebs?"

"He's been shot in the head! Damn right he's dead. Stone dead." Krebs gulped.

"Where are you now, Clyde?"

"I'm at Getts' house. It's horrible, Sheriff!"

"Hang on, Clyde. Stay put. Don't touch anything and don't let anybody in the house, you hear? If anyone shows up, tell them to stay out and you're acting on my orders. You got that?"

"Yep. Just hurry, Sheriff!"

"We're on the way."

Bates hung up the phone and scowled at Reed and Phipps.

"Another killing?" Reed asked.

"Yep. Looks like we've got ourselves another one. The second murder in as many days. It's Sherman Getts. Clyde Krebs says he's deader than a hit squirrel on the road." The sheriff was quick to take charge. " Mel, grab your car and meet Reed and me at Getts' place. We'll go code eighteen with sirens and lights! Ben, you ride with me." Bates rushed out of the office with Reed and Phipps on his heels. They burned rubber out of the parking lot, with tires and sirens squealing. Bates keyed his radio.

"Cletus, can you come out to Getts' place? He's been reported killed."

"I'll be there in a few minutes, Sandy."

The two patrol cars, making enough noise to awaken the entire town except for Getts, careened around the corner and down the street leading to Getts' place. Three miles beyond the turnoff, they slid to a stop. The trio bolted for the back door to Getts' house, leaving their car motors running and lights flashing.

"Hang on there, Sheriff, not so fast!" Reed shouted. The two officers stopped, turned, and looked dumbfounded at him.

"What ya got?" Bates asked.

"May be evidence here, Sheriff." Ben pointed at the ground. "You can barely see them, but those look like fresh tire tracks leading up by the back porch. Someone's driven here recently. We may be able to get good plaster castings of these tire treads where a vehicle drove into the yard. If we're lucky, we might match these imprints with the tires. Could be an important clue about who the perpetrator or perpetrators were."

"You're right. We need to cast them right now," Bates answered. The sheriff ordered Deputy Phipps to start stringing yellow crime scene tape around the house, especially in the back yard. "Watch what you're doing around those tire tracks, too," Bates reminded him. The sheriff and Reed walked carefully to the back porch while watching where they stepped.

Clyde Krebs was sitting on the back porch in a moldy white wicker rocker. At their approach, he stood up. None too steady, Krebs wrung his hands and shivered. He was so pale, he looked like he had wrestled with a jug of bleach and lost.

"Hey, Clyde. You say Getts is in the bedroom?" Bates asked.

"Yep, an' he ain't moved none neither."

Reed and the sheriff entered the bedroom. Getts was lying on a rumpled and sagging bed, with the lower half of his body covered with a sheet. The pillow that had covered Getts' head had been tossed aside onto the floor. The bullet wound in his ear left little doubt about how Getts was murdered.

"He must have been asleep when he was shot," Bates said. "Otherwise, I don't think he would lie here dreaming and let someone shoot him without putting up a fight. Most folks in these parts know Getts was slow-witted, but surely he could think quickly enough to realize he was in danger and then react to protect himself."

"There are a couple other possibilities," Reed suggested. "He may have known the killer or killers and did not feel threatened, or the perpetrator surprised him before he was fully awake and could defend himself."

"That's certainly possible. From the looks of the wound, I'd say the gun was either a twenty-two or a thirty-eight caliber. Anything larger probably would have caused more damage to the inside of his right ear."

"I agree. Hopefully, we'll be able to find the spent slug in or under the other pillow his head is on or in the mattress." Sheriff Bates was busy taking notes, so Ben didn't have to record the scene.

Reed didn't expect to investigate more than one killing when he returned to Flint City. Solving Jeremy Martin's hanging was challenge enough. *Things are slowly getting out of hand,* he thought.

"Well, there's not much else we can do until Cletus gets here and we can roll him over to see if there's anything under his body. Once the ME does his thing, we can lift him up and search around for the wasted slug," Bates said. "I'll grab my camera from my car and start taking pictures. Cletus will have his camera, too. He keeps a camera loaded with film in his van. While we're waiting, I'll get my kit so we can dust the room for prints, but I don't expect to find any."

"So you don't have a special unit here in Flint City to gather evidence and run it through the lab?"

"Naw, that's for big-city cops. Here in this county, the sheriff does it all except for the ME's duties. And then you have to be licensed like Cletus is, who's been at it now for some twenty-five years," Bates replied.

While the sheriff went for his camera and crime investigation kit, Reed studied Getts' body while running all possible scenarios through his mind. Bates returned and began dusting likely places where prints might be found. As he expected, no luck.

Before the sheriff finished dusting, the coroner walked into the bedroom carrying his black bag and camera. "Hey, Sandy, Ben. Looks like we got a messy one this time. Maybe we need to find a different hobby," Poole said with a sardonic smile. "What in hell's name is going on in Flint City? I mean, we haven't had a killing here in—I can't remember when. Now it seems they're coming packed two to the box."

"Cletus, I'm not sure what's going on. Whatever it is, it isn't good for us and sure as hell isn't doing the victims much good either. We need to clear up these killings before the whole town goes nuts," Bates said. "Folks are already hidin' behind locked doors. I reckon those with guns got 'em loaded beside their rockers in daytime and tucked under their pillows at night. Too bad ol' Getts didn't have a gun handy when someone shot him. Cletus, you need Reed or me just now?"

"No. If you got to do something else, go ahead."

"Okay, thanks. Reed and I want to interrogate Krebs before he gets lockjaw or shakes to pieces."

The two of them returned to the back porch.

"Clyde, we got a few questions. Depending on your answers, you may be free to go," Bates said. "How come you know, uh—knew, Getts?"

"Hardly knew the man, but I knew his kind. Didn't cotton much to him."

"You weren't friends then?"

"We weren't friends, that's for damn sure. I done business with him but only one time. I shoulda knowed better. I sold him that there Chevy pickup." Krebs pointed to a rusting blue truck parked in the back of Getts' yard. "Paid me a little down, and he owed the balance for some months now. He'd sit here on the porch in that broken-down swing yonder just easin' back and forth like he owned the world. As far as I knowed, he didn't work regular, but he seemed to have enough bills to get by on. I reckon he picked up some money in payment for odd jobs he done. Said he was expectin' to come into 'big money' real soon. Otherwise, I wouldn't have sold him my truck on part down with the balance in promises."

"So that's how you chanced to find him? Come to collect?" Bates asked.

"Yep. I come here a little bit ago to collect what he owed me—still owes me, come to think on it. Hollered, but old Sherman didn't answer. I figured, like as not he was hidin' to keep from payin' his due. Well, anyway when he didn't yell back, I come in the house lookin' for him, and there he was in bed. Figured he was asleep, but when I lifted the pillow offin his head, I seen he'd been shot. Don't take no big detective to see he'd been killed. Just like I told you on the phone." Krebs paused after giving the longest speech of his life.

"Now think hard, Mr. Krebs. Did he say anything or try to speak? Did he whisper or moan or make any sound at all?" Reed asked.

"Nope." Krebs shook his head although it was hard to tell with his trembling so. "Getts was already a goner when I found him. I was in the army, and I know what dead is when I sees it."

"How did you get in the house?" Bates asked.

"Well, after I yelled several times and Getts didn't answer, I banged on the back porch screen door. Still got no answer. So I tried the screen door and it weren't latched, so I went in and began to look for him. I done told you this once before."

"We want you to tell us again, okay?" Reed tried to reassure Krebs, who was visibly shaken. "Was the back door into the house locked?"

"Well, if it were locked, I couldn't a got in, now could I? I recollect it was standin' wide open. That's when I thought 'twas mighty odd Getts not answerin' my bangin'. Can I go now?"

"Just a couple more questions, Clyde," Bates said. "What did you do after Getts didn't answer your knocking and yelling?"

Krebs expanded on his first version. "When he didn't answer me, I went into the kitchen. He warn't there, so I started lookin' in the other two rooms. Went first into the livin' room, and he warn't there neither, so I peeked into his bedroom kinda careful like. At first, I thought he was asleep, till I lifted his pillow. Oh, Lordy. I'm sure gonna puke just thinkin' about it!"

Reed heard a cough. It was coming from near one of the patrol cars. Deputy Phipps was leaning against a fender, smoking. Reed hadn't missed him until that moment.

"Did you touch anything except to take the pillow off Getts' head?"

"Nope. Who'd want to touch a dead man? Had 'nough of that in the army, too."

"Then you phoned my office?"

"Yep. That's just what I done."

"Was Getts' truck parked where it is now, back there by one of the sheds?"

"Yep."

"Okay, Clyde. We may have more questions later. If we do, we know where to find you. Don't leave the county until I tell you that you can, okay?"

"No fear of that, Sheriff. I got no place to go anyhow." Krebs left the porch, cranked up his truck, and drove away toward home.

The sheriff went back into the house to watch ME Poole while he conducted his preliminary investigation. Poole had also taken pictures before he gathered evidence and before Getts was moved. Ben lit a cigarette and waited on the porch.

The sheriff and Poole came out of the house. Poole sat down in the rickety porch swing with a deep sigh. He also set several paper evidence bags down by the swing. The contents of each paper bag were identified on the front in ink: "Pillow case and pillow," "Top sheet and bottom sheet." Poole would be sending them to the GBI lab in Atlanta for thorough examination.

"Well, from a quick examination, it looks like Getts was killed sometime last night or early this morning because rigor mortis is setting in, which happens between six and twelve hours," Poole reported. "He was shot once in the right ear, probably by a right-handed person, with what I suspect was a small-caliber handgun. The bullet exited the left side of his throat just about at the hinge on his left jaw. The entry and exit areas are too small a caliber for anything large like a thirty-eight or forty-five. I will leave you two to dig in the mattress to see if the spent slug is in there, since I'm not a ballistics expert. I'll have to get Getts to the morgue for a complete autopsy. We'll need to notify his next of kin, too. Sandy, do you know who his next of kin might be?"

"I don't rightly know. I'll ask around. Some of the long-time folks here in town might know. As far as I know, Getts was a loner with just a few acquaintances. We may have to place a notice in the personals section of our newspaper and maybe even in the Atlanta newspapers, see if any next of kin shows up."

Bates called Phipps to come help, and the four of them loaded Getts' body on a gurney and carried it out to Poole's van for transportation to the morgue.

Bates ordered his deputy to go to the office and bring back his mold-making kit. Phipps grudgingly followed orders. While the deputy was gone, Reed and Bates searched Getts' bedroom with a fine-toothed comb. They found the spent slug buried in Getts' mattress. It was a twenty-two caliber, small enough not to cause major outward damage but large enough to be lethal. Bates made a note about the bullet on a paper coin holder, dropped the slug inside, folded it over at the top and carefully put it in his button-down shirt pocket. They moved the bed away from the wall and searched carefully for a spent shell casing. Ben suggested that the killer either used a revolver, which did not eject an empty shell casing when fired or, if the weapon was an automatic which did spit out a spent casing, the killer took the casing with him when he left Getts' house.

"Poole will want to see the slug, and we'll need to get it off to the Atlanta crime lab for ballistics testing," the sheriff said. Outside again, Reed leaned against the front fender of Bates' patrol car, lit another cigarette, and pondered about what he had seen and heard. The sheriff walked through the house, checking to make sure all of the windows were locked from the inside and couldn't be opened without breaking the dingy glass that was mounted in rotting frames. Bates closed and locked the back door to the house using Getts' key, which he found thrown on a table. He attached crime scene seals and tape to the front and back doors.

Meanwhile Phipps, who had returned with two buckets, stirring sticks, and bags of plaster, was waiting outside. Before making the plaster casts, Bates took close-up pictures of the tire tracks with his camera. Then Deputy Phipps carried water from an outside spigot, which he poured into the bucket of dry plaster and stirred the mixture. They poured several casts of the tire tracks in different locations, using Popsicle sticks for reinforcement. The castings were turned over after they hardened to see if there were readable impressions.

"They look good to me," Bates said. "We'll let the lab brush off the dirt on the bottoms in case there are clues hiding there. I'd lay odds it's a truck of some kind because the tire tread is that wide-open zigzag type guys in these parts buy for driving when it rains and gets muddy on these back roads. I'll wager nearly a hundred trucks carry that tread, and we'll play hell ever identifying the vehicle that made those ruts."

Closer examination of the plaster casts showed that the rubber on one tire was chunked out near the edge of the tread like it had been gouged by a sharp rock, a piece of metal, or glass.

"That gash may make it a little easier," Reed observed. "By the looks of those other imprints in the dirt, it's the right rear tire. I suggest we're looking for a truck that is probably no bigger than a pickup, with a fairly large gouge of some sort in the right rear tire." Ben watched as the sheriff gathered soil samples from in and around the tire tracks.

They inspected Getts' truck tires carefully to see if the tread was the same as that found near the house. All four tires carried a different tread, but none matched the tire track left in the dirt near the porch. The spare tire, if Getts ever had one, was missing from his truck so it couldn't be compared with the plaster impressions. The truck cab was littered with crushed cigarette packs, beer cans, scraps of paper, food wrappers, and small hand tools. The bed was a jumble of rubbish, broken bits of lumber, and empty oil cans. Any evidence that might be among the junk would have to be checked out by someone from the GBI crime lab. Reed agreed to drive Getts' pickup downtown, where it could be impounded in a locked garage.

The trio left with Reed following behind the sheriff and his deputy in Getts' balky Chevy, which was running rough on six or seven of its eight cylinders. With a sigh of relief, Ben finally arrived, where he parked Getts' pickup in the garage behind the courthouse and locked the doors. He and the sheriff planned to check it over and dust for prints later. It was almost dark when they arrived back at the sheriff's office. As they shook hands, Reed said, "Call me at the IdaHO any hour—day or night."

"You got it," Bates replied. As he turned to go into his office, Bates said, "Before I forget to tell you, the FBI guy, Doug Williams, called again to tell me he and FEC railroad investigator Tom Kellerman will be coming to my office about ten o'clock Monday morning."

Ben assured the sheriff he would be there, too, and drove back to the motel. As he entered the parking lot, he saw Ida watching out the front window of her office. *Why is she so curious about my comings and goings?* he wondered.

Reed unlocked the door to his room, went in, and immediately crossed to the closet. Opening the closet door, he stooped down to examine his backpack. He looked carefully for the thread he had attached to the strap earlier.

As he expected, the thread was broken.

10

As usual, Reed got up early on Wednesday morning, the day of Jeremy's funeral. He turned on the shower, and as he got in the steaming water, he thought about what had happened in the past three days. *I spent half a night sleeping below a hanging boy; walked along the railroad several miles west of Flint City to the town of Button and hitchhiked back; paid for a murdered youngster's funeral expenses and met the boy's attractive mother, Carol. I bumped into the local sheriff and had a confrontation with his deputy; accompanied the sheriff to the scene of a second killing. All of this in less than seventy-two hours? No wonder I'm worn out; are my age and years riding the rails beginning to catch up with me? Naw—no way!*

After shaving and cleaning his teeth, Ben pulled on khakis, which he had hung in the shower the night before to smooth out the wrinkles. A clean shirt, no tie, sport jacket, and comfortable shoes completed his wardrobe. He wanted to look his best at the funeral home that afternoon at four o'clock when he paid his respects to the murdered boy, Jeremy Martin, and to his mother, Carol. Ben also had an appointment with the sheriff to show Bates where he had slept after arriving on the train.

When he closed the door to his motel room, he glanced at the sky and noticed storm clouds were gathering just above the southwestern horizon. He was aware people set their clocks by the arrival of afternoon showers in the spring. He hoped he would not have to dodge raindrops and slosh through puddles of water.

He drove to Sal's for breakfast. He had more questions to ask her, but she wasn't at work. After he ate, he motored to the switching yard and parked along the street. Before he picked up the sheriff, Ben wanted to be alone to study the scene of the hanging without anybody else there to interrupt his thoughts. He searched the grass in a circle well beyond the perimeter where he had been sleeping. Nothing. He stood under the oak tree where Jeremy's body had been hanging. Nothing. He even walked from the tree in a zigzag path to the switching yard tracks and down them for several hundred feet in all three directions. Nothing. Discouraged but confident he had not missed anything, he picked up Bates at his office and returned again to the grove of trees. On the way, they reviewed the facts of the Martin and Getts killings, but came up with nothing new. Ben parked on the side of the road, and they walked to the hanging tree, ducking under the crime scene tape that was still strung around the site.

"Over here where the grass is all tromped down is where I slept after getting off the train," Ben said. "You can see where I was sleeping in relation to the limb where the body was hanging. I wasn't right under him, but mighty close. I was near enough that the body was the first thing I saw when the dogs woke me up and I peeked out of my sleeping bag. If it hadn't been so dark Sunday night, I might have noticed him before I turned in."

"So you told me before."

"I just want to make sure we're both looking at the same picture—that we're both on the same page—now that we're standing at the site where the boy was hanged."

"Where he was killed, you mean," Bates corrected.

"Well, let's put it this way. Where hanging him may have contributed to his death," Ben suggested. "Either way, it was murder. Nothing less—and premeditated at that. What puzzles me is why the killers took the time to hang Martin upside down like they did. To me, it does not make sense." Then turning to the sheriff, Ben asked, "Where do you think the kid's other tennis shoe got to? He was only wearing one."

"That's a question I've been thinking on ever since we found the body Monday morning."

"And another thing. Suppose those pit marks on Martin's cheek are tiny pieces of railroad ballast? What would that tell us?" Ben searched his pockets for a match, found a folder of "gofers" and lit a cigarette. He smiled, waiting for Bates' reaction, not to his smoking but to Ben's question.

The sheriff looked at the grass, then up into the oak tree, at the nearby siding of the switching yard, then finally answered. "I would say the boy must have been somewhere along the railroad tracks at some point before he was hanged."

"I think that is a sound supposition," Reed said. "His arms and legs must have been bound up at the same time, otherwise he probably would have tried to wipe his face. That's the natural thing to do when something is stinging or burning your skin. People naturally want to get rid of whatever the cause is—a bug bite, wasp sting, or even after someone slaps your face. What do you do? You rub it."

"You're right. He could not brush off or pick off the irritants with his fingers. If he had tried to remove the pieces of rock, they would not be in his face any longer—there would be just the holes. We'll check again with Cletus after he gets the report back from the Georgia lab about what kind of material he dug out of Martin's face. It may prove to be ballast and it may not, but I will tell you one thing, it will be very interesting if the rock proves to be bits of ballast and it matches that kind the Flint River Railroad spreads along their tracks."

"Let's assume it is ballast from around here, and rather than waiting for Poole's report, we do some searching along the tracks from a little west of here to the switching yard. From there we'll look at all of the sidings and tracks going north toward Atlanta and east to Waycross."

"That sounds like a good plan, but to cover that much ground, we'll need more help. Mel and I can't search along that much track in a short period of time, and we need to get moving so none of the clues go any colder on us. I'll see if we can recruit some help from the R.O.T.C. cadets at the high school."

"Great idea. With a good, solid briefing about what we're looking for, the high school boys should be able to spot Martin's missing sneaker, assuming, that is, it was dropped there and is still there."

After their scrutiny of the oak grove, Ben dropped the sheriff off at his office. He still had more questions to ask Sal, but since she was not at the café, his questions would have to wait. He decided to pass up Sal's for lunch and instead drove to Granny's for a hamburger, cola and fries. After he ate, Ben returned to the IdaHO Motel to think about the double murders and to rest until time for Jeremy Martin's funeral.

A few minutes before four, he drove to the funeral home and grabbed a parking space as close to the building as he could in case the still-threatening rain materialized. He had a poncho in the trunk of his car if needed, but he seldom carried a bothersome umbrella, opting for the poncho instead. He left the umbrella in his motel room.

Upon entering the funeral home, a scarecrow funeral assistant dressed in black bowed slightly and forced a smile. In a whisper, he said, "This way, please," while gesturing toward the small chapel where family and friends, mostly the good citizens of Flint City, were gathering. Ben signed the visitor's book on the pedestal outside the door and entered the chapel. As Bates had predicted, the pews were almost full, so Ben had to sit closer to the front than he wanted to. Jeremy's closed coffin rested just below the altar, with enlarged photographs at the head and foot, mounted on raised stands.

Precisely at four o'clock, piped-in organ music began. Carol and an older couple Ben assumed were relatives or close friends were ushered into the chapel. She was dressed all in black and carried one white rose. She held her head erect, although her lovely face was pale and drawn, revealing the stress she was under. She gripped the elderly woman's arm. The three were seated in the first row of pews directly in front of Ben. Before taking her seat, Carol nodded toward him, and a faint smile touched her lips.

The funeral was brief, more of a memorial service with a local minister presiding. After the final prayer was offered and the organ played quietly again, Carol and the elderly couple with her were escorted out of the chapel, followed by the funeral director Granger and the preacher. Reed waited a discreet few minutes, then followed along behind the others who were leaving the chapel. He met Sheriff Bates, who had been standing at the back of the chapel, halfway up the aisle and shook hands silently.

Everyone seemed to be crowded into the vestibule to stay out of the rain, which was falling steadily. There was no sign that the rain would stop, as it poured off the awning covering the sidewalk and already formed puddles in low areas of the parking lot. Ben greeted Carol, touched her hand, and smiled in a way he hoped said, "I understand."

She did not reply verbally, but her eyes signaled she received and understood his message. Turning, she introduced the sheriff and Ben to her Aunt

Grace and Uncle George Martin, who lived in Savannah. She told them that George was her father's brother. Then she added, "They took me in and raised me like their own daughter after my parents died."

Then Carol surprised both of them by asking, "Would you and Sheriff Bates like to come by my house? My aunt and uncle and a few friends will be there for a light snack and drinks. We will be remembering Jeremy and celebrating his life." Ben didn't know about the sheriff, but in his mind he was halfway there already.

"I'd love to," Ben replied, upstaging Bates who muttered he could drop by later, but only for a few minutes. He had promised to take his wife out to dinner that evening.

"Carol, do you have your own car here?" Ben asked, knowing full well Granger had arranged to have the three of them picked up in the funeral home limousine for the service and that he would take them back to her house afterward. Her answer was what he expected to hear. "No, Mr. Granger picked up the three of us at my house, and he will take us home after the grave-side ceremony. Before we depart, I want to thank Mr. Granger for all of his kindnesses."

"I see. Then I'll follow along in my car and see you at the cemetery." He parked behind the hearse and limousine, which were already under the awning of the portico and waited in his car. He had a notion one of the things Carol wanted to talk to Mr. Granger about was Jeremy's funeral expenses. That was a relief because he did not want to be a party to their conversation for fear his face might give him away.

He waited for Carol and her uncle and aunt to come out of the building. She had removed her veil so Ben could easily read the expression on her face. A puzzled look creased her forehead and she tried to stifle the smallest hint of a smile by pursing her lips in a straight line. He wondered if she had had time to digest the news Granger had given her.

Almost on signal, the rain stopped as the burial party drove through the cemetery gates. Ben gathered with the others under the awning, and the minister delivered a brief eulogy.

Afterward, as he walked with Carol to the funeral home's limousine, she turned to him and said, "Curious thing. Mr. Granger told me someone had already paid for all of Jeremy's funeral expenses, flowers, coffin, interment, limousine, everything!" She paused to take a breath and then continued. "I don't know anybody with that kind of money or anyone else who would be—could be—that generous."

"Beats me," Ben replied with a sideways glance of pure innocence. When he opened the limousine doors for Carol and her aunt and uncle, Carol asked if he knew where she lived. He replied that he remembered because she had told him earlier her house was around the corner behind the IdaHO Motel.

"Mine is the second house down on the street," she reiterated.

Ben arrived at Carol's house where he parked his car in her driveway behind her uncle's car, which had been left there before the funeral. The rain had slacked off again, so he made a dash for her front porch. The house was ablaze with lights, and the kitchen was wall-to-wall people who had come to celebrate Jeremy Martin's life. Coffee, soda pop, and lemonade were being served. The dining room table was full of delicious smelling food, which had been brought in by neighbors and friends. Guests were munching hungrily because dinner hour was approaching and many of them had not yet eaten supper.

Ben was aware that alcoholic beverages were not usually offered, especially on these occasions, at least in many areas in the South. He had been on the wagon for two years now and did not want to return to his old nemesis— the hard liquor bottle. He sipped his soft drink, watching Carol discreetly as she tried to be cheerful and smile as she thanked everyone for coming to remember Jeremy. He marveled at how well she was holding up.

Carol's Aunt Grace and Uncle George stood nearby watching, as the latter filled Ben in on the many wonderful attractions in Savannah. George was so enthusiastic in the telling that Reed did not want to spoil his narrative by admitting he had been in the historic city many times during the past two years when he passed through riding as a hobo on rumbling freights. For another thing, he did not want the old man to know he was a drifter roaming the country by hopping railroad boxcars. Ben did not know when Sheriff Bates told Carol about his prior law enforcement career and if he had also told her about his hobo ways. Probably so, but he hoped not. She would find out eventually, but he wanted to be the one to tell her in his own way and in his own time.

And speaking of the sheriff, Bates arrived to the delight of most of those present. He was well known in Flint City and a very popular sheriff in spite of his diminutive size. As soon as Ben was able, he guided the sheriff to Uncle George so he could move away without causing offense and follow Carol, who was now in the dining room. He was amazed at how she managed a broad, if not totally convincing, smile even under stress. She was able to make everyone in the room think they were special. He decided her gentile, cultured upbringing by her aunt and uncle after her parents died had stiffened her resolve, taught her impeccable manners, and how to cope with sadness. Unless someone noticed her rough hands, it was impossible to tell this charming, graceful gazelle was responsible for overseeing huge, noisy, dangerous, and demanding looms at the Flint City carpet plant. *She really is something special,* he thought again.

Soon, but not too soon for Ben, the crowded house began to disgorge people into the street, as those who had come earlier to bolster Carol in her time of grief departed, scattering in different directions. Ben moved his car into the street so Aunt Grace and Uncle George could back their car out and drive to the Hotel Flint where they preferred to stay rather than imposing on their niece. Carol had insisted they would not be a burden to her, but the tottering old couple had their way. Only three or four women and Ben stayed behind to help clean up. He helped so the task would be completed sooner and the ladies would leave sooner.

Then it was over. Carol and Ben were left alone. They sat together on the couch in the living room, with only one small, dim lamp burning. She sat on one end of the sofa and he on the other. Carol leaned her head back on the couch and sighed deeply. She surprised Ben for the second time that day. "Sandy Bates told me you're an ex-cop from Florida, right?" He assured her that was correct. "And what's more, he said you were also a railroad detective before becoming a policeman."

Ben said he was an investigator for the Florida East Coast Railroad for fifteen years before joining the Titusville Police Department. Then he explained what a railroad detective did to earn his pay.

"That's all there is to know about you and your past?"

"That's about all there is to Benjamin Alford Reed's story up to now," he answered. He wondered if this was the right time or place to talk about his wife Mary's fatal accident, especially because Carol had suffered a similar loss of her son only three days earlier. Then again, he might not ever have a better chance to share some of the details about Mary's death. When it came time, if it ever did, the most difficult part might be trying to justify why he had not remarried. The truth was, he had not met the right woman. Until now, maybe.

That story could wait until Carol was back to normal—back on level ground. Years ago, his father had told Ben, "A Southern gentleman does not take advantage of a woman who is in mourning or recently divorced or who has suffered some other traumatic experience in her life." Sage advice, but his dad notwithstanding, Carol was very tempting.

"You know, Jeremy filled a big void in my life, and he gave me something to live for. Now he's gone." Silence. "Oh, I have a lot of friends here in Flint City, and there is always my aunt and uncle, who have asked me to move back to Savannah. But I have a good job now, and besides my roots are here, so I'm not sure moving there is the best thing for me to do." Again silence.

The silence pounded in Ben's head, finally reaching a crescendo. He had to say something, but what? Finally, "I know something about how you feel at this very moment. You see, I had the very same empty, lonesome, and lost feelings after my wife Mary was killed," he said. Carol looked at Ben and expected him to go on.

Sensing the time was right, Ben told her about the tragic automobile accident that took Mary away from him, how he was the first investigating officer on the scene, and how terrible it had been when he looked into the mangled car and realized it was his wife who had been killed by a driver who ignored a stop sign and broadsided her. He told her about his two years wandering around the country as a hobo riding the rails; how alone he felt in spite of his daughter, Lynn, and how only lately was he beginning to deal with the double-headed nightmare of loneliness and guilt.

Before he finished talking, tears began to pool inside the bottom rims of his eyes. Damn, he couldn't help it. His tears came welling up, spilling over, and running down his cheeks. As he wiped his face with the backs of his hands, Carol's eyes glazed over and she also began to cry silently. Ben handed her his handkerchief, while trying unsuccessfully to clear his eyes.

Carol slid across the couch toward Ben. She wiped away his tears with his hanky and wrapped her arms around his neck, pulling his head down so their lips would meet. Ben returned her embrace as their lips and tears mingled.

They parted but still held onto each other. She said, "Oh, Ben, I'm so sorry about your Mary." She locked her damp blue eyes on his and searched within them.

All he could manage to do was whisper, "Thanks, Carol." Among the other things he admired about her was her empathy, her ability to offer solace to him while she had her own loss to endure. "I'm sorry to have put on such a display of emotion in front of you," Ben admitted. "Grown men aren't supposed to cry. You see, Mary was my whole life, just as Jeremy was yours" He paused waiting for her to say something—anything. They sat looking at each other and tried to read what was in the other's mind. Carol nervously twisted Ben's handkerchief around her fingers.

Finally, straightening both her black dress and her resolve, she said: "I can see how much Mary means—meant to you. I do feel the same way about Jeremy. But, Ben, we must go on somehow." Then she surprised him for the third time with her wisdom and sensitivity. "Life has dealt us both a terrible hand. It's the only one we have, though, so we must play it the way we see it. Don't you agree?"

What a turnaround! Here he was a rough, tough ex-cop who thought he could handle anything and had done so many times in the past. But here he was drawing strength from someone who was willing to share her resolve and determination to take life's hard knocks without whimpering—without giving up. Ben knew Carol was right.

"You're right. I guess we've got to give life our best shot always, all ways. Maybe it's time for me to quit hopping boxcars—to quit running away. Maybe I should go back to Titusville after the sheriff and I catch the people who took your son away from you."

"You *are* going to catch him then?" she asked hopefully.

"Them, Carol, them," he corrected her gently with a smile. "You see, there had to be more than one individual involved, perhaps two or even three or more," he ventured, choosing not to explain how he arrived at that conclusion. "Yes, we'll catch them," he said with conviction. He really was not so sure how soon the killers would be apprehended, if at all, but for Carol's and Jeremy's sake, he prayed it would be certain and soon.

"It's getting late. I must be going. Thanks for inviting me to celebrate Jeremy's life and most of all just for your company. You've helped me a lot this evening, and I appreciate your sharing what you did with me," he added as he stood up to leave. He did not tell her the two reasons he had accepted her invitation to the reception after Jeremy's funeral. First, it was an opportunity for him to be near Carol again. Curious how his feelings toward her were changing. And second, he wanted to size up the people who were there to see if anyone acted uneasy about the boy's death. Unfortunately, he did not score on the second reason.

Carol rose. "I'm so glad you came. When will I see you again?"

Not *will* I see you again, but *when* will I see you again? Ben was quick to pick up on her nuance and broke into a wide smile below his crooked nose.

"How about if I telephone after you get off work tomorrow. What time will you get home from the mill?"

"My shift ends at five o'clock, so I should be home by five-thirty at the latest." Then she remembered. "Nope, wait a second. Even with all of this food from this afternoon, I still need to stop by the grocery to pick up a few things, so it'll probably be six or six-fifteen before I'm home."

"You don't have to stop by the grocers. Why don't I pick you up here around five-thirty, and we'll go out to dinner? But tomorrow night, not at Sal's." They both laughed.

As Ben turned to open the door, Carol caught hold of his coat sleeve and brushed his cheek with a light kiss. As he opened the door to leave, Carol handed his handkerchief back, which he decided to keep to remind him of her just as he had kept Mary's wedding ring on a chain around his neck.

"Thanks again for coming," she whispered.

"Four steam locomotives couldn't have kept me away." Ben noticed the sky had cleared completely and the stars were out fully when he walked to his car, cranked the engine, and drove slowly around the block to the IdaHO Motel, where he parked in his usual spot in front of the door to Number 10. He killed the engine and sat quietly for a few minutes, mulling over the day and particularly their earlier conversation that was shared on the couch after the reception. He said, "Yes, sir, she's quite a gal. Am I falling for her? Well, so what if I am—maybe it's time for me to put Mary's loss in perspective and return to being a human being. If that's what Carol is making of me, so much the better. I like it!"

He locked the car and dug into his pants pocket for the room key. Distracted by his thoughts of Carol, he unlocked the door and pushed it open. Then he froze.

Chzzz—chuuzz—chzzz! The unmistakable sound warned Ben that somewhere in the dark room was a coiled rattlesnake waiting to strike!

11

H AIR STOOD UP ON THE BACK OF Reed's neck as he fought to control his near panic! His years of experience dealing with emergencies of all kinds taught him to remain calm in dangerous situations. Ben had enough presence of mind to settle himself down, back out of the door slowly—ever so slowly—shutting it securely behind him. He leaned against the motel wall and lit a cigarette, his hands shaking slightly from the close encounter with possible death. Inhaling deep puffs, he blew the smoke out, wondering how best to deal with this threat aimed directly at him. For threat it was. Ben thought he knew why the rattler was planted in his room. He got the message loud and clear: *Don't stick your crooked nose into Flint City's business!* The why was evident, the who wasn't. Not yet anyway.

How to remove the dangerous reptile from his dark room without causing a ruckus and, more importantly, avoid getting bit was another unanswered question. He considered getting his gun out of the trunk of his car, barely cracking the door, then reaching carefully into the room to turn on the light. If he was lucky, he would see the snake in time and shoot it before it could strike. There were three problems with this solution. First, whoever put the snake in his room in the first place was probably aware there was not an overhead light in the room and may have pulled out all of the cords on the lamps, so flipping on the switch by the door did not necessarily mean the room would be lighted. Second, even if the lights came on, he only had a fifty-fifty chance of seeing the snake before it saw him and struck. Not good enough odds. And third, if he did see the rattler first, shooting it would make such a loud noise the sound of the report would surely arouse Pug and Ida, if not the whole neighborhood. Taking another long drag on his cigarette, Ben realized he must find some safe way to deal with the snake, or did he? He had been in tighter situations than this and survived. Slowly a solution formed in his mind.

From where he was standing, Ben couldn't be seen from the motel office. He snuffed out his cigarette in the parking lot gravel and, leaving his car parked in front of Room 10, he eased back into the darkness and slipped quietly away from the motel. He felt as if two sets of eyes in the dark motel office were watching and waiting for some kind of ruckus when the rattlesnake struck its intended victim. He walked the long way around into downtown Flint City and took a room for the night at Hotel Nagel rather than the Flint because, although he liked Carol's aunt and uncle, he did not want to bump into them and have to explain why he was not staying the night at the IdaHO Motel. Of course, Ben didn't have luggage, but the night clerk did not seem to notice or, if he did, to give a damn. He would have to sleep in his underwear, but that was not a problem. He had done so many times before.

Just before daybreak on Thursday, a gang of wailing banshees invaded Reed's subconscious. The sound of sirens approaching from a block away managed to scream Ben into wakefulness. Aroused, he tried to unwind the cobwebs woven between the rafters in his confused head. What the hell! What's that sound? Where was he? In a moment, the cotton candy in his brain began to dissolve as he recognized he was in a room at Hotel Nagel.

Ben dressed quickly, combed his hair, and headed for the elevator. He rushed out the front doors and ran in the direction where he thought the sirens were coming from. Sheriff Bates' patrol car was sliding to a stop in the parking lot in front of the IdaHO Motel office, with an ambulance riding his back bumper. Ben arrived on the scene, breathless after running several blocks through downtown.

"Ben, I'm glad you're here!" Bates shouted. "Come in the office. Ida called to tell me Pug has been bitten by a rattlesnake and he's about to go into shock!" They pushed passed Ida Wainright, who was standing with the office door open. It wasn't easy to squeeze past her ample figure, but they managed. On their heels were the ambulance driver with a folded-up stretcher and hospital staff doctor lugging his medical emergency kit.

Pug was slouched in a wicker chair, pale, wild-eyed, and in danger of slipping into unconsciousness. Bates and Reed stayed out of the way while the doctor injected antivenin into one of Pug's arms. After the injection, the doctor helped put Pug on the unfolded stretcher and hustle him to their waiting ambulance. On the way out the door, the doctor told Ida that he felt they had arrived in time and that Pug should recover because rattler bites are seldom fatal as long as the victim receives the proper medical treatment immediately.

Pug was mumbling something about seeing a snake just as it struck him. "Big around as a stove pipe," he muttered. "No warning, but I seen for sure it was a rattlesnake that bit me." As he was helped into the back of the ambulance, he moaned again and said that the snake didn't rattle until *after* it bit him. "Just clamped his fangs into my leg, and it hurt like hell." Pug was nearly delirious. The doctor said he would sit with Pug in the back of the ambulance to monitor his pulse and breathing. As the ambulance pulled out of the parking lot, the driver told Sheriff Bates that the doctor probably would admit Pug to the hospital at least for one night in order to keep him under observation.

Just before shutting the ambulance door, the staff doctor asked Ida if she was going to ride with her husband to the hospital.

"Not likely. Someone has to stay around to run this here establishment. There's only the two of us, ya know. Anyway, I'll have to finish his chores on account of Pug quit sweepin' the walkways and emptyin' trash after that snake bit him," Ida whined, thinking selfishly about herself rather than poor scared and hurting-like-hell Pug.

"Two murders and now a sneak snake attack." Bates launched into a rampage, directing his outrage at the parking lot and motel building. "What's happening in Flint City all of a sudden? Seems all hell's broken loose, for sure! We've prided ourselves in being a quiet, rural, friendly Southern town. But now I don't know." Taking off his hat, the sheriff wiped the inside hatband then his forehead with a handkerchief, although it was still early on a cool spring morning.

After Sandy Bates calmed down, Ben turned to him and put his hand on the sheriff's shoulder. "I know where the snake is, or was. It was in my room last night. I think Pug must have gone into my room early this morning, but I don't know why. That rattler may still be in my room and it may not."

Bates interrupted, "I'd forgotten Room 10 is yours." The questions tumbled out like a slot machine paying off quarters. "Didn't you sleep here last night? Where was the rattler when you went to your room? How come it didn't bite you? Who put the snake in your room? Why? How come old Pug opened the door to your room so early?" The sheriff's asking the right questions confirmed Ben's belief about him knowing how to do his job.

As they walked toward his motel room, Ben turned to the sheriff. "I think I can answer all of your questions except one or two. The rattlesnake was put in my room by someone sometime late in the afternoon, obviously while I was out. The snake didn't have a chance to strike me because when I unlocked the door and took a step into my room, unlike with Pug, it warned me with a loud, long rattle. It must have been asleep or groggy and didn't sing out for Pug." Ben lit a cigarette, his first of the day, and continued. "I look forward to asking Pug if he was in my room earlier this morning to clean up and how he knew I was not in there asleep unless he knocked and I didn't answer the door. Someone has been in my room before. The thought has occurred to me that perhaps the person or persons who hoped the snake would bite me would then return to see if I was lying dead on the floor. Pug took the venom intended for me, although I don't think he's the one who wanted me dead."

Ben paused to collect his thoughts then went on. "In answer to your most important question, I don't know who put the rattler in my room or why, but I'm sure as hell going to find out if I have to hang around in Flint City for a year! And in answer to another one of your questions, no, I didn't stay at the motel last night. After the snake threatened me, and I couldn't see how I could deal with it in the dark without causing a commotion or getting bit, I shut and locked the door, then walked downtown to Hotel Nagel, where I spent the night."

They walked to Room 10, their boots crunching on the graveled parking lot. Ben unlocked the door and then cautiously opened it. No rattlesnake warned them to stay out. They entered and looked carefully under the small table and chairs, the knee-hole dresser, and end tables, but they gave the bed a wide berth. Bates looked in the closet and kicked Ben's backpack with the toe of his boot, trying to arouse the rattlesnake if he was behind it. No snake there. Nor was it in the bathroom. Bates suggested to Ben that the sheriff go to his car and fetch a flashlight before they looked under the bed. When he returned, Bates made sure the rattler wasn't under the bed by shining his powerful flashlight under the side that was away from the wall.

"Seems it's gone," Bates observed, getting back to his feet. "Pug must have panicked when the snake struck him, and his only thought was to get away and go to the office so Ida could help him. Mostly, he just wanted desperately to get out of your room, I expect. I agree with you that Pug didn't put the snake in your room, or he would have been watching out for it and not gotten bit because he would know it was in here."

The sheriff walked back to his patrol car and keyed his radio to call Deputy Phipps and order him to hustle on down to the IdaHO Motel to search for the snake around the outside of the building. Bates also ordered the deputy to start knocking on doors near the motel to tell residents to watch out for a rattlesnake that may be hiding in their yards. Turning back to Ben he said, "We'll be damn lucky if someone else doesn't get bit before it's caught."

Reed and Bates stood looking at each other, thinking. Ben glanced up at the sky while lighting his second cigarette of the day. The morning coolness was beginning to surrender to the Georgia sun. Puffy white clouds were hanging like cotton balls ripe for picking in a field of deep, blue sky. It was another one of those perfect spring days in South Georgia if a person only had time to kick back and enjoy it.

"By the way, have you arranged with the Flint City High School principal for the R.O.T.C. class to meet us down by the switching yard?" Ben asked. "I hope they can come after their last class this afternoon to help us search for Jeremy's missing sneaker. Perhaps the principal will consider having them work with us as an official field trip. Jeremy was hanging in a tree down there by the tracks, so I figure that's the most logical place to start hunting for his shoe."

"I phoned him yesterday, and he confirmed they're coming this afternoon. A lot of them knew Jeremy and will be anxious to help in the search. Surely they can bring the cadets down in a school bus. Their R.O.T.C. class is around twenty youngsters—give or take one or two—who should be mature enough to be responsible and follow orders. Twenty pairs of eyes ought to be enough to do a thorough search up and down the tracks for a mile or so in each direction and around the yard, don't you think?"

"That'll probably be plenty, but we don't want too many. We don't need a bunch of eager boys running over each other or making a game out of what's serious business."

"No, we sure don't."

"You will be briefing them when they get off the bus?"

"Sure. I'll get their attention if I have to knock their heads together." Bates laughed. "These R.O.T.C. cadets seem to be a little more serious about life than most kids do at their age. I've worked with them before on some projects, and they're a real fine bunch of young men."

Both men walked back to the motel lobby to console Ida, if she needed consolation. Bates assured her again that Pug would recover—that he would survive the snake bite just fine and would be fit as a fiddle in a couple of days. He might have to limp around some while cleaning the rooms and carrying out the trash, but once the poison was out of his system, he'd be his old self again. Ida sat at her desk petting her cat, cigarette smoke swirling around her head like a forest fire. A pile of crushed cigarettes overflowed the ashtray on her desk, while another lighted one dangled from her painted lips. Ben wondered what else she had on her desk underneath all that clutter. Cigar butts? Betting slips? Last week's mail? A half-eaten pizza? A handgun?

Looking at Bates while she tried to stifle a cough, she said, "If you say so, Sandy. I hope he'll be back here on the job tomorrow. Lord knows, I got all I can handle around here and more. You don't know how much there is to do," she complained. Both men wondered how much she really had to do with only one room rented and that to Reed. Ben glanced at the motel room key box; the key to Room 3 was back on its hook. Curious.

"Now, now, Ida, quit feeling sorry for yourself. You ought to be thankful we got a hospital of sorts close by to take care of ol' Pug. What if he had to be hauled all the way up to Macon or Valdosta or somewhere like that? Like as not, he would have expired from the venom along the way, being such a distance and all." He told her he and Ben had to go because they had a lot of work to do to solve two murders and the rattlesnake business.

Bates and Reed left. The sheriff headed back to his office, while Ben walked through the parking lot to his motel room. After having another look around his room to make absolutely sure the rattler was gone, he shaved, showered, and put on fresh khakis and a matching shirt. Although he had just talked to Lynn the day before, he sat down on the edge of the bed and dialed her office number at Canaveral.

"Port Canaveral, good morning, this is Sue, how may I direct your call?"

"May I speak to Lynn Reed, please? This is her dad."

"Just a moment, please, I'll transfer you to her extension."

"Hey, Daddy. You just called me yesterday—is something wrong? Are you okay? Have you and the sheriff solved the murder already?"

"I'll fill you in in a moment, but first how are you doing?"

"Oh, about the same. Working hard, swimming some, playing a little tennis when I'm not at work. I miss you terribly, Daddy." Lynn's voice was barely above a whisper. Ben could tell she was trying to choke back tears.

"I miss you too, baby. I still hope to be home soon, but I may be hung up here longer than I had expected. I can't leave here in good conscience until I see these two murders solved and the perpetrators brought to justice. You of all people know how I am about people being wronged."

He took a couple of deep breaths then said, "I didn't tell you yesterday, but I'm in Flint City, the small town in South Georgia I told you about. I'm staying at the IdaHO Motel." He gave her the telephone number at the motel and at the sheriff's office in case she needed to reach him.

"You're not in any danger, are you?" Lynn asked. As always she was very perceptive. Ben had not mentioned the rattlesnake incident. *Did she deduce he was in some danger?* he wondered. *How could she possibly know only from hearing his voice?* He thought he had hidden any uncertainty in his voice.

"No, no, honey. I'm fine, really. I really called to tell you I met the murdered boy's mother; her name is Carol Martin, and she's the first woman I've been attracted to since we lost your mother." He described Carol in some detail, hoping against hope he was not overdoing it. Primarily, he wanted Lynn to know about Carol and how he was beginning to feel about her.

"Carol sounds like a really neat person," Lynn said, much to Ben's relief. "I'm so happy you have met someone nice. I truly hope your relationship makes you happy."

"Yes, I'm happier now than I've been for a long, long time."

"Speaking of time, it has been, how long—over two years now—since you've been gone, and I miss you something awful. Grandma is fine. She asked me to give you her love when we talked again."

"Be sure to tell Mom that I hope to see both of you before too much longer, and I send a boxcar load of love to her and to you." She returned his love, and they hung up. He was glad he had not mentioned Pug's rattler bite. Lynn would just worry.

Ben decided to eat a late breakfast at Sal's again. The food was plain but filling. He drove downtown and parked across Bond Street from the café. A light breeze was blowing in from the southwest and might bring some more rain later in the day. He noticed as he entered Sal's that Penny was waiting tables. She followed him to his customary back booth, carrying a pot of coffee. She turned Ben's mug right-side up and filled it to the brim.

"Hey, you're near 'bouts a regular in here, ain't ya?" She grinned, pulling her pencil from behind one ear and retrieving an order pad from the front pocket in her apron.

"Like a bad penny, Penny." Ben smiled back and searched the menu that was already on the table for something that sounded good. He had totally forgotten breakfast when he ran from the Hotel Nagel to the IdaHO earlier in the morning. Was it only this morning, he wondered? It seemed like a year ago. He ordered number two: bacon and eggs with toast, grits, and coffee. Penny scribbled his order on her pad, then swished away toward the kitchen. She returned with his order, poured him another mug of coffee from the pot, and sashayed away again.

When he looked up from the table, someone was sliding into the other side of the booth. It was Sal. A frown, unusual for her, wrinkled her forehead, showing she had something other than the weather or idle gossip on her mind.

"Ben, you and Sandy Bates are looking into these killings, right?" she asked.

"Yep."

"Got very far along yet?"

"Nope."

"Wanta know what my idea is?"

"Yep."

"Well, suppose somebody around here has been doing something they got no business doing, and supposing—just supposing, you understand—that whoever hanged Jeremy Martin also killed Sherman Getts. That's what I'm thinking."

"What makes you think that?"

"Well, I see and hear about things going on in this town."

"For instance?"

"Well, like vehicles driving around after dark with only their parking lights on, and one of the sheriff's cars cruising up and down streets early of a morning before daylight."

"Beyond the sheriff's car, you got any descriptions you'd like to share with me?"

"Not right off. But if you want to know what I think, I have an idea the Martin kid being hanged the way he was sure wasn't a high school prank. It might have been a warning for someone. That's what I think, anyway," she whispered.

"What kind of warning would that be?"

"Well, suppose Jeremy's hanging and the Getts killing were both in revenge for something that happened earlier?" Sal whispered. Ben had to lean forward on his elbows to hear what she was saying.

Ben smiled at her. "Frankly, that angle was in the back of my mind, although I can't figure out who would want to take revenge on a teenage kid." He and the sheriff already had the *means,* and if Sal's theory was right and revenge was the *motive,* then only the *opportunity* factor of the three "m.o.m." ingredients needed to be figured out. No doubt about it, he would have to think more about Sal's ideas.

"Think on it, Ben," she suggested.

"You bet I will," he promised.

Sal returned to the front counter to ring up other customers' meal tickets. Ben finished his breakfast, drank the rest of his now-cold coffee, and stood in line to pay. When his turn came, he said, "Sal, you may just have something in your ideas. But better keep your thoughts between us two, okay? I'll share what you told me with Sandy."

As she handed back his change, she said, "Sure, Ben, mum's the word." Ben hoped she would not also share her *supposes* with others around town, although she was known as the town crier when it came to spreading news . . . or rumors. Even if she did broadcast her ideas around Flint City, maybe, just maybe, her suppositions would help flush out a suspect or two. He had witnessed many times before in numerous cases when loose talk had stampeded suspects, causing them to panic and make mistakes that later proved to be their downfall. Maybe it would happen again.

Deputy Phipps was in his office reading the morning newspaper when Ben arrived looking for Sandy Bates. The sheriff was not in, and Reed would be damned if he would ask Phipps where he was. He greeted the deputy with a smile and got a surly "hey" in return. Ben sat down in a rickety chair beside the sheriff's desk, crossed his legs, and reviewed some entries he had jotted down in his notebook about the two murders.

Sheriff Bates' car pulled into the parking lot. "Hey, Ben. I dropped by the high school on the way back from breakfast and talked to the principal. It's all set. He will have the R.O.T.C. troop at the rail yard after their last class this afternoon. That will be around two-thirty. Will you be ready to head down there after a bit? We can go a little early and maybe talk to the yardmaster while we do some looking on our own before the troops arrive and tromp all over the place. In the meantime, we can review what we know about these two cases, or one case if they're related."

The two discussed Jeremy's hanging and Getts' murder. Ben told the sheriff about his conversation with Sal and what her ideas were about the murders. They explored ways in which the two crimes might be related. Were the murders only coincidences? They had happened only a couple of days apart. Was that meaningful? Who had reasons to hang Jeremy Martin? What would Poole's autopsy show or confirm? Who was driving the truck that was parked behind Getts' house unless it was Getts himself? Why was Getts killed? Who put the rattlesnake in Ben's room and why? Had they missed some clues that were important to their investigation? Meanwhile, Deputy Phipps kept up the pretense of reading his newspaper, but his attention was obviously directed at their conversation, which lasted until after noon.

"Mel, go grab some lunch, then hurry back to hold down the fort while Reed and I go to grab a snack and meet the high school cadets who are helping us look for the Martin kid's missing sneaker," the sheriff ordered. Phipps nodded, tossed his newspaper on the corner of the sheriff's desk, and slouched out the door to his car for lunch.

When the deputy returned over an hour later, Bates retrieved Jeremy's sneaker from the evidence bag. He and Ben got into his patrol car and stopped at Granny's drive-thru for hamburgers and colas. The sheriff then drove to the rail yard, where he parked near the yardmaster's hut beside the tracks. They ate their hamburgers in the car. The yardmaster wasn't in his shanty. No trains were due within the next couple of hours, and he only had to report when one was expected to arrive. They needed to interview the yardmaster, but that would have to wait until after the search was completed. If the sneaker was not located along the railroad tracks, they might not need to question him anyway.

Bates moved his squad car to another location in the yard. After he stopped, the two of them got out, leaned against the hood, and looked back down the road in the direction of the school house. Ben lit up a cigarette.

"Here's where we're to meet the high school cadets," Bates said. "In fact, I think I hear their bus coming now."

The bright yellow school bus drove slowly into the yard, where the driver parked alongside the sheriff's car. Before Bates could board the bus to brief the cadets, the front door swished open, and a stream of teenagers looking sharp in their dress uniforms began to flow out like green water from a broken main. Twenty eager faces smartly formed in military style in two ranks of ten and stood at attention in front of their bus. Their instructor, a tall, braced-up and stern-faced officer wearing captain's bars, greeted the two waiting investigators.

"Wilson. *Captain* Wilson, at your service!" All very proper and more than a little pompous. Wilson had a big nose, no chin, thin lips, ramrod posture, and wore a highly starched and unwrinkled uniform and a matching, billed military-style cap. He looked like a staunch British officer. Indeed. Ben expected the captain to salute and was surprised he was not also sporting a monocle in one eye. No, monocles were German, not English. No doubt the students in his troop were all well-trained and disciplined. They had better be!

When Ben introduced himself, the captain looked at him as if he was a Martian. Bates needed no introduction, but he caught the expression on the captain's face and thought he should clarify who Reed was by saying he was from Florida after all, not Mars. The captain did not understand the remark. "Mr. Reed is here helping us out with the murder investigations." Bates told the captain he would take only a couple of minutes to brief his troops about what they were expected do.

"Attention! Dress right, dress!" Wilson shouted in a gruff, authoritative voice. His command brought immediate silence, except for some shuffling feet that scuffed the ballast as twenty youngsters held out their arms first to the side then the front to measure the correct space between each other. They looked like an experienced military unit about to be reviewed by their commanding officer. "Now listen up!" As if they had an alternative.

After the shuffling feet stopped and the boys looked up at Bates, he stepped in front of the ranks and told them why they were there and what he wanted them to do. "You're here to help us find Jeremy Martin's missing sneaker that is the mate to this one. Many of you knew Jeremy personally, and I am sure you are as anxious as we are to help discover why he died the way he did. We will be dividing you up into five squads of four each. One squad of four will walk down the tracks to the west, two men on each side of the main railroad line. Another squad will be walking north, and one will go east along the main lines. The rest of you will cover all of these sidings both ways from where they branch off from the main line to the place where they intersect again. Any questions so far?" Bates asked.

The stern look on Captain Wilson's face when he glared up and down the ranks signaled to the youngsters that not one of them should say a word.

"Okay, then." Bates continued, "We're looking for a sneaker just like this one." He held Jeremy's sneaker up again for the entire troop to see and then handed it to the first man in the front rank. "Here, pass this through your ranks. Everyone take a good look at it." He paused while the shoe was handed up and down the front and back ranks. Taking the sneaker back from the last cadet, he said, "Whichever squad finds the shoe, don't pick it up! Hear me, don't touch it! Stay away from it! Don't even go near it, except to see if you think it matches this one. You are unlikely to find another sneaker or tennis shoe similar to it along the tracks, but if you do find a shoe of any kind, and I repeat *of any kind,* send one of your squad members back here immediately to report to me and to your captain. You got that? Any questions?" he asked again. Silence.

Looking first at their captain and seeing him nod, the kids responded in unison, a loud *"Yes, sir!"*

Captain Wilson ordered the troop to count off in squads of four. Then Bates selected squads and assigned each team to their search areas. Nobody moved until Captain Wilson shouted "Dismissed!" The cadets broke up, silently heading for their respective areas to tackle their assignments.

Forty-five minutes later, one of the cadets raced up, flushed and excited, to where Sheriff Bates, Ben Reed, and Captain Wilson were waiting.

He saluted and reported breathlessly, "Sirs! I think we found the shoe, sirs!"

12

GOOD MAN. YOU DIDN'T TOUCH THE sneaker, right?" Bates asked the R.O.T.C. cadet.

The boy panted. "No, we didn't. We surrounded it, but nobody touched it, just like you told us not to."

Sheriff Bates reached into the back seat of his patrol car to grab his camera and Jeremy's other shoe he had put there after showing it to the students. "Okay, young soldier, lead on!"

The cadet's chest swelled with pride as he led the way, with Bates, Reed, and Wilson following close behind. He led them down one of the sidings running east from the main line toward Waycross and Florida. Flint River Railroad used the siding when it shuffled freight cars for later pick-up by another train. The other three cadets stood in a circle a half mile down the siding from the yardmaster's shanty.

The trio snapped to attention when the investigators and their captain approached. "Well done, men," Sheriff Bates commended them in a loud voice. He and Ben stooped down to look more closely at the sneaker lying by the tracks not far from the switch stand.

"Ben, it looks like a perfect match to me," Bates observed. "What do you think?"

"Yes, they seem to match up. Little doubt this sneaker also belonged to Jeremy Martin."

Without touching the shoe, Bates pointed out several similarities: style, color, and manufacturer. "We'll have to check the size and any signs of identical wear patterns on the sole after we pick it up, but I'll lay you two to one we'll find they are identical in every way. With both sneakers, the right one he was wearing when we found him hanging and now this left

93

one, we may be able to reconstruct what might have happened to Jeremy on the night he was killed," Bates said.

"Perhaps. But I think it may be best not to discuss any possibilities or probabilities here in front of the troops."

"I hadn't planned to."

Bates said he wanted to take photographs of the shoe before anyone touched it. He asked the cadets to move away while he snapped pictures from several angles. Then he placed the shoe Jeremy was wearing, tagged as evidence, next to the one lying by the tracks and shot more photos of the two together. There was even less doubt the shoes were a matching pair when laid side by side. He tagged the second sneaker and marked the date, time, and place where it was found and slipped it into a brown bag. He initialed the tag and asked Reed to do the same.

"Captain Wilson, let's go back to your bus," Ben urged. He suggested the captain might send these four cadets down the tracks to recall the other three squads.

Back at the bus, Bates waited for the other youngsters to return so he could thank all of them for their help. He and Ben shook hands with Wilson and thanked him warmly again for his and his troop's assistance.

"Now, it may take us some time, but I think we better split up and take a good look up and down these sidings for a ways to see if we come across anything else that might be connected to Jeremy's death," the sheriff suggested. He had thought of asking the cadets to help, but even with some instruction about what to look for, their lack of experience in crime detection might cause them to overlook a vital piece of evidence.

They walked in different directions down the tracks, searching the ground for anything that might be linked to the teenager's murder. Ben wondered why the Martin kid's left shoe was laying out here in the switching yard. He thought to himself, *Could be Jeremy was killed out here by the tracks, but we haven't found blood or buttons or any other shreds of clothing that indicate he was struggling when he was attacked. All we have is the shoe.*

When the two joined up again, Ben pushed ballast around with the toe of his boot and reported he hadn't seen anything yet. He said there likely had been a lot of foot traffic along the path beside the tracks since the murder probably occurred, either late Sunday night or very early Monday morning. "Any traces of blood, unless it was a lot, chances are would have been worked into the ballast and dirt by now, I would imagine," Ben said. "For the sake of argument, let's suppose whoever killed Jeremy surprised him near where we found the shoe, ran him down, then tied him up in their truck and carried him in their vehicle to the grove of trees and hanged him by his heels. Obviously, he was still alive and able to walk when he entered the yard but, apparently, not able to move freely or leave on his own. He sure wouldn't have left one shoe behind." Sheriff Bates remained silent, waiting for Ben to continue. After a pause, Ben kicked more ballast around and said, "I doubt Jeremy would try to walk very far on these rough sharp stones without both shoes on. Then again, it could have fallen off. The laces aren't untied, but they are loose enough."

They discussed what the chances were for a loose shoe to come off unnoticed during a struggle, assuming there had been a struggle in the first place. They also were curious about how someone, or perhaps two people, could tie him up and carry him away in their car or pickup truck without noticing Jeremy had lost one of his tennis shoes. Bates said it must have been somebody who was mighty stupid, dim-witted, or scared and in a big hurry to take off. Then, too, it could have been too dark to see his shoe come off.

Ben picked up on Bates' remarks. "It sure looks like the railroad is tied to Martin's killing somehow. All we have to do now is figure out how."

After their search along the tracks had turned up no more clues, Bates returned to the marker he had left where Jeremy's sneaker was found and took several photographs, focusing up and down the siding in both directions. As they walked slowly back to the patrol car, Ben shook his head and glanced at the sheriff. He reminded Bates they needed to catch up with the railroad yardmaster as soon as possible because he may have seen or heard something on the night Jeremy was allegedly abducted and hanged.

Bates replied that the yardmaster was shy and a little closed-mouthed. "Could be that's why he's good at his job. He has only one helper and rarely talks to other people except when freights come through, and then only when they're switching cars to be set out." Then after a pause to cough, "I doubt he ever says two words to the engineers or brakemen. If he can get by with a wave of his hand after receiving or passing along train orders, that's good enough for him."

"Has he been with the railroad very long?"

"Forever. Last name is Corey. I don't even know his first name. He's clean. I never had an occasion to pull him in or lay a charge on him. Not even speeding tickets that I know about, and I haven't been called to his house for any kind of domestic dispute either. Appears to me he's a quiet soul and a solid citizen who never misses his shifts at the yard and who doesn't cause trouble. He takes care of the railroad's business here in Flint City, and I've seen in the local newspaper where he has received several awards over the years for his outstanding work."

Ben mulled over what the sheriff had said about Corey. *If he's as clean as Bates thinks, then there's probably no reason to suspect him of aiding and abetting in the killing of Jeremy Martin,* Reed thought. *But then again . . .*

After walking a little further along, Ben said, "Another thing we need to do is drop by the hospital to see how Pug is getting along."

The two men slid into the front seat of the patrol car. The sheriff cranked up the engine and drove slowly along toward the hospital. Neither man spoke until they had parked in one of the slots reserved for law enforcement vehicles in the parking lot. The sun was playing hide-n-seek with boiling gray clouds, heavy with spring rain that was building up in the southwest.

As he got out of the patrol car, Ben said half to himself that it would be interesting to know how a fellow named Bertram Wainright got the name "Pug." They entered the hospital, and Bates asked the lady in pink at the information desk what Wainright's room number was. She told them he was in Room 304. The elevator took them to the third floor, and after spotting room direction signs, they walked down a hall where they found Pug's room and stepped inside.

Pug appeared to be asleep. The two visitors quietly backed out the door without disturbing him, and they retreated back down the hall to the nearest nursing station, where Bates asked a nurse about Pug's condition.

"Oh, he's fine," the busy but patient nurse assured them. "I think he's sleeping just now, but if you want to visit with him, I can wake him up," she offered.

Bates was quick to assure her they didn't want to disturb his beauty rest. He told the nurse jokingly that anyone who looks like Bertram Wainright probably needed all the rest he could get. "So the old rattler didn't do him too much harm," Bates added.

"No. As soon as he arrived in the ambulance, we checked on his tolerance to the antivenin the doctor gave him, and he is reacting positively to the injection. We're keeping him overnight, though, just to make sure all of his vitals are back to normal before we discharge him, probably in the morning. Mr. Wainright will be fine, except he'll have a large ugly bruise in and around the area where the snake struck him, and his tissue will no doubt die there, as well. But that's to be expected in these snakebite cases," the nurse said, smiling in an effort to reassure the two men even further. They thanked her and left the hospital, relieved that Pug should recover.

The two men returned to Bates' patrol car, got in, and drove away toward the sheriff's office. Neither commented on Pug's condition, except to say they were pleased he would be okay. As they parked in the sheriff's parking lot, Bates asked Ben if he had talked to Carol yet about the details of Jeremy's death.

"Not really, Sheriff. We've touched on Jeremy briefly, but I've been delaying that task until she's gotten over the initial shock and better able to talk about it. I hope to broach it with her sometime over this weekend. I'm taking her out to dinner tonight, but I'm not sure then will be the time or place to open such a painful subject. It may still be too soon, then again, maybe not. I'll have to see how the evening goes."

A barely noticeable smile crossed Bates' lips as he shook his head in agreement. "I think you've been wise to wait a little longer. You sure don't want to turn her off by coming at her too soon," the sheriff cautioned. Ben didn't see Bates' smile, so he had no way of knowing what was hiding behind it. The sheriff was thinking that Ben was beginning to come on mighty sweet with Carol.

Ben headed for his rental Ford. As he opened the door, he turned to the sheriff, who was about to enter his office, and asked, "Think you can catch up with yardmaster Corey and question him about what he may have heard or saw the night Martin was assaulted in the freight yard?"

Bates replied that he would do his best.

Reed started his car and headed back to the IdaHO Motel. He figured Carol Martin would be home from work by the time he got there. It was after five-thirty. He parked, unlocked the door, and entered his room. No snake greeted him this time. He sat on the edge of the bed, picked up the telephone, and dialed Carol's number.

"Hello."

"Hi, Carol. It's me, Ben, how are you?"

"Well, okay under the circumstances. I was hoping this call would be from you," she said in a voice close to choking up. "Maybe I shouldn't have gone back to work at the mill so soon. I had a really hard day today. We had a loom go down, and I was asked to help the technicians get it back on line. Those looms are getting so old they need to be replaced because there seems always to be something wrong with one of them."

"Perhaps you shouldn't be working at all. From what I hear you saying, your frustration at work is being magnified by your loss." After a pause, "Why don't you take some time off? I'm sure your boss would understand and agree you need some down time to put your life back together. If you want, I'll go talk to him."

"I'm okay, Ben, really. The boss gave me tomorrow morning off and besides the work keeps me busy, even if it is drudgery keeping those darn looms on line. At least my mind is somewhere else for most of the day, you know. You have to stay focused or you could get hurt . . ." Her voice trailed off and there was another pause.

After a moment, "Carol, we can call off dinner tonight if you're too stressed out or tired. If you want to postpone our date, please say so. I'll understand."

"Oh, no, Ben, I'm not that tired or upset and I can rest up tomorrow morning. I shouldn't have said anything about that old loom breaking down. Forgive me for complaining, alright?"

"Hey, that's okay. I have broad shoulders, so any time you need one or both of them to lean on, they're at your disposal."

"Thanks for understanding. But there's another thing I have to tell you."

"And that is?"

"Well, you'll have to understand and forgive me if I burst into tears without any warning while we're having dinner. I cried a couple of times while we were under the loom banging on the gears and levers, but it was so noisy my coworkers didn't hear, I don't think."

Silently, Ben promised himself that he would take it slow and easy with Carol, out of respect and a feeling that she was vulnerable. "If it's not rushing you to change, what about picking you up at seven-thirty, that's about two hours from now?" Ben asked.

"Plenty of time," she replied.

Ben showered, scraped off his five o'clock shadow, applied some after shave, and dressed casually in khakis, a white shirt open at the collar and no tie. A dark blue blazer topped his wardrobe. On his feet, he put casual tan leather moccasins on over brown socks. As he dressed, Ben noticed he needed a haircut and hoped Carol wouldn't see it. He left his motel room, locked the door behind him, and drove around the block behind the motel to Carol's house. He parked in her driveway and knocked on her front door at seven-thirty on the dot.

A blue angel opened the door. Carol was dressed in a shimmering blue sheath dress that looked like she had been poured into it. Around her neck was a single strand of glowing white pearls. Her hair was up, swept back and held by a small Spanish-style comb. Each ear was adorned with matching pearl earrings. Her long, graceful legs were hugged by blue stockings that matched her dress, and she had put on blue pumps with just a touch of white to highlight her pearls. When she opened the screen door and hugged Ben, he noticed a slight scent obviously sent from heaven. Perfect.

"Hi, Ben," the angel greeted him with a wide smile. "Please come in. I've poured us each a small glass of white wine that we can sip before leaving for dinner. Okay?"

Ben felt he had dressed far too casually and was a little embarrassed. But his embarrassment was soon erased by an overwhelming feeling that he would not hesitate to do anything Carol might ask, including jumping off the Empire State Building. "Sure, Carol," he stuttered. "We have the entire evening before us, and I have a notion the restaurant will hold our reservations until we show up. If they don't, well, we'll just take our appetites somewhere else."

Although he hadn't had a drink in two years, Ben couldn't resist sharing a quiet, intimate moment over a glass of wine with this lovely lady. The thought struck him like thunder that it wouldn't be all that hard to spend more than an evening with her. They sat down close together on the living room couch as she handed Ben a glass of chilled golden Chardonnay. Holding up her glass toward his, Carol offered, "Cheers."

"Skol," he replied, as they clinked their wine glasses. After a small sip and a smile, he said, "You're exceptionally beautiful tonight." As soon as he had said it, Ben was afraid he might have hurt Carol's feelings because she always looked beautiful, not just tonight. Apparently, she didn't take offense. To be sure, Ben added, "What I meant to say is, you are lovely always, not just tonight."

"Thank you," Carol answered with a coy smile. "I know what you meant. A gal like me always likes to be complimented, even if it's just for one night. I did so want to look nice for you, Ben, and I guess I succeeded."

"Indeed, you did." *How good to see her smile after all she has been through,* Ben thought. So he decided to tell her what he had been thinking about.

They finished their wine and left for the restaurant. Carol locked her door while Ben waited by the open car door. "Thank you, kind sir," she teased, smiling again. He noticed her smile again, and it pleased him.

He walked around to the driver's side, slid behind the wheel, started the engine, and backed out of the driveway. He headed for the Old South Restaurant, which was the best in Flint City, located on the outskirts of town. Neither one said much on the way, except to chat about what each might order for dinner.

He parked the car at the restaurant, went around and opened her door again, and taking one of her hands, gallantly helped her out then escorted her on his arm into the restaurant. Ben felt like a teenager on his first date. It was after eight o'clock, but their reservations were still being held for them. The waiter ushered them to a large, secluded booth near the back of the restaurant. Carol slid into one side of the booth, and rather than sitting across from her, Ben slipped in next to her on the same side. A candle burned in a small holder on the table, contributing to the romantic atmosphere.

"Cozier this way," he observed.

"Yes, I like it."

The waiter brought menus to their table. Ben asked Carol if she would like another drink of some kind. She gracefully declined, which pleased Ben because he didn't want another drink either. They studied their menus in silence until Ben asked her if she minded if he ordered for both of them. She replied that it would be nice, telling him she trusted his tastes, especially in women. She giggled.

For appetizers, Ben ordered shrimp cocktail, followed by cups of minestrone soup then by porterhouse steaks cooked medium. To accompany this concert, he selected twice-baked potatoes and *Spinace Italiana*. He asked the waiter for two cold iced teas to be served with the meal.

While they ate their shrimp, Carol asked about his past. There wasn't much more to tell than he had already shared with her. He told her sketches from some of his experiences while investigating crimes in Florida, hoping his remarks might encourage her to open up to questions about her son Jeremy's background and his hanging. After a while, she seemed more ready to talk about her son. She shed a tear, which distressed Ben.

He waited for her to gather herself and then asked if she would like to tell him a little about Jeremy—who he was, what kind of child he had been while growing up, and so forth. Carol wasn't ready yet to talk much about Jeremy. At Ben's gentle urging, she did say he was a good boy, and heaven knows, she had done her best to raise him without having a father around to help out. She admitted he had been in a couple of scrapes but nothing serious, and he seemed to be getting along okay in school, making good grades and all. At least Carol didn't have to be called to the principal's office more than a time or two, which told her his overall behavior was not that bad. She said she had known about several parents who had been telephoned from the principal's office about their kids on a regular basis, almost monthly.

The night Jeremy disappeared, she knew he was going to the friend Billy's house, but he had been invited to spend the night, then walk to school on Monday morning with his buddy. She had no idea he had changed his mind about staying overnight, so she did not worry or get upset when he didn't come home after dark. "I certainly had no idea his plans changed and he intended to come home Sunday night," Carol said. "If I had known he had even thought about cutting through the railroad tracks, I would have told him not to take that shortcut. All kinds of weird characters hang out down there," she said, forgetting Ben was one of the weirdos. Tears began to roll down her cheeks, which she dabbed with a tissue. Ben was curious about Jeremy's minor scrapes at school, but he decided not to open a subject that would undoubtedly add to her distress.

Carol declined the dessert tray, which was all right with Ben who was feeling a bit stuffed himself. Two Italian cappuccino coffees topped off their dinner. Ben paid the check and gave the waiter a handsome tip. He saw lots of male heads turn in their direction as he escorted Carol out of the restaurant and through the parking lot to his car. Whether their stares were curiosity or jealousy, he couldn't tell, nor did he give a damn. At the moment she was his!

As he drove back to Carol's house, they talked. About halfway there, she slid over next to him on the front seat and locked her arm through his. When Ben parked the car in her driveway and turned off the ignition, Carol turned to him and looked up, inviting a kiss. Ben was only too delighted to oblige.

"The dinner was lovely," she said. "Thank you very much for taking me out for a wonderful evening."

He told her he was happy she accepted his invitation to go out to dinner. Then after a pause he said, "I enjoyed the evening in your company. It's a shame our date has to end so soon." With that comment, and in spite of his previous vow, Ben was venturing into deeper water with Carol, and he well knew it.

The rain that threatened earlier had failed to materialize, and the Georgia stars were shining brighter than ever. It was one of those balmy nights when Ben would liked to have stripped naked and plunged into the Atlantic Ocean off the beach in Titusville. He chased those thoughts to the back of his mind as he got out of the car and opened the passenger door for Carol. She stepped out almost directly into his arms. She was so close, Ben began to tremble. Was it Carol, or the enchantment of the spring evening in the South, or both?

To his surprise and pleasure, she said, "But does the evening have to end? Surely you don't have to go back to that run-down motel so early, do you?" she asked, feigning a pout. "It's only a little after nine-thirty. Did you forget that I don't have to go in early tomorrow?"

"No, I guess not," he replied, hiding his pleasure.

"Well then, stay for a while, and I'll make us some coffee," she invited. "I've known you now for what, three or four days, and I haven't even cooked a meal for you yet. All I know so far from the rumor mill down at the mill is that someone had been bitten by a rattlesnake. You can tell me all about that while we drink our coffee. If you can tell me the details, that is."

"There's nothing secret about Pug being struck by a rattler," Ben said. Then he asked Carol if she knew who Pug was; she shook her head yes, and Ben said only vaguely, "He's in the hospital right now, and the doctors are keeping him overnight for observation. He's expected to recover, but he'll have a sore calf on the back of his leg for a while." He told her what he knew about the circumstances of the snake attack, which wasn't much because old Pug was too disoriented and scared to make sense right after he was struck. When he and Bates went to interview Pug in the hospital, he was asleep so they decided not to disturb him until morning. Their questions would have to wait until he was discharged.

"I don't think Pug is going anywhere very soon, or very fast for that matter," Ben said. "He'll be doing good just taking care of his chores at the motel. From what I've seen, Ida doesn't cut him a lot of slack, and she showed very little compassion when the rattler bit him. She didn't even go with him to the hospital this morning, using the excuse she had a business to run. Seems to me she could have had someone come in for an hour or so, but she didn't." Ben followed Carol into the kitchen as she put the percolator on the stove.

She said she heard people say that Ida seems to ride in a different rodeo than the rest of us. "She doesn't miss much that goes on up and down the road in front of the IdaHO. These same people have said they think she has the motel rooms bugged, and she may have small cameras hidden in indiscreet places," Carol suggested.

"Curious," Ben mumbled.

"Would you like cookies?"

"No thanks. I'm still full from dinner."

The coffee began to perk, filling the kitchen with its roasted aroma. Carol filled two white café mugs and added sugar and cream to hers. Ben said he drank his black. They walked back into the living room and settled on the couch. A floor lamp lit on low bulb made the room seem all the more cozy and to Ben's eyes very romantic. They chatted until midnight, refilling their coffee mugs a second time.

Ben changed his mind about talking to Carol about Jeremy. He took his courage firmly by the handles and asked if she was ready to talk about her son and to hear what he knew. "Yes, of course," she answered, clutching tissues she took from a box on a nearby end table.

Ben eased into his narrative by telling her what he and the sheriff knew and suspected. Although they still had a long way to go in finding out exactly what happened to Jeremy, he assured her once again that they would eventually get to the bottom of the circumstances surrounding his demise. Even though Ben was trying to be gentle, Carol began to cry. Her shoulders shook, and she bent over with her head in her hands. Ben tried to be soothing by wrapping his arm around her and gently pulling her toward his chest. They sat that way for several minutes while she composed herself. "Sorry," she whispered.

"That's okay. You need to release your feelings, and crying is the very best way to do that," Ben whispered.

After a while she looked up and tried to smile. "I'm okay now," she murmured.

He told her Jeremy had on only one of his sneakers when he was found in the tree, and his other shoe had been recovered near a siding in the railroad yard.

She listened to Ben's words with tears welling up in her eyes from time to time. She didn't ask any questions, just sat quietly and stared at him. Finally when Ben ran down, she said she also was convinced he and Sheriff Bates would solve Jeremy's mystery. What's more, she hoped the criminals would be prosecuted to the fullest extent of the law. "I know that won't bring back my son, but they deserve what they get," she said with conviction. Ben assured her he would personally see to it that the person or persons now unknown were identified, arrested, and fully prosecuted.

With those remarks, Ben said he had better be going. "You've had a long hard day at the mill, and I've been running around Nagel County most of the day, so we both need to turn in. Tomorrow is Friday and you have the morning off, so stay in and rest."

"If you want to drop by, I'll cook you some breakfast in the morning," Carol offered. "The coffeepot will be on, and you can come whenever you like and have a hot cup while I'm whipping up bacon and eggs. Deal?"

"Indeed. Thank you for the invite."

"Until tomorrow then. . . ." Carol's voice trailed off.

"See you in the morning," Ben promised. "Bright and early but not before sunup." They kissed goodnight, this time on the lips. Carol watched as he walked to his car, started it up, and backed out of her driveway, waving as he pulled away from the curb.

Although the hour was late, fifteen minutes after midnight, Ben's instinct told him Ida Wainright was on guard behind the curtains in her office even at this hour, keeping tabs on his comings and goings. He drove into his parking space at the IdaHO Motel but resisted waving to let her know he was aware that she was spying on his movements. No sense in antagonizing her. After all, she made a better friend than enemy, he reasoned. Then too, one enemy was more than enough if that enemy was a deadly rattlesnake.

Sandy Bates had told Ben earlier in the day that Deputy Phipps did not find the rattlesnake around the motel during his search, and as the sheriff ordered, he had knocked on doors to warn homeowners to be careful because the reptile could be anywhere in the neighborhood. Nonetheless, Ben cautiously opened the door to his room. No rattling sounds greeted him this time, but he reached in before entering and flipped on the light. A careful check of his room turned up no snakes, poisonous or of the more dangerous two-legged kind. He double locked his door, undressed, tugged on his pajamas, turned out the lamp by his bed, and slipped under the sheet. He fell asleep instantly.

At four-fifteen on Friday morning, Ben's phone rang insistently.

"Ben, my house is on fire!" Carol shouted into his ear.

13

"HELP ME, BEN! CAN YOU COME? I've called the fire department and they're on the way. But I need you, Ben!" She sounded hysterical. Justified after waking to a house ablaze and rooms beginning to fill with smoke.

Ben yelled harshly at Carol. "Get out of the house, *now*! Don't bother to hang up the phone, just run! Go—Go—GO!" Ben shouted. He heard the phone hit the floor and the front door slam. Later, when he asked her why she had bothered to shut the door, she could not even remember closing it. Ben was relieved. She had understood what he told her, and she was getting out of the house—getting away from the fire, from burns, smoke inhalation, and possibly worse.

By now he was on his feet and fully awake. He banged down the phone, grabbed his trousers, and tugged them on hurriedly over his pajama bottoms and did not take time to change out of the top. He jammed one hand into his front pocket to make sure his room key was still there and his wallet was safely in his back pocket, then slipped bare feet into loafers, pulled on his jacket, and bolted out the motel door, pausing only long enough to be sure it was fully shut and locked.

While he dressed, Ben had decided it was too much bother to take the car. Much faster on foot. He ran full tilt around the corner past the IdaHO to Carol's house on the next street, practically over the motel's back fence. Her house was an older one in Flint City, built in the 1930s in the popular craftsman style and situated on a narrow fifty-foot lot. The houses were so jammed together on one side that rain water running off the rooftops dripped in pockmarked lines only a few inches apart. Driveways leading to back lot garages allowed for more separation on one side.

The closeness of houses in these older neighborhoods presented special problems for fire departments, and Flint City was no exception. The fire brigade had its hands full trying to extinguish a blaze in the house that was burning, while at the same time trying to keep the adjoining structures from catching fire.

A fire truck careened around the corner, followed by Sheriff Bates driving his patrol car, with their sirens blaring and every light flashing. They stopped just as Ben dashed through the front yard of the house next door to reach Carol's. The rotating red lights on top of the fire truck highlighted her as she stood on the front lawn wearing a white robe. She seemed to be transfixed, with her tear-streaked face focused on the smoke billowing out the rear of the house.

Firemen streamed from the truck and labored to drag one end of their hose to connect to the water hydrant, while their colleagues ran to Carol's house, unreeling the loose end and attaching a nozzle as they hurried down her driveway around to the back. After shouting they were ready, the hose swelled with water. The firemen began to douse the fire, which was by now crackling angrily and pouring smoke out through a broken kitchen window.

Ben ran to Carol, pulled her into his arms, and held her tight to his heaving chest. He cupped her head in both hands and covered the streaming tears on her face with kisses. "You're safe. Thank God. I was so worried when you called. It seemed like it took me a year to get here. Even though the motel is just around the corner, it seemed like I ran a mile at least."

Ben's breathing slowed. Tears dampened his cheeks, too, but he didn't care. *Sometimes it's okay for a man to cry,* he thought.

"Ben, whatever shall I do? How awful to stand here and see your house go up in flames!" More tears. "Thank you for coming so quickly. I needed . . . need you," she sobbed. "Breaking glass woke me up, and then I smelled smoke so I panicked, I guess. It was a nightmare! I'm better, now that you're here."

"Come with me. Let's sit on the front porch steps of your neighbor's house next door. I'm sure she won't mind." Ben guided her across the lawn with his arm around her shoulders. "Sit here on the porch steps with me. Let the firemen do their job. They'll have the fire out in no time, and then we'll decide what comes next."

Sheriff Bates stood a few feet away from the porch, watching Carol and Ben. He was dressed uncharacteristically in an undershirt with the tail out, jeans, and house shoes. He saw that Ben was soothing Carol, so he simply nodded toward them, holding out his hands palms up in a gesture of bewilderment. In return, Ben tossed him a brief smile and a look of understanding. The sheriff could do nothing but watch the firemen work the fire, so he returned to his patrol car and sat down.

"Carol, you're shivering," Ben whispered. He took off his jacket and slipped it around her shoulders. She was trembling as much from shock at the fire as from the temperature on this still chilly spring night.

Carol's neighbor opened her front door. She had been aroused by the commotion and sirens. She was tall, slim, and stood erect despite her advanced age. Her white hair was earned honestly over time, and her chiseled face was as sharp and hard as a railroad spike, but it softened considerably when she recognized Carol hunched over on her front steps. She stepped out onto the porch and looked down at the couple huddled there.

Ben got to his feet. "My name is Ben Reed, and I'm a friend of Carol's. She's cold. Do you have a sweater or jacket or even a quilt I could wrap around her? Obviously, she can't go back into her house until the fire is extinguished and maybe not for a while after that." Ben was babbling, but he didn't care. Carol needed to be warmed up and wrapped in something better than his jacket to help ward off the dampness and chill.

"I have just the thing to warm her," she said, directing her remark at Ben. Then to Carol, "Just you hang on a minute, honey, and I'll have you warm as toast in no time." Within seconds, the neighbor lady returned to the porch with a large, warm knitted afghan, which she wrapped around Carol's shoulders over Ben's jacket.

Smiling slightly for the first time, Carol said, "Thank you, Mrs. Laramie."

"Yes, thank you, ma'am," Ben said. "I hope it's okay for us to sit here on your steps until the fire is put out."

She surprised them both by saying, "No, you can't sit here!" Then she added with a wide grin, "You two come inside out of the night air. I'll brew us up a hot pot of coffee that will help take the chill out of Carol's bones."

Mrs. Laramie's invitation for coffee didn't include the sheriff, so he stayed in his patrol car waiting for the firemen to douse the blaze. He realized there wasn't a lot he could do to help Carol or Ben. Mrs. Laramie seemed to have them in tow, and Chief Furnace and his men had the fire contained, so to speak. He thought it best to go back home, shower, and change into his uniform. He had to be in his office at the jail at daybreak, and morning was rapidly approaching. Chief Furnace motioned for the sheriff to join him on Carol's front lawn.

Had just Ben needed sanctuary, he would have declined because he did not want to impose on Mrs. Laramie's good graces. However, for Carol's sake he accepted her invitation gratefully and graciously. He helped Carol up from the porch steps by tugging gently on both of her arms and led her into Mrs. Laramie's warm and inviting living room. They sat down close together on a couch, while Mrs. Laramie scurried to the kitchen to start coffee brewing.

Before coming out on the porch to see what was going on in front of her house, Mrs. Laramie had turned on a table lamp in the living room. From what Ben could tell in the dim light, the living and dining rooms were like a veritable antique shop full of neatly arranged furniture and attractive pictures and knickknacks collected during her early days. Ben recognized that some of the furniture dated around the turn of the century or even before.

Returning to the living room, Mrs. Laramie expressed her sympathy to Carol about Jeremy's death. "He seemed such a nice boy, and I know you miss him so," she whispered. Carol only nodded and buried her head deeper into Ben's warm, secure shoulder.

"I don't believe I know you, Mr. Reed. Have you been in Flint City long?" Mrs. Laramie asked, looking kindly at Ben. She sat down opposite them in a well-worn, high-backed bentwood rocker.

"Just a few days, that's all. I'm here helping Sheriff Bates investigate Carol's son's death and the Sherman Getts killing as well."

"Land-a-Goshen. I don't know what Flint City is coming to. All this murdering going on and fires in peoples' houses. Well, it just scares me something awful, me being alone and a widow." She wasn't complaining, just making a statement of fact as she started her rocking chair in rapid motion.

"Yes, Mrs. Laramie, I hear what you're saying. Some strange things are going on in town, and the sheriff and I intend to get to the bottom of them as soon as we can."

"Funny you should bring up these strange goings on. I'm a light sleeper, and, you know, the other night, well, I guess it was around midnight or a little before, I heard what I thought was a car going slowly up and down my street. I got up and looked out my bedroom window."

Ben interrupted. "Excuse me, Mrs. Laramie, what night was it that you heard this car?"

"Well, it was Sunday night. I had trouble falling asleep and was still partially awake when I heard this car cruising up and down. I can see the street and clear down to the corner if I look out my windows on the driveway side. I saw a smallish truck rather than a car go by and turn around at the corner and come back by in this direction. I thought nothing of it at the time. I figured somebody got lost, and they were just trying to find their way somewhere."

She paused. Ben didn't interrupt again because she seemed to be collecting her thoughts. "You know, now that I think back on what I saw, it was silly of me to think they were lost because before I got back to my bedroom, you see I sleep in that one," she said and pointed at the front bedroom facing the street. "I guess I should sleep in the back bedroom where it is much quieter—don't know why I don't."

Her thoughts began to drift, so Ben chanced interrupting her. "I see. Please go on about the truck." Ben was trying to get her back on track.

"Well, as I was saying or thought I was saying, just as I got back into bed another vehicle of some kind drove slowly back up the street toward my corner."

"And . . ." prompted Ben.

"I came back in here and peeked out that window." She pointed at a living room window facing the street. "I could see it was the same small truck, but this time when the driver got to the corner he turned left toward downtown."

"You said he. The driver was a man, then?"

"Oh yes, I saw him, not clearly mind you, but I know it was a man. He had on a red ball cap. I could see that."

"What kind of truck was he driving? Was it a big truck or a small pickup? Did you notice what color it was? Could you hear it? Was it loud like the muffler had a hole in it? Anything at all unusual about the truck?" Ben's questions came rapidly, too quickly for Mrs. Laramie to comprehend and answer all at once.

"Goodness, so many questions at one time!"

"I'm sorry. Let's take them one at a time. Why do you suppose you woke up when you did? Do you usually wake up when cars or trucks go down your street?"

"No. Not normally. It must have made some unusual noise to disturb me, but as I said before, I'm a very light sleeper."

"And tell me again. Which night was this?" Ben asked again to see if Mrs. Laramie was sure about the time and night or if she might be a little confused and change what she had told him earlier. He jotted down notes with a stub pencil in a small pad he took from his pocket.

"Well, as I said before, I recollect it was sometime after I went to bed Sunday night. I didn't look at the clock like I usually do, but I would say it was probably around midnight." Mrs. Laramie's rocker was in overdrive, and the motion set both it and the floor to emitting subtle squeaks.

"That's good enough for now. Can you describe the truck?" Ben asked in the hope she had seen enough to remember and describe what she saw.

"Let's see. I remember it was small, like a pickup, and sort of a light color. Maybe gray or light green or blue. You see, I sometimes have trouble telling the difference between those three colors, and under the corner streetlight, well, I'm not really sure."

"Anything else you can remember? Was it banged up or rusty, for instance?"

"I couldn't tell if it was dented or rusty, but I know it was older, maybe ten years old. I wouldn't swear on the Bible about when it was made, but I know it wasn't one of those new fancy ones like people are driving now. I'm afraid I haven't been much help to you, Mr. Reed," she said, glancing at Carol to see if she appeared to be calmer.

"Nonetheless, what you've given me is the kind of information that is very helpful." Ben made more notes in his notepad.

"Come to think of it, that truck may have been the same color as the car you drove when you came to Carol's the other day." She giggled, hiding her mouth behind one hand. "Maybe I shouldn't be looking, and I wasn't spying, I just happened to look out and saw your car parked out front. Carol's driveway is next to my house on that side, so I can't help but notice when there's a car there." Her face flushed red and she looked down at the oriental carpet partially covering the living room floor.

"That's okay, Mrs. Laramie. I'm happy you're alert to what's going on in your neighborhood. You're being a lot of help to the sheriff and me."

"Oh my, I'm about to forget the coffee." She asked how Carol and Ben drank theirs, then toddled to the kitchen to pour the coffee and put in the fixings.

"Carol, how are you doing?" Ben asked.

"I'm much better, now that you're here. I'm worried, though, about how much damage has been done to my house." She looked up at Ben with tear-stained cheeks.

Ben told her not to worry about her house. There was not one thing in the house that couldn't be repaired or replaced. He would see to that. "The only thing in your house that cannot be replaced is you. You're here now, and you're safe—nothing else really matters."

Mrs. Laramie returned to the living room carrying three cups of steaming coffee on a serving tray, which she placed on a low table in front of the couch. She picked up a cup and handed it to Carol then another one, which she handed to Ben. Taking one herself, she sat down again in the high-backed rocker.

"Is your coffee all right?" she asked. Carol only nodded, so Ben assured her it was. Actually, it was a lifesaver for Ben, who was beginning to need a cup real bad. Carol hardly touched hers. To do so, she would have had to peel herself away from Ben's embracing and secure arms. Instead, she drifted into a doze, brought on by being absolutely worn out from stress and lack of sleep.

"Where were we?" Mrs. Laramie asked.

"I think we've about covered everything, unless you can think of any other details about the car you dreamed about on Saturday morning," Ben prompted.

"Listen, Mr. Mead, or Reed, or whatever your name is!" Her shackles were raised, causing her momentarily to forget Ben's name. This time, Mrs. Laramie's face turned crimson, but she wasn't embarrassed. She was justifiably angry. Some of her ire was dispelled on the rocker as she increased her rapid rocking. "I didn't say it was a car! I didn't tell you I *dreamed* about seeing that truck on Saturday morning! It was a truck, and I saw it big as life when I woke up sometime on Sunday night." She was staring right into Ben's eyes and not at all kindly. He quickly found out she could be a bundle to contend with when she was crossed.

"Allow me to apologize, Mrs. Laramie. This is an old trick investigators pull once in a while to find out if witnesses really saw what they first reported seeing, or if they are liable to recant later, say in front of a jury," Ben confessed through a wide smile.

"I know what I saw! No one can change that." Mrs. Laramie seemed to relax a bit after Ben's apology and stopped her rocking chair long enough to take another sip from her coffee cup.

A knock at the front door of Mrs. Laramie's house interrupted Ben's interrogation. The elderly woman, still light on her feet despite her age, sprung from her rocker, set her coffee cup down on the table, and crossed the room to answer the door. Fire Chief Gabe Furnace, dressed in full firefighting regalia, except for his helmet which he held tucked under one arm, stood holding open the outer screen door. He was sweating profusely from fighting the fire in Carol's house and from the weight of his heavy yellow waterproof rubber suit. Sheriff Bates stood behind the fire chief with one foot on the top step and the other planted on the walkway.

"Ah . . . ma'am," Furnace stammered as he always did around women, "I'm Chief Furnace from the Flint River Fire Department. Are Carol Martin and Ben Reed here, please?" He craned his neck to peek into the living room.

"Yes, Chief Furnace. They are both here with me."

"Ma'am, if I could, I would like to speak to Ben or her for a moment."

By that time, Ben had removed his arm from around Carol's shoulder. He approached the door, accompanied by Carol who was gripping his right arm tightly. Ben greeted the firefighter with, "Good morning, Chief. What's with the fire?"

"It's out entirely. I'm happy to say there's not too much damage. Didn't burn through the ceiling or walls, only scorched them some. They'll need to be scrubbed, sealed with an odor-stop of some kind, and repainted." Carol's sigh was audible, and Ben grinned at her reassuringly. Furnace went on, "We tried to keep from hosing down the rest of the house beyond the kitchen to minimize water damage, too. Unfortunately, we couldn't save the appliances, and they're shot. I must say it'll be a while before you'll be boiling up spaghetti and meatballs, I'm afraid."

"We thank you for being careful, Chief, and considerate. When do you suppose we'll be able to get in to begin cleaning up the mess?" Ben asked.

"Well, we'd like for you to wait until the fire inspector has finished combing through the kitchen for the cause of the fire. He'll be here in about an hour. We had to get him out of bed."

"Chief, you're a very kind and caring man. Thank you," Carol said.

"Well, you're certainly welcome, Mrs. Martin." With that, Chief Furnace glanced at Ben and nodded for him to come out onto the porch.

Before he stepped outside, Ben urged Carol to sit back down on the couch, finish her coffee, and chat with Mrs. Laramie while they waited on the fire inspector to conduct his investigation. She gratefully took his suggestion. Mrs. Laramie, kind and sympathetic soul that she was, took Carol by the arm and led her back to her seat on the sofa and slipped into the kitchen and returned with fresh cups of hot coffee. She handed one to Carol. Mrs. Laramie knew fresh coffee would help distract her for a few moments and might help revive her spirits a tad.

Ben stepped outside onto the front porch and down onto the sidewalk, where Chief Furnace and Sheriff Bates were waiting. Furnace motioned him down the walk toward the street. As soon as they were sure they were out of earshot, Ben asked, "What's up, Chief?"

"To tell you the truth, Mr. Reed, even at this early stage, we're pretty sure someone threw a fire bomb through Mrs. Martin's kitchen window, filled with some kind of accelerant in a bottle and probably with a rag for a wick to start the fire. From the looks of things, it was started on purpose by somebody. May even have been more than one person."

The sheriff interjected, "You know, if it pans out that it was started by an individual or individuals, this elevates the fire from accidental causes to arson with criminal aforethought and intent, which is, of course, punishable by strict laws."

"So, now we have two murders, a snake attack, and arson on our hands!" Ben said.

"It seems that's about the size of it," the sheriff agreed. "And we had better start finding some solutions real quick, the way these crimes are gaining on us."

"We're not one hundred percent sure at this point, but there is a suspicious-looking hotspot right in the middle of the kitchen floor. Something no doubt burning at the time and already hot landed there after crashing through the window. That's what's got us spooked," Furnace said. Then he added, "We know for sure it wasn't house wiring or faulty appliances that started the fire. That's pretty clear even to us, and we're not trained fire investigators." The chief explained that his men had thoroughly inspected Mrs. Martin's refrigerator and stove for evidence that one of them malfunctioned or overheated enough to ignite a blaze. "Neither of them was to blame, but as I said, they will have to be replaced. The appliances are scorched and beyond repair, I'm afraid."

"Why do you suppose anyone would want to torch Carol's house? And even more importantly, why do so with a fire bomb when there are simpler ways?" Ben asked the fire chief.

"Don't know, Mr. Reed. Your guess is as good as mine. As I said, we think now that the blaze may have been ignited on purpose and, again, maybe not. We expect confirmation when the fire inspector gets here and does his thing."

"Thanks, Chief. Will you let the sheriff and me know when his inspection is completed and official?"

"Count on it, Mr. Reed."

The three separated. Bates toward home and a late breakfast and Chief Furnace back to his truck and the fire station. Ben returned to Mrs. Laramie's living room and sat down on the couch beside Carol. He explained to her that the fire was extinguished, but it would be later in the day before hired workman could start cleaning up the kitchen. In the meantime, it was safe for her to go home and change out of her bathrobe into something suitable so they could go shopping.

"Shopping? For what?" she asked.

"We're going to buy you some new appliances, including a refrigerator, cook stove, kitchen table and chairs, the works. We'll have them delivered on Tuesday or Wednesday after the kitchen is all dolled up. What do you say to that?"

"I can't afford new appliances, and I don't have insurance," Carol admitted.

"Don't worry about that right now. It'll all work out, you'll see," Ben assured her. He was already planning to return to the bank and transfer sufficient funds to buy new appliances and to pay workmen for cleaning up and painting the kitchen.

"We'll buy a couple of big box fans this morning and turn them on to air out your house, assuming Chief Furnace approves."

Mrs. Laramie, the epitome of Southern grace, hospitality, and warmth, walked over to the couch and took Carol by the hand. "Carol, listen. You come and stay with me now for a few days or as long as necessary for your house to be put back in order. I have that extra bedroom in the back that's quiet, and you're certainly welcome to stay right here with me. I'll not take no for an answer."

Looking through misty eyes, Carol smiled at Mrs. Laramie and at Ben. "What good friends you two are. I mean, really. Thank you both from the bottom of my heart."

14

B EN ALSO THANKED MRS. LARAMIE FOR her hospitable offer and urged Carol to accept her invitation, which she did gratefully. Now there were two displaced persons who walked next door to Carol's so she could retrieve some of the belongings she would need for her stay at Mrs. Laramie's house.

The smell of scorched paint and wood greeted Ben and Carol the moment they opened the front door. The odor was not overwhelming, but it was strong enough to be repugnant. Both of them coughed and sneezed at the same time. They turned to each other and smiled. For Ben, it was good to see Carol smile again.

When they peeked timidly into the burned-out kitchen, a stranger unknown to Ben acknowledged their presence with a nod of his helmeted head. The fireman's helmet had breathers of some sort attached, which furnished him with fresh air. The man walked into the dining room from the kitchen to greet Carol and Ben.

"I'm Fire Inspector Bert Graves." Graves removed his helmet. Ben guessed that Graves was about fifty years old. The inspector's long-waisted torso was supported on legs that were too short. He was heavy, with graying hair cut in flat-top military style. His black eyes were set wide apart and almost hidden by bushy, untrimmed eyebrows. "I'm here to determine how Mrs. Martin's fire started."

"Glad to meet you, but not under these circumstances. I don't suppose you've had a chance to complete your work yet?" Ben asked. "Any early ideas?"

"Well, from what I've seen already and from samples I've taken, I would almost guarantee this fire was started on purpose. We have a clear case of arson here, I think," Graves said, shaking his head. "We'll have to take these samples down to our lab to see what was used as an accelerant. At this stage, I would guess probably gasoline. That's what a lot of arsonists use because it ignites immediately, is cheap to buy, and easily available at every corner gas station. Hard to trace, too. What most of these arsonists do is buy gas for their cars, then siphon off enough to fill a bottle or container of some kind."

"You found a bottle?" Ben asked.

"Not the whole bottle, of course. It exploded on impact and spread the burning contents into nearly every corner of the kitchen. I found a thick, curved chunk of glass, which must have been the bottom, over there between the stove and the wall. Although it survived the intense heat of the fire, the piece is melted some. We've got enough sample, I think, so we can figure out what kind of bottle it was and maybe even what it held originally. If we're lucky, we might go so far as to discover where it was made and who in Flint City sells liquids in this kind of glass container."

"What's the matter?" Graves asked Ben. "You have a frown on your face that would rival gullies in the Grand Canyon."

"A thought just struck me." Carol had quietly slipped away from them earlier to go to the bedroom to gather her belongings to take to Mrs. Laramie's.

"And . . ."

"And what I'm wondering is if Carol's fire, which probably *is* arson, Jeremy's hanging, the rattlesnake in my room, and the Sherman Getts killing are all connected in some way."

"I wouldn't know, of course, but it does seem odd that all of these things happened within the past few days," Graves agreed. "We never have had so much crime around here and certainly not buckets full and in such a short time. However, if you want my opinion, I would say, yes, they are probably connected. Without more details, though, to base my judgment on, I can't see how." The two men stood quietly, thinking about what Reed had just said. When Ben realized Carol was missing and he saw she had left the kitchen, he figured she had gone to pack. He excused himself from the fire inspector and followed her to the bedroom, where he leaned against the door jam and watched as she selected dresses, shoes, and other garments. She sensed he was there and looked up.

"Carol, it isn't all that bad. Your house is damaged, yes, but it isn't a total loss. We can have your kitchen back shipshape in a couple of days, you'll see." With that, he walked into the living room, found the telephone book under the phone and turned to the yellow pages to look up the names of companies who specialized in home repairs. In a loud voice Carol could hear, he asked if she had any particular company she had used before that he could call. Ben hoped the question might help direct her thoughts in a more positive way.

It worked—to a degree. She came to the bedroom door, looked at Ben and replied, "Not really. But people tell me that a company called Hearth and Home is honest as well as dependable, they do good work, and they work quickly. Why don't you try them?" It was time for the company to be open for business.

Ben dialed the number and used his most persuasive powers to explain the circumstances of Carol's fire and how desperate she was to put her house back in order. Finally, he hung up and turned to Carol. "Good news! They can send a man over today to look the situation over and give us an estimate. The owner said his men usually don't work on Saturdays; however, he might be able to make an exception under the circumstances and because they know who you are and about Jeremy's loss. If we approve his estimate for repairs, he has a crew he can send over to start cleaning up this afternoon. When the owner shows up, I'll pin him down about working again tomorrow and see if he thinks the job is manageable enough that they can finish up sometime on Monday or for sure by Tuesday."

"At least it's a relief to know they can complete the work that soon," Carol said, as she crossed the room to hug Ben tightly. He hugged her back, and their lips touched lightly. They read in each other's eyes what they wanted to see. While she finished putting her belongings together, Ben walked back to the kitchen to see if Fire Inspector Graves had completed his work. "Any interim diagnosis, Mr. Graves?" Ben asked.

"Just finished here," Graves replied. "As I said earlier, I'll have to run these samples back to the lab at the station to see what they reveal. Should be done with that analysis later this afternoon. Would you like for me to call you when we have definite results?"

"Yes, thanks. I'll let Sheriff Bates know as soon as I hear from you. Carol, er . . . Mrs. Martin and I are going shopping for new appliances. It would be better if I telephone you from one of the stores because I don't know where we're likely to be at any one time. Would later this afternoon after lunch be okay?"

Graves assured him he would have his lab work done by then.

Ben helped Carol carry her personal items, now packed in a suitcase, to Mrs. Laramie's house, where she placed them carefully and neatly in a dresser and wall closet in the back bedroom. They thanked Mrs. Laramie again, to which she replied, "Think nothing of it, honey. I'm happy to help you out."

Carol told Mrs. Laramie they were going shopping. Ben walked back to the motel, where he showered, shaved and changed into more presentable clothes before driving his rental car back to Mrs. Laramie's house. When Carol came out, he opened the passenger door and waited while she took her seat. While he went around to the driver's side, Carol slid ever so slightly to the middle of the wide bench seat to be closer to him. He cranked the engine and drove into downtown Flint City, where he parked the car in the only open space in the lot beside the largest department store. Carol had told him the store carried a wide selection of kitchen appliances in various price ranges and qualities.

The Georgia sun was beginning to make itself felt. Ben suggested they leave the car windows open a little so the heat would not build up inside while they were in the store.

By noon Carol had made her decisions, including new paint colors for the walls. Ben arranged for all of her appliance purchases to be delivered late on the following Tuesday afternoon, or earlier if the kitchen was ready before then. He pulled the store manager aside to make arrangements for paying the bill while Carol was wandering the aisles. Ben wanted to pay with cash first thing Monday morning, but he had to wait until after the bank opened to present his letter of credit. He explained his circumstances to the manager, that his home bank was in Titusville and he could transfer funds on Monday to cover Carol's purchases. "You'll have your money before you make delivery," Ben assured him. The store manager confirmed that holding everything until Monday would not be a problem and he handed Ben an invoice to sign, temporarily charging the purchases.

"Ben, those appliances are very expensive," Carol said, as they left the store. "I really don't know how to thank you for helping me out this way. If you hadn't come along when you did, I would surely be miserable."

He only smiled and said, "You're entirely welcome."

Even with the windows rolled partway down, the car was hot from sitting in the direct spring sun for nearly two hours. Luckily, the car Reed had rented was air conditioned, and with it running full blast, the small Ford began to cool inside by the time Ben parked again, this time outside Sal's Café.

"What do you say we have lunch? A tall, cold glass of Sal's iced tea would go down really good right now," Ben suggested. Carol agreed. They rolled the car windows down partway again and entered the café, where they were greeted warmly by an ever-smiling Sal.

"Hey, you two!" Sal hugged Carol and threw a wink at Ben over her shoulder. They followed her to a booth, the same one Ben had occupied on his first visit to Flint City. When he reminded Sal of his first time to be in her café, she said she remembered and also recalled Ben's confrontation with Mel Phipps. She thought they were going to fight right there and then. She changed the subject. "I am sorry to hear about the fire in your house, Carol. Is there anything I can do? Can you stay at home or do you need a place to bunk down for a few days?"

Carol thanked her for her concern and said she and Ben had everything under control and that she was staying at Mrs. Laramie's house until her kitchen was put back in shape.

"You two are becoming quite the talk here in town. Did you know that? Or care?" She handed them menus, displaying her widest toothy grin.

"What are the good citizens of Flint City saying about us?" Ben asked.

"Oh, just that you make a handsome couple, and you've been seeing a lot of each other lately." Twinkling devilish eyes searched their faces.

"Yeah, we are, and we have. Is that enough to keep those local tongues wagging?"

"Well, it doesn't take much around here to start the blabbermouths flapping their lips, but always discreetly and behind their hands. That way, if a rumor turns out to be just a rumor or hearsay, the guy who started it can claim to be innocent." With that, Sal threw her head back and guffawed, which quieted the café and turned customers' heads in her direction. Attracting attention was the last thing Ben wanted to do, so Sal's outburst did not make him happy.

Quieter now. "Tell me, Sal, what are folks saying about Pug's snakebite and Carol's house fire? And don't try to tell me you don't know anything about those events or about Getts' murder," Ben chided, halfway teasing but also with a serious tone in his voice. The scowl on his face showed how displeased he was to hear there was gossip around Flint City about his relationship with Carol and about the recent increase in criminal activity.

Sal slid into the booth beside Carol and patted her arm. "To be honest, they aren't saying much about Pug being bitten by the rattlesnake. Only most people are of a mind that he was dumb as a carpet tack. They think he wasn't the one who dumped the rattler in your room at the motel because otherwise he wouldn't have gotten himself bit in the first place if he had known it was there."

"And being my best source for rumors, what do you think, Sal?"

"To be truthful, I don't think Pug put that snake in your room. To be direct, Pug really isn't a dummy like most people around here think he is. He's dumb like a fox in a hen house who knows when it's time to catch chickens and when he'd best get out of the chicken coop."

"Could you translate that into English?" Ben asked. They had not ordered lunch yet, and he was getting hungry. The smell of food cooking in the kitchen did nothing to quell his appetite. He flipped the pages of the menu in the hope Sal would take the hint and also take their orders.

"To simplify, he does what Ida tells him to, when she tells him to, and how she tells him to. But he's got eyes and ears and sometimes only makes out like his licker jug is uncorked. He knows more than Ida or anyone else in these parts gives him credit for."

Sal suddenly stopped talking as Penny approached with two glasses of water, which she set on their table. Carol gave the waitress her order of a bacon, lettuce, and tomato sandwich, potato salad on the side, and iced tea. Ben said to make it two, with unsweetened iced tea. Penny wrote their orders on her pad of checks and flounced away toward the kitchen.

"Sheriff Bates and I plan to interview Pug later today or tomorrow," Ben offered. "I understand he's home from the hospital now, and he should be able to talk—to remember better what happened the day he got bit. At least, I hope so. About Carol's house fire. What's the scuttlebutt about that?"

Sal sucked in her breath. She shook her head slowly from side-to-side and looked grim. "That's a real shame, that fire. I hear it was set on purpose by someone who wanted to intimidate Carol," she replied and patted Carol's arm.

"Intimidate me? Why, for heaven's sake?"

"To be real frank, they—whoever they are—don't want you asking around or talking about your son or about what else has been going on lately in Flint City."

Carol protested. "But, Sal, I don't know anything about what's been going on. I tried to raise Jeremy up right, and now he's gone. I just don't understand. I work hard five days a week, keep a clean house, pay my bills on time, and hardly ever take a vacation. I'd like to know when people think I have time to poke my nose into their business. Give me a break!" The last a desperate plea.

"To be plain, I guess if you don't know what's going on, you're better off. Maybe those guys who set your house on fire will come to realize you're the victim in all of this and leave you alone. At least I hope so, Carol," Sal said, as she glanced across the table at Ben Reed.

Curiouser and curiouser. Sal said "guys." I wonder if she knows more than she's telling me, he wondered.

Ben reached across the booth and held Carol's hand. He waited for her to regain her composure before he asked Sal if she thought Jeremy's and Sherman Getts' deaths, his own near miss with the snake, and Carol's house fire might be connected in some way. Sal gave Ben a cagey sly smile, which belied what she said next. "I got my suspicions, Ben. Whether they're related or not, when I know more about what's happening—who might be responsible— you and Sheriff Bates will be the first to know," Sal promised. With that, she patted Carol's arm again and said "See ya" to Ben and returned behind the front counter, where she took money from departing customers.

About the time Ben stared inquiringly toward the kitchen door, Penny brought their BLTs, sides of potato salad, and iced teas. She set them on the table unceremoniously, smiled, deposited the check alongside their food, and remembered to remind them to let her know if they wanted refills of tea or anything else. She swiveled away to wait on other customers.

"What do you make of that?" Carol asked.

Ben wasn't sure whether she meant what Sal had said or Penny's walk, but he reckoned she meant Sal's comments. "I'm not sure. I have a notion Sal knows more than she's telling us. I hope whoever has committed these crimes doesn't get wise to what she knows, or thinks she knows, or we may have another tragedy on our hands," Ben whispered just loud enough for Carol to hear. They ate their sandwiches and potato salad, drank their teas, and walked to the counter to pay. As Ben paid the tab, he leaned over close to Sal's ear and whispered, "Sal, you best hold your peace. I'm urging you again to keep quiet about what you know or even what you think you know. The bad guys won't take it kindly if they even suspect you're talking to anyone—particularly the sheriff or me—about what they're up to."

"Come on, Ben, do you take me for a complete idiot?" Consternation was loud and clear in her tone of voice. "I haven't said a word to anybody, not even to my kinfolk, about what I think might be going on. You and the sheriff are the onliest two people I am likely to share my thoughts with."

"I'm surprised you're telling me, of all people, anything. You've hardly known me—what—about a week now, or even less?" Ben reminded her.

"When Sandy had lunch here yesterday, I asked him about you. He told me you're on the up and up and I can trust you. So . . ." Sal still sounded a little miffed.

"It's good to know Sheriff Bates feels I can be trusted and you feel you can share your thoughts with me. But I'm telling you again, don't breathe a word about your suspicions to anyone else, or you might find your café on fire," Ben warned. As he retrieved his change and opened the café door for Carol, Sal said, "Not to worry. Mum's the word."

Ben seated Carol in his rental, cranked it, and took her back to Mrs. Laramie's house. They said good-bye, and Ben drove around the corner to the IdaHO Motel to confront Pug. Just as he parked, Pug came out of Room 9 next to Ben's with his mop, a bucket, and dirty linen. His cleaning cart seemed way too large for the small number of towels, sheets, pillowcases, and bathroom supplies on it. Ben figured Ida had probably picked it up cheap, even though it was about twice the size the motel really needed. From the way he limped, it was obvious Pug's leg was still sore from the snakebite. Ben noticed he leaned forward, with both hands firmly grasping the cart's push bar as he struggled to move the cart from one room to the next.

Ben turned off the ignition and got out of the car. "Hey, Pug. How you feeling?"

"Well, Mr. Reed, I ain't up to this here work yet, but Ida—she insists I get my chores done anyway. She's a real slave driver, she is," Pug complained, moaning loudly enough to make sure Reed would hear him and be sympathetic.

"You need to take it easy if you can, Pug. If you will, please come into my room. I have a few questions to ask about the rattlesnake that bit you." Ben unlocked the door to his room and held it open for Pug. Pug put his bucket down just outside Ben's room, leaned his mop against the door jamb, and followed close behind, leaving the door open.

"To tell you the truth, Mr. Reed, your room gives me the creeps."

"I can see why, and I sympathize with you, Pug. You know, it could have been me that was struck. The snake rattled right away when I first opened the door. That's why I didn't come on in. He was singing as loud as a room full of startled crickets."

Ben gestured for Pug to sit on the edge of the bed nearest the door while he pulled open the drapes. He sat down on the one and only chair in the room. Pug sat down slowly on the very edge of the bed, extending his left leg. It was obvious to Ben from the way Pug moved that his leg was hurting him considerably. The thought entered his mind that fat Ida must be unfeeling or even inhuman if she expected her husband to do the motel's cleaning while he was obviously in such pain.

"Tell me, Pug, how do you suppose the rattler got into my room?" No reason to beat around the bush. Ben's first question was to the point.

"Beats me, Mr. Reed. I hope you don't think I put it in here. I know what people say about me, that I'm dumb and I have one wing that's short a feather. Well, maybe so, but I ain't that stupid. I'm not crazy enough to put a poisonous snake in your room or anyone else's then walk right up on it and get bit! Now am I?"

"No. I'm convinced you didn't put the snake in my room. Nobody I know of would be dumb enough to let a snake bite him, especially if he knew ahead of time where it was. But if you didn't put the rattler in here, then who do you think did?"

"I got my wonders." Pug sniffed, looking everywhere in the room except directly into Ben's eyes.

"Who do you wonder about, then?"

"Can't tell you, Mr. Reed. I'm just supposin' now, same as you. I see things, hear things, and I know things that I daren't spill 'cause they might not be right."

"Is someone threatening you?"

"No. It ain't that. I got brains enough to keep my mouth shut, though. Don't reckon it'd pay to be talkin' nor takin' chances, I say."

"If you know something, you better come clean now. Look what's happened to Mrs. Martin's house and to her son, Jeremy. She doesn't know anything, and look what someone did to her and her boy!" Ben was becoming exasperated with Pug's reluctance to talk. "Do you want me to take you down to the jailhouse and let Sheriff Bates or Deputy Phipps grill you for a few hours? Is that what you want?"

"No." Pug's face was painted with fear, and he began to shake uncontrollably. "I seen a few things here 'n there that I probably shouldn't have, that's all, like Room 3 that's been locked up this last few days. Ida won't give me a key for it. She says it don't need cleanin'. Other comin' and goin' happen at night, like on Sunday night before you checked in here."

"When I checked in, I noticed the key to Room 3 was missing from the key cabinet in the office, so I assumed the room was rented. What's in Room 3, anyway? What happened Sunday night, Pug?" Ben probed.

Pug looked at his feet and out the window, avoiding Reed's burning stare. "Beats me. Room 3 was locked Sunday night before you got here and it's still locked. Your guess is as good as mine. That's all I can tell you right now," Pug responded so timidly Ben could hardly hear him. "I may be in trouble for talkin' to you this little bit. If Ida seen me come into your room like this, and stay for a while like I have, unless I was cleanin' up . . . well, there'd be hell to pay, I'll tell you that."

"I sure don't want to place you in any danger, Pug, believe me." Ben thought over what Pug had told him, but he didn't want to press the issue just then because he figured there would be plenty of chances to talk to the handyman again. "You go on about your chores, clean in here if you want to, then if Ida asks you why you were in my room so long, you can tell her I was extra messy and it took you this much time to clean up after me. Okay? I'll be leaving again in a minute."

"Thanks, Mr. Reed," Pug said, as he tugged at his clothing nervously like he had a big grasshopper crawling up the pant leg on his bum side. He struggled to get up off the bed. As he reached the door, Ben said, "Sheriff Bates and I will want to talk to you again in a day or two. You're not planning to leave town any time soon, are you?"

"Nope. With this leg, I can't even walk regular! Now where would I be traveling to?" Pug asked, not expecting an answer. And he didn't get one. With that, Pug picked up his scrub bucket and mop, gathered fresh towels and cleaning supplies from the cart, filled his bucket with water from the shower, and began to mop the bathroom floor.

Ben got back in his car and drove to Sheriff Bates' office at the jail. Bates and Deputy Phipps were both at work. Phipps was reading the morning paper, while the sheriff was reading ME Poole's official written autopsy reports on Jeremy Martin and Sherman Getts. With a nod, the sheriff handed the boy's report to Ben and continued reading about Getts' killing.

Ben read the preliminary entries about the boy's address, next of kin, height, weight, age, and sex. His general physical condition was excellent until he was murdered. He skipped most of the basic data, until his eyes fell on Cause of Death. Here, Poole had written:

"Delayed subdural hemorrhage likely caused by a severe blow to the left temporal lobe region of the cerebral cortex of subject's brain causing intracranial pressure. Clotted and fresh blood were found inside the superficial temporal vein of the skull, indicating he sustained a traumatic head injury, which only rendered him unconscious. The blow occurred two to three hours before he succumbed. He experienced limited bleeding at that time, but he was still alive. Perhaps as much as three hours later, and maybe as long as four hours, the temporal vein released a sudden and rapid increase in intracranial pressure, magnified by blood flowing from his body trunk to the top of his head, probably aggravated from hanging upside down. Expiration of the subject was almost immediate."

Poole's earlier assumption had been correct. Good man and skilled pathologist. Reed checked to see if there might be clues hidden in what the boy had on his person when brought into the morgue. Nothing. His pockets were empty. Nothing?

Curious? Pool did note minor bruises were found on Jeremy's wrists and ankles, as well as scrape marks on the right side of his face, and his arms from the elbows down. His supposition was that Jeremy had run and fallen on rough ground covered with some kind of rocks, probably rail ballast, before he was knocked unconscious. He also listed the clothes the boy was wearing, making special mention of the missing left sneaker.

Ben had read enough. He exchanged autopsies with Bates and read about Sherman Getts' murder. Not much he didn't already know. Getts was shot in the right ear with a small-caliber weapon, either a revolver or an automatic. He died instantly. Bates had retrieved the slug from Getts' mattress and guessed it came from a .22 caliber revolver. Small as the bullet was, it did major damage inside Getts' skull. Poole reported that whoever killed Getts must have held the gun close to Getts' ear. There were minute traces of gunpowder in his ear, and the impact of the bullet inside Getts' skull caused major damage on its pathway through his brain tissue. The bullet Bates retrieved had been dispatched to the ballistics lab in Atlanta for analysis.

Deputy Phipps excused himself, saying it was time to make his daily rounds of downtown. He shot Reed a malicious look that could have knocked down an incoming missile and slammed out the door. Ben merely smiled and winked at Sheriff Bates as if to say Phipps was a pain in the ass. Which they both knew he was.

"Not really much new here, is there, Sheriff? Poole's reports confirm his earlier suspicions when he first examined the Martin boy and Getts," Ben observed, rubbing his chin and frowning. When Bates finished reading Jeremy's autopsy for the second time, he laid it on his desk and asked Ben if he had anything new, especially concerning the fire at Carol's house. Ben said he had nothing new on her house fire and that he had collared Pug just before coming to the office. Ben was of the opinion Pug knew more than he was telling.

"The really interesting thing Pug said during our conversation was that Room 3 at the motel was locked the night I arrived in Flint City and it is still locked. Beyond that tidbit, he was very tight-lipped. We need to take a gander inside Room 3—what we find in there might be very interesting," he said.

"We can get a search warrant issued when the judge opens up on Monday," Bates agreed. He reached over to write a note on his desk calendar pad for Monday to call the court. Ben also filled the sheriff in about his conversation with Sal at lunch. He stressed that Sal seemed to be holding back information, just like Pug probably was. Reed said Sal agreed with him that it wasn't likely Pug planted the rattlesnake in Ben's room at the motel. She did not say much about Jeremy's hanging or Carol's house fire because Carol was having lunch with Ben and Sal probably would not have said much in front of her anyway.

"Why is it everyone in Flint City except the two of us seems to know what's going on?" Ben wondered out loud. "We're doing our damnedest to get to the bottom of these killings and the fire but, if the good citizens— and I use the term good loosely—of Flint City won't cooperate and help us, how are we ever going to find the killers or arsonists?" Ben's frustration and pent-up emotions were beginning to show through his usual calm, calculating demeanor.

"Did you talk to the yardmaster Corey?" Ben asked the sheriff.

"Yes. I meant to tell you about that. I went to see him this morning after I left Carol's house and ate breakfast. I caught him at home and questioned him pretty good. He said he didn't see or hear anything the night the Martin kid was killed. He was back on duty at his tower when the second north-bound freight train you were riding on came in."

"He didn't see me either?"

"Apparently not. Said he chatted some with the engineer and conductor, then threw switches while they set off cars for later pick-up by the eastbound freight. He went back home to grab some sleep after the northbound train completed its drop and cleared the yard and before the early morning eastern came through. Didn't see anything then, either."

"Well, somebody saw something—sometime—somewhere! Surely not everyone in Flint City is blind! Otherwise, we wouldn't have a dead boy, a man's corpse, a planted snake, and a burned-out kitchen on our hands." He sat down wearily in the chair Phipps had vacated, and after asking the sheriff if it was okay he lit his first cigarette of the day. No ashtrays in sight, so when he was sure the match was extinguished, he dropped it in the wastepaper basket beside Bates' desk.

"I guess there isn't much more we can do at this stage. We'll get back on the case first thing Monday morning when Williams and Kellerman get here," Ben said.

"I have to go back to Carol's now. I want to be around while they're cleaning and fixing up her kitchen." With that Ben got up to leave, and as he went out the door he turned to the sheriff with a determined look on his face. "We better solve these crimes real soon, Sheriff. As you well know, the longer it takes us, the colder the trail becomes. It will be a week on Monday since you found Martin's body, and a week is a long time."

Bates responded with a wave of his hand. Ben flipped his cigarette onto the walk, stomped it out, cranked up his Ford, and backed out of the parking lot.

When Ben arrived at Carol's house, the workmen were already ripping and pounding in her kitchen. He had called Hearth and Home earlier to approve their estimates and to authorize any necessary overtime. He also needed to remember to telephone his bank in Titusville first thing on Monday to request a transfer of funds to his account in Flint City to cover costs of the repairs and new appliances.

Their trucks and vans were parked haphazardly and took up the driveway and most of the lawn, which only left room for Ben to park at curbside in front of Carol's house. As he walked around the front of the car, he caught sight of an object lying in the gutter beside the right front tire. He squatted down to pick up whatever had attracted his attention. The object was a small pocketknife, along with a couple of coins. He spread his handkerchief out on the pavement and, using his open gofer match pack as a shovel, carefully scooped the knife and coins onto the cloth before gathering up the four corners and picking the bundle up in a hobo-style pouch. Maybe it belonged to one of the workers. He would ask.

15

WHEN BEN ENTERED CAROL'S HOUSE, the kitchen reverberated with sights and sounds of workmen tearing out the old, scorched cabinets and removing the appliances so new items could be installed, hopefully on Tuesday. Thoughtfully, the workers had hung sheets of plastic over the door leading from the kitchen into the dining room to keep out the dust particles stirred up by their sanding, hammering, and ripping.

He stood peering in through the plastic barrier, waiting to catch the attention of one of the carpenters. Before long, a sweating worker noticed him and pulled the plastic door aside and motioned for Ben to come into the kitchen. Ben did not have a dust mask on, so his lungs immediately filled with dust. The taste in his mouth almost choked him. Stifling a cough, he shouted in a workman's ear to ask which man was their foreman and where he was. The pounding was so loud the carpenter merely pointed at one of their number, who was helping to carry the kitchen stove out the back door. Ben breathed as shallowly as he could, then crossed though the kitchen and followed the boss and his helper outside.

After they set the stove down out of the way under a tree, Ben introduced himself to the head man, who said he was Tony, and then asked, "How's it going?"

Removing his gloves to shake hands, Tony replied, "Not bad. We should have all of this out of here before quitting time today. If not, I'll work them overtime." Tony paused to cough and spit aside in the grass. "I've got two of my men lined up to come in real early tomorrow morning and on Sunday, to clean up, finish scrubbing down the walls and ceiling, and coat them with a sealant to cover the smell of smoke the fire left behind and then paint. That's if you're willing to pay more overtime." Tony took Ben's silence as approval. "With an accelerant drier mixed in, the paint should dry quickly enough that the crew can begin laying linoleum on the floor Monday morning. After that's done, which shouldn't take them long in this small kitchen, we can begin hanging the cabinets, install the counter-tops, and sink. Mrs. Martin's new appliances will be the last thing to be set in place, and we plan on doing that sometime on Tuesday. Installing appliances is really more a matter of carrying them inside and plugging them in," he added.

"I've already called your office and authorized overtime, which includes Sunday if need be, so that's taken care of. You feel you'll definitely be ready to set the new appliances then on Tuesday?" Ben had made all the necessary arrangements at the store but would call them again to reconfirm the time the manager would have Carol's stove and refrigerator delivered.

"Sure—barring any hitches, we'll have the cabinets up before we quit on Monday if it takes till midnight. Once the cabinets are in, we'll get our plumber over here to hook up water to her sink and reset the drain. The electrician is coming in on Monday to inspect the electric and to hang her new ceiling fixture. While he's here he'll test the kitchen wiring, and if he finds any problems, he'll run new wiring to the outlets. I doubt she'll need much new wiring strung, if any, because the wires in these older houses are shielded in conduit, which provides some protection from weather and heat. They both should be able to do their thing in three or four hours and be out of here before lunch when the appliances are delivered."

"Good man. Oh, by the way, does this pocketknife belong to you or to any of your workmen?" Ben unfolded his handkerchief and showed the workman the knife he had found at the edge of the street in front of Carol's house.

"Not mine. You'll have to ask my men if it belongs to one of them." Tony shook his head, then turned away to go back inside the kitchen to help his men lift the refrigerator onto a wheeler so it could be rolled out the back door. The foreman was working just as hard as his crew, which pleased Ben to no end.

He asked each workman in turn, not interrupting their labors any more than necessary, if the knife was his. Each in turn said nothing but shook his head no. From outward appearances, the knife's casing was not rusty, nor were the edges of the blades, so Ben had an idea—even with the recent rainfall—it hadn't lain in the street very long before he found it.

Curious.

With a shrug and a sigh, Ben carefully wrapped the knife back into his handkerchief and slipped it into his pocket for more thorough examination and fingerprinting later.

Before walking back to Mrs. Laramie's house, Ben used Carol's telephone to call Fire Inspector Graves. "If you've had time, what's your verdict?" he asked.

"Well, it's arson, just like I suspected. Someone used a bottle filled with gasoline and probably used a rag for a wick that was lit and hurled through the kitchen window. Luckily, the whole house didn't go up before the fire department got there." While Ben listened, Graves explained that the glass fragment he had recovered showed traces of a petroleum residue in sufficient quantity to determine what flammable was used to make the fire bomb. "A Molotov cocktail—that's what it was," he confirmed. Then as an afterthought, he added, "We haven't been able to determine yet which plant made the bottle and where it is, but we're not giving up."

"I see," Ben said. "Thanks, Graves. Sheriff Bates and I are much obliged to you for your work, although I must say, knowing it was arson doesn't make me a very happy camper." In fact, he was appalled. Infuriated! Livid! He would have strangled the person who threw the firebomb single-handedly if he had had the arsonist in his grasp in the few seconds before he hurled the firebomb into Carol's house!

After hanging up the phone, he sat for a few minutes in Carol's living room, a boxcar full of emotions welling up inside. Slowly, anger trickled from his tormented thoughts, leaving him in a cold sweat. What injustice! What an overwhelming set of circumstances surround these crimes! Two murders, a rattlesnake used as a weapon, and an arson fire, all in less than a week! "What will come next?" he wondered aloud, shaking his head in bewilderment.

In control of his emotions once again, Ben walked back to Mrs. Laramie's house, examining the curb along the street more closely. He didn't know what he was looking for—maybe the solution to this mess. But he didn't find anything else. *Seldom works out that way,* he mused.

He knocked on Mrs. Laramie's door and was greeted by Carol, who was all dolled up in a cool spring dress dotted with small, colorful flowers that accentuated her figure, above as well as below her waist. Her hair was pulled back in a ponytail, which made her look ten years younger, almost like a girl young enough to be wearing bobby socks.

"Hey, Ben," she said, smiling as she opened the screen door for him. "How's the remodeling going in my kitchen? I was over there earlier this morning, but the workers had just arrived, so I got out of their way pronto. Didn't want to be in their way and hold up their progress."

"They're coming along more quickly than I would have expected. They have removed almost all of the cabinets and appliances and will begin cleaning up after a while." He filled her in on details of the foreman's schedule, adding, "If they can stick to his schedule, you'll be back in your house and kitchen by late Tuesday evening, or for sure before noon on Wednesday."

He brushed her lips with his and told her how lovely she looked. She didn't draw away. "You look refreshed and like a young girl," he teased with a broad smile.

"Well, now, what would you be knowing about young girls?" Carol teased in return. She held his hand tightly, even after Mrs. Laramie came into the living room to see who had knocked on her front door. She greeted Ben with her usual Southern charm and asked for a report about the progress on Carol's house. "Not that I'm trying to get rid of her, mind," she said, a wide grin lighting up her face.

He filled her in as he had Carol, but not with as much detail, ending with, "How about I drive the three of us over to Button tonight for dinner? There's a great barbeque restaurant near the railroad just this side of downtown." He could see by the smiles on their faces and their quick affirmative nods that his invitation had been accepted.

"I'd hoped you might invite us. That's why I'm all dressed up," Carol said. It wasn't true, but again, who cared?

"It's all arranged then. I'll go back to the motel, spruce up, and change my togs. Be back in a couple of hours. How does that sound?" Both women agreed two hours would be just right, so Ben left and drove around the corner to his room at the IdaHO Motel. Again, he felt rather than saw Ida's glaring eyes watching him. He had paid for a week in advance, which would be up on Tuesday. He would have to pay again if he intended to stay any longer. Then an idea struck him about how he might kill—not a good word—three birds with one stone. If only . . .

He was back within two hours and knocked once more on Mrs. Laramie's front door. The ladies were ready, so the three of them set out in Ben's car for the town of Button for good ol' Southern barbeque with all the trimmings. They arrived as the sun was turning the western sky from blue to pink, parked near the front door, and entered the barbeque shack, where they were seated promptly in a booth. Ben and Carol sat together on one side of the booth, and Mrs. Laramie sat facing them. After their orders for barbeque pork, onion rings, fried okra, and iced tea were taken by a waitress, the conversation became warm and intimate. People who didn't know probably thought Carol was Mrs. Laramie's daughter. They did look enough alike to be related.

Just before ordering identical desserts of sliced peaches topped with whipped cream and a cherry, Carol turned to Ben and asked, "What were you looking for so intently in front of my house earlier just before you came over to Mrs. Laramie's?" Her question didn't sound like she was grilling or accusing him of anything, simply asking with a woman's unfathomable depth of curiosity.

"Oh, well, I found a pocketknife and a couple of small coins along the edge of the street in front of your house when I came by to see if the workmen had arrived and started to work yet."

"And?"

"I thought perhaps I might have missed something, so I looked again more carefully on my way to Mrs. Laramie's."

"And?"

"As luck would have it, nothing else was there. I don't know what I expected to find, probably nothing. I wasn't disappointed, really," he said with a wide grin, trying to be reassuring and to pass the incident off as unimportant. Carol was noticeably relaxed now, and Ben didn't want to stir up unpleasant memories or emotions, particularly tonight when he had an important question to ask her.

But Carol would not let him escape so easily. She persisted. After a moment, she asked, "Who do you suppose the pocketknife belongs to."

"Well, none of the workers, that's for sure. I showed it to each workman, but nobody claimed it. You don't have sidewalks in front of your house, so it could have been dropped by someone walking down your street." He hoped Carol would leave it at that, but she didn't.

"May I see it, please?"

"Sorry, my dear, I didn't bring it with me tonight. It's in my room at the motel, wrapped up in a hanky. Come to think of it, maybe I should have brought it or at least locked it up in the trunk of my car. I doubt it's important, but you can't tell because it was found in front of your house. I plan to ask Sheriff Bates to fingerprint it on Monday, anyway." Ben could not help but wonder why Carol was so interested in the pocketknife. No special reason as far as he could tell. Just curiosity, he decided.

They enjoyed their barbeque and desserts. Ben asked for the check. After the waitress left their bill on the table, Ben fished some bills out of his wallet for her tip and paid their tab at the cashier up front. That done, the trio departed the restaurant for their return to Flint City. On the drive, they talked about the weather, how prices seemed to be always going higher, and other small talk, apparently in a conscious effort to avoid discussing the recent crimes or the fire at Carol's.

They parked in front of Mrs. Laramie's house. On the trip back, she had mentioned being all tuckered out and said goodnight. Ben escorted her to the front door, unlocked it, and saw her safely inside while accepting her warm thanks for dinner and a delightful evening.

Ben returned to his car and crawled into the front seat beside Carol. He leaned over and asked if she was tired and needed to call it a night. While he waited for her answer, he gathered up courage to make a suggestion. One that might very well change the rest of both of their lives.

"No, Ben, I'm fine, really. I'm just enjoying being near you—with you—and I'm in your capable hands as long as you want me around."

He was unsure exactly what she meant by that statement. He had thought long and hard about what he wanted to suggest to her. His concern was the right way to broach the subject. If he took the wrong approach, he could blow the deal right from the get-go. He steeled his nerves, took Carol's hand in his, and began cautiously, hoping he would not upset her with the idea he wanted to propose.

"Listen very carefully to what I'm about to say. Please don't interrupt me or reply until you've heard me out. Promise?"

"I promise," she whispered. "This sounds like something serious, something I may not want to hear. Tell me now, you're not leaving Flint City or anything like that?" Her voice was quiet and barely audible.

"No, I'm not about to leave Flint City or you. Nothing like that. In fact, it's just the opposite," he assured her. After a silence in which he could hear his heart beating and what must have seemed an hour long to Carol, he began to explain what he had in mind.

"To start with, I don't want you to be frightened, but I think someone is out to harm you," he said quietly.

"Ben, you *are* scaring me!"

"I'm sorry. Please don't be scared. You haven't heard yet what I have to say. And remember, you promised not to interrupt." At that, she said no more but gripped his hand even more tightly.

He continued, "Unfortunately, I don't have any ideas right now about who may be a threat to your safety or even if there is a threat. I don't know what this person—or these persons—might try to do or when he could try to do something or what that something could be. One thing I'm fairly sure of is where the attempt, if there is one, will come. He, or they, will go after you again at your house or when you're on your way to or from work at the mill." He paused to let this soak in. He could see the streetlight reflected in her eyes, and they were eyes of a frightened person. She kept quiet though.

"You need someone watching over you night and day except when you're at work. To be really blunt, you need around-the-clock protection. Your safety is my major concern and reason number one why I'm going to suggest a solution to you in a minute. Reason number two has to do more with my situation than yours, but it ties into reason number one. I'm positive old lady Wainright—Ida that is—watches every movement I make." Carol took in a deep breath as if she was about to say something. Ben held up his left hand as a signal to wait. "The other evening, I'm sure she eavesdropped on the telephone call I placed to my daughter in Titusville. The phones at the motel go though the switchboard, which makes it a snap for her to monitor my calls. What's more, I suspect she reports everything I do or say to someone else, who I don't know. I'm not paranoid, but the bottom line is I need to get out of the IdaHO as soon as possible."

He paused again so Carol could digest this last bit of information. She sat silently, staring at Ben with wide, expectant eyes. He was encouraged because she had not bolted from the car to run to Mrs. Laramie's. At least not yet.

"So, here's what I think we should do to resolve both of our situations. I'm paid up at the IdaHO until Tuesday. Your house should be ready for you on Tuesday. If you agree, I could check out of the motel, come to your house, and sleep in Jeremy's bedroom. This way, I would be nearby if anything happens and I can escort you back and forth to work." That was all. He had said what was on his mind, and he hoped Carol would be receptive to his suggestion.

A quick glance at her face told him her fear had dissipated somewhat. He didn't add anything more. She slowly withdrew her hand from his and dropped both of them in her lap. She looked down—her eyes closed. Ben sat punishing himself for being so forward. He had known Carol for less than a week, and here he was asking her to take him into her home. What was he thinking? Unconsciously, he pounded his fist on the steering wheel, which frightened Carol, who flinched noticeably. She jerked upright and looked at him with wide eyes.

He thought she wasn't going to say anything more—just get out of the car and run to Mrs. Laramie's house. After a moment, she said slowly, choosing her words carefully, "Oh, Ben, it's so soon after I lost my son, my Jeremy. Then someone sets my house on fire, and you tell me I may still be in danger. I'm so confused. Please let me think about your suggestion for a couple of days," she pleaded. "I promise to give you my answer sometime early on Tuesday morning if not before. If I decide your idea is a good one, I'll let you know in plenty of time to check out of the motel. Whatever I decide, you'll have my answer."

That was all Ben could expect or hope for. At least she hadn't turned him down flat. She was considering his proposal. With a nod in her direction, he got out of the car, went around to open the passenger door for Carol, and walked her to Mrs. Laramie's porch. Mrs. Laramie had left a table lamp lighted in the living room. *A nice, friendly touch,* he thought. They kissed goodnight before Ben opened the door for Carol to enter.

She looked back at him through the screen door and said, "Goodnight, Ben."

To which he replied, "Good night, my dear. Be sure to lock the door behind you."

He drove back around the corner to his motel, parked his rental, entered cautiously, undressed, and hit the sack.

On Saturday, Carol and Ben spent some time in the morning watching Tony and his workers as they continued their assault on Carol's kitchen. Tiring of the noise and turmoil, the couple drove in Ben's car to the local hardware to replace pots, pans, utensils, hand towels, and other small kitchen equipment ruined by heat from the fire. They returned to Carol's house before noon and unloaded their purchases from the car, stacking everything in neat piles in the living room.

Carol told Ben that Mrs. Laramie had invited them for lunch. He felt like he was imposing and mentioned that as they entered her house, but Mrs. Laramie said, "Not at all, young man, come in here, you're entirely welcome."

After lunch, Ben and Carol went to see Cecil B. DeMille's gigantic production of *The Ten Commandments,* starring Charlton Heston as Moses and Yul Brenner as Ramses II, which lasted over three hours. On the way back to Mrs Laramie's they stopped off at Granny's Diner for hamburgers, fries, and colas.

Mrs. Laramie had left a lamp burning dimly in the living room for Carol's return. "How thoughtful of her to leave a light burning for me," Carol said. "She really is a sweet person." Ben agreed wholeheartedly.

They embraced each other tightly and prolonged their goodnight kiss. Carol thanked Ben for the movie and hamburger. As she opened the door to go in, Ben distinctly heard a lady's voice inside the living room say, "Good night, young man."

Ben chuckled the entire way as he drove back to the IdaHO. At least her eavesdropping was well intended, unlike what he figured Ida Wainright's motives were.

After checking on the workmen Sunday morning to be sure they didn't have any questions, he decided to telephone Carol and see if she was still speaking to him. He wanted to pick her up and maybe even drive somewhere out in the countryside where they could find a cool, shady spot to have a picnic lunch. Was he beginning to take her for granted? He hoped not. Rather than knocking on Mrs. Laramie's front door to ask if Carol wanted to take a little drive, he decided to telephone her from his room at the motel.

In answer to his invitation, Carol said, "That would be lovely." Her earlier remoteness had seemingly diminished. "Yes, I can be ready by noon. Will that be okay?"

He assured her that would be fine and he would come to pick her up then.

After he showered and shaved and dressed in his usual khaki attire with a tan knit shirt, he opened the curtains of his motel room and sat down at the table near the window to review notes he had made in his notebook about the crimes he and Sheriff Bates were investigating. After perusing them for some time, he came to the conclusion that he had few clues to go on. All he had were suppositions from Sal and Pug, which were not based on facts. Even their suspicions didn't put much meat on the bones. Hopefully, on Monday, when Kellerman and Williams arrived, they would get down to cases. That is, if the two of them had information that would help piece together a complete puzzle.

Ben picked up Carol at Mrs. Laramie's a few minutes before noon. She was dressed in bright red Bermuda shorts, with a red-and-gold checkered sash of the same hue tied around her waist. As a top she had slipped into a sparkling white blouse and on her feet wore white sandals. Her hair was pulled back in the ponytail again like it had been earlier and held with a red-and-white ribbon.

He had brought the pocketknife with him. As soon as they were comfortable in the front seat of his car, Ben unwrapped it and held it out in front of her. She stared at the knife for a moment, then reached over to take it from Ben's hand. He quickly closed his fingers around the handkerchief to keep her from touching it.

She sat motionless and stared at his folded-up handkerchief, even though its contents were no longer visible to her. "Carol, what's wrong?"

"Oh, Ben," she said. Her eyes were misty. "That's Jeremy's pocketknife! I gave it to him on his sixteenth birthday, and he has carried it with him every day since."

"Carol, honey, listen to me. Are you sure? There's no doubt?"

She told him there was no doubt at all. The knife was definitely Jeremy's. She asked him to unwrap it again, and without touching it, she pointed out a little nick in the edge of the tortoise shell handle where he had dropped it one time on the pavement. "Ben, it's—it was—his," she insisted. "Why do you keep asking me?" She sounded exasperated.

"All right, Carol, forgive me. I'm sorry I've upset you. Like I told Mrs. Laramie, it's just an investigator's way of making sure what he hears, or thinks he hears, the first time is what a person actually said. I'm truly sorry," he apologized again.

Carol had partially regained her composure, enough to say, "It's not you I'm upset with, Ben. I thought Jeremy's knife would have been among his personal effects when Mr. Poole returned them to me. But he sent only Jeremy's clothes. The knife wasn't in any of his pockets, so I thought maybe it had been lost or stolen and Jeremy was afraid to tell me." She paused to take a deep breath and to dab her eyes and nose with a tissue. "Now here his knife is. It turns up when I least expect it. It's like having a part of Jeremy right here in the car with us. Can you understand that, Ben?"

"Yes, I can. I know from my wife's tragic death how it is to feel the presence of someone—someone who seems to be there to help us get over the rough spots."

Carol said maybe Jeremy was telling them something about his death, how he was killed, and perhaps even who did it. Hopefully. Ben assured her he would do his very best to find out why Jeremy's knife was in the street in front of her house, when it got there, and how. Also he would have it fingerprinted to see if there were any traces of prints. Ben doubted they would find a full set of fingerprints because the handle was so narrow, but he didn't tell Carol about his misgivings.

Their picnic was dampened somewhat by circumstances surrounding Jeremy's pocketknife. Nonetheless, they both tried to present brave, sober fronts, eating and enjoying the scenery as well as the beautiful, sunny, warm spring afternoon in South Georgia. They returned just before dark, kissing again in the car, then on the porch as Carol bid Ben goodnight.

Another restless night for Ben, tumbling and tossing. Murder, bodies hanging in trees, guns, and fire raced in and out of Ben's mind. When he couldn't sleep, he sat up in the side chair in the dark just thinking about Carol and the case. By morning, nothing had been resolved about events of the past week or about the case, or about her.

16

Monday morning. Ben awakened to what at first sounded to him like another rattlesnake singing. *Oh, no, not that again!* he thought. Slowly, he realized the sound was his alarm clock. He reached over and banged his hand down on the button on the clock, which had been trying its best to disturb his peace.

He rubbed his eyes with the backs of his hands as he stared at the ceiling of his motel room. Slowly, his gaze roamed to the far corner of the room above the door where paint was surrendering its hold on the ceiling and had begun to droop down like fall leaves. He hadn't noticed that before. What a dump! True, Pug did his best to keep the place clean, but his room could use some fresh paint and wallpaper, not to mention new furniture. This realization only strengthened his resolve to move in with Carol, assuming she agreed, which helped to satiate his misgivings.

As he reluctantly crawled out of bed, Ben chided himself for ever choosing the IdaHO Motel in the first place. But on second thought, had he not stopped off there he would not have been close enough to Carol's house to help when her house was set ablaze. He probably would not have known about the mysterious Room 3 at the motel, either.

Showered, shaved, dressed, he drove around the block to check again on the workmen at Carol's house. It was after seven-thirty, and he knew she would have left for work at the mill before he arrived. Her car was not in the driveway. Inside a sealed envelope he found on the dining room table, there was a note to him in Carol's handwriting. *Dear Ben, I have decided not to wait any longer to tell you that I agree it would be best for both of us if you moved in with me today rather than waiting until tomorrow. You can bring your things over whenever you want to. Love, Carol.*

Faithfully, the workers were on the job. He shifted the plastic sheet aside and stuck his head into the kitchen. The linoleum had been laid late Sunday, and workers were installing new cabinets and counter-tops. Another carpenter had replaced the broken kitchen window. With a wave of his hand and a big grin, Ben indicated he was happy with them and their progress. Repairs were going as planned.

After a quick cup of coffee and a couple of donuts at Sal's, where eating had become habitual, Ben headed for the River City Bank to alert the head teller to expect a rather large fund transfer later in the afternoon from his home bank in Titusville. He further instructed the teller to deposit the funds into the checking account he had already established. He used the bank's courtesy telephone to call his Titusville bank and request a sum to be transferred to his River City Bank account. He gave them his account number.

He left the bank and drove to Sheriff Bates' office at the jail. He wanted to be there before the Florida East Coast Railroad detective Kellerman and the FBI agent Williams arrived at ten o'clock.

Sheriff Bates was already on duty, as he had expected, but Deputy Phipps was not around. After a cordial greeting, Ben unwrapped Jeremy Martin's pocketknife and told the sheriff where and when he found it. He also told Bates about Carol's reaction when she saw it, confirming that the knife indeed was her son's. No doubt about it from the way she recoiled and became misty-eyed.

"I have a theory about how the knife got there and when," Ben said as a matter-of-fact.

"Which is?"

"It could have dropped out of the kid's pants pocket into the bed of the pickup Mrs. Laramie saw make a one-eighty and come back up her street. There is a possibility, however remote, that Jeremy's knife slid out of his pocket while he was being loaded into the back of the pickup and was jostled and bounced around during the rough ride along the railroad tracks, then dropped in the street on one of its passes by Carol's house," he theorized.

"Poole didn't find anything in Jeremy's pockets during his autopsy. They were empty," Bates reminded both of them.

"And the good Poole was right. Whoever caught the boy by the railroad siding must have banged him on the head, tied him hand-and-foot, loaded him into the back of their pickup, and then drove around with him while they tried to decide what to do with the boy. I would guess at the time, they thought he was still alive. We do not yet know where they ended up. Maybe whoever was in that truck also took him to the grove and hanged him," Ben suggested.

"But why, and why upside down? Those are the big questions. Why would two or more persons, presumably men, knock the kid out, tie him up, and haul him up and down Carol's street before hanging him where he was bound to be found at daylight?" Bates asked. "And what's more, killers usually go to great lengths to hide bodies of their victims, or they just leave them lying where they died. I don't know of a single case where killers displayed their victims' bodies for the public to admire."

"Doesn't make sense, but all the same, I think that's just what happened. It's the only explanation we have that ties the shoe we found in the switching yard, the pickup truck Mrs. Laramie saw, and the boy's knife together."

"I confess, you just may be right."

Ben sat down, lit his first cigarette of the day, ground out the match on the floor with his shoe and said that maybe they should go over all the facts or suppositions one more time about Jeremy Martin's hanging.

"First, somebody—probably two men—caught the boy in the switching yard when they were down there robbing the boxcar," Ben said. "We do know why Jeremy was in the yard. According to Carol, he was cutting through on his way home from his buddy Billy Kleggin's house."

Then Bates took up the review. "Second, we know he was forcibly held down with his head pressed in the rocks. The minute grains of ballast embedded in his cheek tell us that." He paused to think, and then continued. "The same perpetrators hit him on the side of the head hard enough to knock him unconscious, and the force of the blow caused hemorrhaging to start inside his brain. We don't know why they hit him on the head, unless he was hollering and they wanted to shut him up. If they had wanted to kill him, they would have done it right then and there. If we're on the right track with this—ah, pardon the pun—two or more men must have loaded him into their truck of unknown size and description. In their apparent haste, they did not notice one of his sneakers had dropped off."

Ben said, "Up to now, most of what we've gone over is nebulous guess-work at best, but I'll bet it is fairly close to what actually took place. I first saw the Martin boy when I woke up after sleeping in the grove overnight. You were summoned early Monday morning by a good citizen, Emma Lake, who heard dogs barking. Besides the dogs, Emma, the killers, and me, you must have been the next person to see him hanging in the tree."

"And he was already dead."

"He was already dead. Killed from the hemorrhage inside his head."

"What about the rattlesnake in your room? Don't forget him."

"You don't have to remind me about the rattler, Sheriff," Ben said grinning. "It seems funny now, but it wasn't when it happened. We don't know who put the snake in my room, but we're pretty sure Pug was not the guy."

"Suppose that episode was some sort of warning that you are not welcome in Flint City and you better get the hell out of town?"

"As clear as one of the springs that feeds Flint River!" Ben agreed.

"Then four days later, Carol Martin's house is set on fire by a person or person's unknown. We do know from Furnace's report that it was arson, but that's all we do know at this point."

Ben nodded. "It was definitely arson. And what's more, I think the fire was a warning to Carol to keep her mouth shut, if she saw anything or knows anything, which she doesn't. Strange, though, Sal has an idea the fire was set as revenge and maybe Carol's boy was murdered for the same reason. If that's so, then we have motives for both crimes."

"Revenge is a strong motive for killing," Bates agreed. "This morning you bring me a knife that Carol has confirmed was Jeremy's, which you found in the street in front of her house. How it got there is still a mystery."

"Well, the bottom line is, we have a few facts and a lot of suppositions. If we're right about revenge, we have motive, means, and opportunity for Carol's fire and her son's hanging. What we don't yet have is a motive for Getts' killing. In fact, we don't even know if the three crimes are connected. I have a notion that somehow they are."

A car pulled into the jail parking lot precisely at ten o'clock, just as Sheriff Sandy Bates and Ben Reed were about to review the facts, or suppositions, about the Getts murder. Ben got up to look. In the car were two men he did not know, but since it was time for their arrival, he assumed they were Kellerman and Williams.

"I think they are the Florida East Coast Railroad investigator and the FBI," he told the sheriff. "And they're right on time. I like punctuality in people."

The two came into the sheriff's office and introduced themselves to Sheriff Bates and Reed as Doug Williams, Florida FBI, and Tom Kellerman, Florida East Coast Railroad investigator, both with offices in Jacksonville. Ben did not know the FEC railroad detective. Williams was around six feet tall, pale-skinned, bald-headed, with no neck and rounded shoulders that barely supported suspenders that were holding up his trousers. Like most FBI types, Williams was wearing a white shirt, tie, and black unbuttoned jacket.

Kellerman was the opposite—short, almost dumpy, a head of dark curly hair, with a bulbous nose that would shame a light bulb. He was wearing a long-sleeved shirt, although the morning was warming up. After a few minutes exchanging pleasantries about the weather and how summer was just over the horizon, they got down to business. The sheriff grabbed two folding chairs out of his closet and invited the men to sit down. They did so carefully because the chairs were obviously old and wobbly. Williams explained that Atlanta had assigned a Florida agent to the case rather than someone from Georgia because the crates were found missing at Port Canaveral in Florida.

"You two are the full complement who run this office?" Williams asked.

"Well, not exactly." Bates explained about Ben being a former Titusville cop and railroad bull with the FEC railroad and that the sheriff had a deputy who was not due in until after lunch.

That out of the way, the sheriff asked, "So, what can we do for you two gentlemen?" He was sizing up his visitors at the same time. Kellerman didn't resemble what a railroad bull was expected to look like, but then neither did Ben. Williams, on the other hand, was spit-and-polish, very much a typical FBI agent.

Kellerman led off. "We, the Florida East Coast Railroad that is, had a burglary reported by our unit at the Cape. Sometime during this past week a boxcar from the Redstone Arsenal in Huntsville, Alabama, was apparently broken into and burgled. Hell, there is no *apparently* about it. Someone took a very important shipment out of that boxcar. We're checking back down the route the train followed to find out where the theft happened.

"We don't know if the cargo was stolen while the train was at Flint City. It was one of our LCL cars. An LCL car is one with less than a carload lot, meaning it is usually loaded with other consignments going to different locations along the train's route, only this car had just one specific load for only one unique destination," Kellerman explained.

"I see. And one of the stops on the route was here in Flint City?" Ben interrupted.

"Exactly. It was set off with some other boxcars to be picked up by an eastbound freight to Waycross then through Jacksonville to the Cape. You see, we interchange with the Flint River Railroad in Waycross. That was a week ago yesterday—last Sunday night." Kellerman referred to his notes. "There were four wooden crates of equipment consigned to the Cape, two big ones and two smaller ones. The two smaller boxes have gone missing."

"What is—or was—in the crates?"

"I'd rather not say. In fact, I cannot say."

Agent Williams butted in. "That's classified information! Classified top secret!"

Bates ignored Williams. "Come on, Mr. Kellerman," Bates pleaded. "How can we help you if you don't level with us? We are all professionals here and we know how to keep our mouths shut about ongoing investigations. Fact is, just now we have more than we want, or need for that matter, what with double murders, poisonous snakes, arson fires, and the like right here in Flint City."

Williams took the conversation away from Kellerman. After a long pause to reflect about how much he could or should reveal, he said, "These two crates contain certain guidance components of a highly secret system destined to be delivered to the space port at Port Canaveral. These systems are vital in readying one of our nation's most important protective defense devices. But that's hush-hush you understand! It's absolutely essential—no, more than that—imperative that we recover those two crates immediately. As you can imagine, all hell has broken out all the way from the Pentagon to the Cape."

Ben and the sheriff both blew air at the same time through pursed lips. "Whew. It does not get much more expedient than that," Ben observed. "Tell me, why weren't they shipped by commercial air or by military cargo direct to the Cape?"

"I'm told the manufacturer was running way behind time on his contract and was already facing stiff fines. He did not want to wait around for air or alternate truck transport to be approved by the brass in the Pentagon."

"But Mr. Kellerman, if the contractor was already way behind in making his contract, couldn't the Cape have waited a few more days for air transport to be approved?" Ben asked.

"Who knows," Williams replied. "Washington works in mysterious ways it's a miracle to perform."

"So, what makes you think the boxes were stolen while the boxcar was parked for only a few hours in our yard here in Flint City? Was there a shipment to drop off here?" Bates asked.

"Two things. Although the crates were in an LCL boxcar, as I said before, this car was dedicated solely to this shipment. No other freight was in the car, so there wasn't any reason for it to be opened anywhere between the point of origin in Alabama and the Cape. The cargo was highly classified, so no one was even supposed to know what was inside. The shipper and those at the Cape felt safe in having the boxcar sidelined only once for a brief time before being picked up again," Kellerman answered.

"I was wondering about that. Seems illogical to me to leave a top secret, top priority, sensitive shipment sit around anywhere on a siding for very long, if at all. I sure wouldn't do it if it were me." This from Ben. "Seems to me, a special unit train could have been assigned, or at least have a car with armed security coupled behind to guard the shipment."

"Same answer; too long for the government approval process to go through," Williams answered.

"The boxcar was secure and sealed. That's another thing. The seal that was on the car when it arrived at the Cape had been tampered with. Besides, as I said, there was no reason for it to be opened by anybody," Kellerman pointed out. "That's one of the things that leads us to think the burglary took place on your siding. Along the entire route from Huntsville to Canaveral, the boxcar was only delayed here in Flint City and then only for a few hours before it was scheduled sometime around daylight next morning to be hitched to the string headed east and down the Florida coast."

"It's obvious to me that someone found out somehow what the boxcar contained," Bates observed. "And they made the best of it."

"Unfortunately, that's true," Williams admitted, rubbing his forehead. "We have agents working on that end of it this very moment across southern Alabama, Georgia, and down the east coast into Florida. We suspect an inside job, and the railroad tends to agree with us. And with only one layover here in Flint City, it meant the burglars had enough time in six or eight hours to open the car, steal the crates, and get away without worrying about a consignee or anyone else showing up bright and early in the morning to claim the shipment. They would have had most of the night to take the goods—almost at their leisure, you might say."

"You said there was another thing?" Bates asked.

"This seal." Kellerman dug a metal railroad seal out of his pocket and handed it across to the sheriff. "As you can see, it's a far cry from what it was. It's not even the seal the railroad issued to the manufacturer in Huntsville. We checked first thing on what the number had been before it was defaced like that. It came from a batch in our FEC offices in Jacksonville."

Ben explained, "You see, Sheriff, shippers have a supply of seals that railroads issue to them. The numbers on each seal are registered and carefully tracked. With a mixed load carried in a typical LCL car, that's the only way any railroad has of knowing who has entered their car, when, and for what purpose."

"So, what is so special about this seal?" Bates asked.

"Look at it closely, Sheriff," Kellerman said, as he got up and looked over Bates' shoulder. "Do you see anything unusual?"

"No, not really, except it's a little rough, kind of like it was beat on. Here, Ben, you're more experienced at this than I am." Bates handed the seal to Ben.

"Someone has cleverly tried to hammer down some of the numbers so they couldn't be read. Whoever did it hoped its origin could not be traced. It was a futile effort because when the shipment arrived at its destination the first thing employees at the Cape would do is look at the numbers on the seal and record them before they removed it from the door to open the boxcar."

Williams took up the narrative. "That's exactly what the Cape people did. On Monday when the boxcar was set off on the siding at the Cape, the men responsible for opening the car recognized immediately that the seal had been tampered with, so they wisely did not touch it. Instead, they called my office in Jacksonville and asked for a special agent to be sent down to supervise removal of the seal and to be present when the boxcar was opened. We sent a man down immediately, and he applied a chemical on the seal that brought out the numbers so they could be read and recorded. He reported the numbers to FEC officials, who looked at their record of seals issued to the system's manufacturer in Huntsville. As it turns out, the seal the railroad issued to the Huntsville contractor is missing. After receiving permission from the Pentagon, our agent opened the boxcar and discovered the two small crates were missing."

"Have you found out to whom this altered seal was issued?" Ben asked.

"Yes. We did trace the numbers on the seal to another company, which will remain unnamed. However, I can tell you that records indicate it was issued about a year ago from Jacksonville," Kellerman said.

"Jacksonville? How could a seal issued in Jacksonville twelve months ago get attached to the door of a boxcar before it ever arrived at the Cape?" Bates was learning. And he was asking the right questions.

"It seems a known ex-con was hired by this unnamed company about a year ago, and he works in the shipping and receiving department. That is what brings us to Flint City."

"Does the ex-con live here?" Ben asked.

"No, but his cousin does." Kellerman referred again to his notes. "The cousin's name is Getts, Sherman Getts."

Bates and Reed were flabbergasted, and they both whistled through their lips. The sheriff pounded his fist on the desk. Without saying anything, the two looked at each other, exchanging nods and wide grins. Both men thought this news might just be the break they needed to solve a couple of murders and maybe even arson.

Like a small boy on Christmas morning, Bates was unable to contain his excitement. "Well, Getts did live here. He's dead! Murdered in his own home in bed by an unknown assailant or assailants sometime last Monday night or Tuesday morning."

It was Kellerman's turn to show his surprise by exclaiming, "I'll be damned! You mean, after all of this I'm almost a week late in catching up with this guy and sweating him under bright lights! I can't believe it. Damn and damn again! Are we sure we're talking about the same Sherman Getts?"

"Yes, Kellerman, there is—there was—only one Sherman Getts in Flint City, and I'm mighty thankful for that," Bates said. "Any more like him, and our crime rate would be blown off the chart! Well, maybe through the ceiling at least. We have been watching him ever since he showed up here from Jacksonville a while back but hadn't been able to pin anything on him. Mostly petty things, like window peeping, poisoning neighbors' dogs, stealing tools and tires from service stations, that sort of thing. Nothing really big until now *if* he was involved in this train burglary."

"Seems all you can pin on him now is a lily to his chest," Williams observed with disappointment painted on his face.

Sheriff Sandy Bates and Ben Reed told the two visitors about the double murders, the rattlesnake incident, and the arson house fire that had recently happened in Flint City. Kellerman and Williams were silent for a few minutes, digesting what they had heard. Finally, Williams asked, "Do you suppose they're connected in some way to the burglary of our shipment?"

"We're working on that as a possibility," Ben replied. "You've brought us a new ingredient we have to add to the mix. It may change the way we look at these cases."

"Well, keep us informed on your progress," Williams said, handing Ben and Bates his card. "For now, we'll go back to our superiors and report that you two good men are checking into the possibility Getts may have been one of maybe two persons who probably burgled the boxcar." The two got up to leave after firm handshakes all round. "I'll leave it in you gentlemen's good hands to find out who the other perpetrators were. There has to be at least two, the crates being so awkward to handle and fairly heavy. I don't have to remind you that we need to clear this theft up as soon as possible and find those damned systems!"

"One more question, Williams. Do you have any idea why the systems were stolen and where they may be headed?" Ben asked. The question had been bothering him all along.

"We think we know why they were taken. The answer lies in where they may be headed, or should I say where they *may be* already. Enough to say, someone wants to sell them somewhere abroad, probably to an unfriendly country that is secretly developing their own defense program," Williams replied grimly. "That's a secret, too, you understand?"

"Well, gentlemen, we'll certainly keep you informed. I guess it's kind of late to be asking if you found any fingerprints anywhere in or on the boxcar?" Ben inquired.

"We dusted it and found nothing," Kellerman replied. "They must have been wearing gloves. At least they were savvy enough to do that because the crates were wooden and bound to have splinters. The trick with the seal was dumb." They nodded and left the jail, backing out of the parking lot to return to their respective offices.

The two investigators stood for several seconds just looking at each other, thinking. Ben's arms were akimbo, while Bates stuffed his hands deep into his pockets. Both were grinning from ear-to-ear like a couple of Flint River catfish. Then, as if on cue, they burst out laughing and began to shake hands vigorously, sensing they may have just gotten their first break in four very baffling cases.

"So, old half-wit Getts was flirting with and flaunting the law," Bates said. "Well, he won't give me any more trouble now, unless he tries to pry the pearls out of the Pearly Gates!" They began to laugh again, not at Getts, but rather at their possible good fortune.

"Since we obviously can't question Getts personally, it seems to me our only alternative is to question some of Getts' close friends and associates," Ben suggested.

"I agree." The sheriff pulled a file from his bottom drawer and opened it on his desk. "And I just happen to have a list of them here. We did pull

Getts in from time-to-time on suspicions of petty thefts and tried to wring confessions out of him without any luck. But I kept a list of all the names he mentioned when he was trying to deflect our questions."

"Who on your list seems most likely to be involved in this kind of thing? Burglarizing a train is a federal offense. Pretty serious stuff. Do you have on your list any priors, perhaps former state felons now out on the streets, or men who have done hard time in federal prisons anywhere? Good place to start."

"I hear what you're saying. If a guy commits a federal offense, doing time won't necessarily cure him, and he probably won't hesitate to repeat a similar crime again sometime. It's usually the first prison time that gives some guys pause, but then they're apt to repeat some similar crime even after they've done hard time." Bates ran his finger down the list of known offenders who had been mentioned by Getts.

"There are two or three known lawbreakers here. Only one who comes to mind immediately. In fact, he sticks out like a sore thumb. He's a guy named Milo Scroggins. Lives here in Flint City. Close buddy and known associate of Getts. Scroggins was sent up to Leavenworth, Kansas, for ten years for attempting to rob a bank over in Mobile, but he was released after six years for good behavior and previous time served. Moved here about five years ago and took up with Getts almost immediately. Spends a lot of time swilling beer and runs up tabs at Shakey's Pool Hall then manages to pay them off in a lump sum. Getts didn't know where Milo got lumps of money all of a sudden to pay off his debts. Scroggins does odd jobs, carpentering, mowing lawns, tree trimming, and helping when moving companies need day laborers. That last job got him into peoples' houses, and we think he used the knowledge to go back later and burglarize them. Couldn't prove anything, though." Bates looked up from the file as Ben lit a cigarette, exhaling smoke toward the ceiling.

"Criminals are all on good behavior when some guard is standing over them. They're not so goody-goody though after they're paroled."

"Neither of them were Sunday school teachers, that's for sure. Funny. It says here that Getts was in Mobile at the time Scroggins pulled the bank job, but the locals couldn't pin him as an accomplice in the robbery."

"A prime prospect, anyway. Let's start with him, Sandy."

"Good idea. While we're at it, we can stop by the judge's chambers and pick up the search warrant for Room 3 at the IdaHO Motel. Let me get my hat. We'll take your car, if you don't mind, because mine might spook Scroggins, and he could threaten us with a shotgun or worse, an ornery rattlesnake!" Bates laughed at his own attempt at humor. Ben didn't.

They left hurriedly after Bates scribbled a note for Deputy Phipps, telling him to hold down the fort until they returned. The note didn't say where they went, or why. On purpose.

After Bates obtained the warrant, they drove first to the IdaHO and presented the document to Mrs. Wainright. She stared at them in disbelief. After reading and rereading the search warrant, she questioned them about why they wanted to interfere with her business and why they wanted to look inside Room 3.

The sheriff did not answer either of her questions. He smiled and asked her calmly to give him the key to Room 3 so he and Ben Reed could take a look inside. Ida dug into a pocket of her apron and begrudgingly handed over the key.

When they opened the door to Room 3, it was empty. There was not one stick of furniture in the room. However, the sheriff did find two short wood splinters embedded in the carpet just inside the door. He dislodged them, and they went into his shirt pocket for safekeeping.

Sheriff Bates relocked the door, and they returned the key to Ida Wainright. With another big smile aimed in her direction, he asked the motel keeper, "Have you been remodeling—or are you about to fix up—Room 3? We see that it's empty, like you might intend to change out the bathroom fixtures or repaper the walls or something."

"If it's all the same to you, Mr. Smarty Pants Sheriff, we are replacing the carpet. The people are supposed to be here later this week to lay it," she growled back at him.

"Interesting," Ben observed, as they walked back to his car. "We find splinters in an old carpet that she is replacing. Makes one really suspicious about where the wood splinters came from and why she's installing new carpet this week only in Room 3. Curious!"

"It may be coincidence, but I doubt it," Bates answered. "I'll bet you ten bucks that they match the wood on the two crates missing from the boxcar. If so, the splinters add a whole new dimension to our investigation. We'll have to look further into that angle."

"For sure," Ben agreed. He cranked his car's motor, and they headed for Milo Scroggins' house.

17

THEY WERE IN LUCK. SCROGGINS was at home, and his radio was blaring so loudly Sheriff Sandy Bates and Ben Reed could hear it half a block away. They turned into his driveway and killed the engine. Parked in front of their car was a light blue pickup, which matched the description given by Mrs. Laramie. Obviously, the truck belonged to Scroggins.

"Before we disturb the good Mr. Scroggins, let's take a peek at the right rear tire on that pickup. I'll bet you five bucks to a hole in a rolling donut it has a chunk missing on the outside tread of one of his tires, probably on the back," Ben said. Without replying, the sheriff got out of the car, put on his hat, and walked to the back right-hand side of Scroggins' pickup with Ben close on his heels. They knelt down to inspect the tire. There was no sign of a chunk missing from it or from the front tire on the same side.

Just then the door slammed open, and Scroggins came charging at them. Red-faced. Angry. Thankfully, without a weapon.

"What in the livin' hell do ya think yer doin', Sheriff!" Scroggins shrieked. "Leave my truck alone and get the hell off my property!" He stopped in front of the intruders, feet spread wide apart, hands on hips, threatening. Ben was relieved. He had never known a man, no matter how angry, who could throw a punch with any force while he was standing with his legs planted wide apart.

"Now, Milo, just simmer down! Mr. Reed and I just want to ask you a couple of questions. If you don't have anything to hide, they'll be easy to answer. Then we'll be on our way." Sheriff Bates was good, real good.

The rotund Scroggins glared at Bates, but the diminutive sheriff stood up to him, resolved to take the heavier man on if need be. Scroggins saw the determination in the sheriff's face, and with the stout, well-muscled Reed to back him up, Scroggins began to cool down. He looked at the ground, kicked the dirt with the toe of his run-down-at-the-heels cowboy boot. "I ain't done nothin'!" Scroggins shot back. Challenging. Not all of the fire in his two hundred fifty pounds of flab gone out yet.

"I didn't say you did, Milo," the sheriff almost crooned back at him, smiling.

"Well, you ain't pinnin' nothin' on me. I don't know what ya want, but you'll find I wasn't involved, whatever it were."

"Oh, were you involved in something we didn't know about?" Bates inquired, picking up on Scroggins' opening. He continued to smile directly into Scroggins' face, disarming him all the more.

"I didn't say that, and you know it, Sheriff." Scroggins' face flushed bright red, and this time it wasn't from anger. His face told the experienced sheriff that he was on the right track. But he was skilled enough to back off a little and let Scroggins cool down some more before launching into the meat of his questions.

"This is Mr. Benjamin Reed. He's an ex cop from Florida. He's here helping out with a couple of cases I'm working on." Bates turned to Ben still smiling, "Ben, meet Milo Scroggins—Mr. Scroggins." Showing a suspect a measure of respect, especially in the early going, never hurt when about to ask questions.

Ben picked up immediately on the sheriff's ploy. "Pleased to meet you, Mr. Scroggins." He recoiled from the smell emitting from Scroggins as he reached to shake hands. The man had not bathed for a couple of days, Ben guessed. *Fat slob!* he thought. His kind always talk tough until things get tough, and then most of them turn to jelly and cave in.

"Huh." Scroggins barely acknowledged Ben Reed's presence. Not very friendly, but under the circumstances little else could be expected. Scroggins evidently was not speaking to Reed, or if he was, he limited his remarks to one-syllable words. Well, there would be time enough for Ben to grill Scroggins under his own terms and in his own way. *Just you wait,* Ben thought.

Turning back to Scroggins, the sheriff suggested the three of them go into his house where they could sit a spell and talk about some recent events. Scroggins, belching and spitting, purposefully in Ben's direction, only nodded, turned on his heels, and headed inside. Once there, the sheriff turned off the radio. After they sat down, not comfortably but seated nonetheless in sagging furniture, Bates advised Scroggins that he didn't have to answer their questions; that the sheriff was alleging nothing, and that Scroggins had the right to have an attorney present even though he was not under arrest. Not yet, anyway.

"What'd I need a mouthpiece for? I ain't done nothin' wrong," Scroggins said.

The sheriff asked Ben to make a note that Scroggins had refused counsel while he was being questioned. Sheriff Bates took up the questioning.

"What you been up to lately, Milo?"

"Not much. Same old six 'n seven," he stammered. Still not running off at the mouth.

"Been in town the last few days, have you?"

"Yep."

"Tell us where you were last Sunday around midnight or a little after."

"I don't rightly remember, Sheriff. That's the shameful truth."

Sheriff Bates figured Scroggins wouldn't tell the truth even to save his own mother's life.

"Now come on, Milo, everyone remembers where he was and when. It's been just a week ago. Level with me, hear?"

"Well, iffin you insist, I was home here listenin' to my radio until late, then I went to bed directly."

Scroggins would not look Bates in the eyes. It was obvious to the sheriff that Scroggins was hiding something. Was it something to do with the Martin kid? He meant to find out one way or the other, short of tearing him to shreds. Couldn't do that anymore, even though he wanted desperately to knock the truth out of the lying bastard.

"So, you got sleepy and went right to bed? Is that what you're telling me? Is that what you want us to believe?" He noticed Ben had his notebook out and was taking notes. Good man. He could concentrate on trying to pry the truth out of Scroggins, if he even recognized it when it jumped up and bit him.

"I don't suppose you have someone to back up your story? A gal, for instance." Bates could hardly keep from smiling as he asked the question.

What woman in her right mind would even consider going to bed with this gross, smelly pig?

"No—no gal." Enough said, certainly.

Bates took another tack to keep Scroggins off balance. "Where did you go when you tore that chunk out of your tire, Milo?"

"Ah, which tire? I didn't cut no damn tire. I'd'a knowed it if I did!"

Ignoring Scroggins' denial, Bates persisted. "Oh, Milo, admit it. You had a big chunk missing from the outside of your right back tire. I'll accept the fact that you may not have noticed it, but we know it was cut."

"So?" Scroggins was beginning to overheat again, his complexion and temperature bubbling up beneath his grubby shirt collar.

"And, my friend," smiling again, the sheriff continued, "we know where you were when you cut your tire, how it came to be sliced, and when you did it. Fess up, Milo."

"If you're so damn smart, why don't you tell me! Shit, Sheriff, so I had a chinked tire. That don't pin nothin' on me!" Scroggins began to protest just a little too much and too loudly in Ben's opinion. "Besides, the right rear began to leak, so I put on the spare. The old one is somewhere in the city dump where I threw it." Later Sheriff Bates sent Deputy Phipps to the landfill to search for the cut tire, but he could not find it—or reported that he couldn't.

"Okay, Milo, since you asked me polite-like, I'll tell you. Just you keep your mouth shut and listen!" Sandy Bates was beginning to run out of patience.

"Crap on you, Sheriff!" It was evident to Scroggins that Bates had something on him from the sound of his voice and the way the sheriff stared threateningly into his face. Scroggins began to tremble, slightly at first.

"You were down in the freight switching yard sometime Sunday night or very early Monday morning. You were driving on the edge of the rail ties and cut a piece out of your tire. You and someone else, probably Sherm Getts, broke into a boxcar parked there and stole two wooden crates, which you loaded into your pickup—the same one parked out there now in your driveway." Bates was letting it all hang out. Leaning forward in his chair, the sheriff pinned Scroggins to the wall with his glare that shot out sparks!

Scroggins now began to shake visibly. The first signs of panic began to ooze out around the edges of his eyes.

"Sometime, maybe when you first got to the yard or when you were leaving, you saw Jeremy Martin—Carol's boy. You knocked him unconscious and kidnapped him."

"We . . . I didn't kidnap nobody, Sheriff!" It was Scroggins' first slipup.

"We? Who was with you, Milo? We know somebody was because the crates were too big and heavy, and you could not have moved them all by yourself."

"Nobody! I wasn't down at no railroad yard, no time, no how!" Scroggins protested. His nervousness increased to the point where his stammer produced saliva in the corners of his mouth and he started to drool.

"Yes, you were, Milo." Bates was tenacious—you had to give the sheriff credit. "You and your accomplice were caught by the boy stealing those crates of merchandise, so you knocked him out, put him in the back of your truck, and left the yard. Where did you go with the boy?"

Ben could see by the expression on Scroggins' face that he was beginning to wonder if someone besides the Martin kid had seen Getts and him rob the boxcar. He looked at the ceiling and all around the room except at the sheriff or Ben. Scroggins could have played drums with his shaking hands if he had sticks. Now the sweat began to appear on his forehead, and he was about to hyperventilate.

Bates kept up the pressure. "After kidnapping the kid, the two of you could not decide what to do with him, so you drove up and down the street in front of Mrs. Martin's house arguing, didn't you? Then you figured the best thing to do was to hang him, right?"

"I want a lawyer," Scroggins begged.

"Okay, we will get you a lawyer right after you answer that last question," Bates pressed.

"No! No! Sheriff! Tweren't me and Sherm that hung him." Scroggins had cracked under pressure as Ben and the sheriff had expected.

"If it were not the two of you, then who hanged him?" Bates asked.

"I ain't answerin' no more questions till you get me a mouthpiece!"

"Ben, I think we have enough to charge Milo with murder, or attempted murder, don't you?" the sheriff asked. He and Ben knew damn well they had Scroggins dead to rights, and it would only be a matter of time before they could wring the whole story out of him.

"Yeah." The first words Ben had said since the questioning began. "But you had better arrest and charge him formally. If we don't let him get an attorney at this point, he may have cause to dodge this charge just as he's done before."

Bates looked back at Scroggins, who was nearly in a catatonic state. He was staring straight ahead, almost comatose. "Milo Scroggins, you are under arrest on suspicion of kidnapping and murdering one Jeremy Martin on Monday last. Do you understand what I am charging you with and the implications?"

Scroggins only nodded dully. He was in duck soup again. If the accusations were proven in court and he was found guilty, this time it would mean Leavenworth or Alcatraz for life, or even the noose. Sheriff Bates asked him again, "Milo, do you hear me? Do you understand these charges against you?"

"Ah . . . I reckon so. I'm innocent though," Scroggins insisted again.

"Don't think we'll need the cuffs, Sheriff," Ben said. He recognized that all the fire and fight had gone out of Scroggins and that he would go along with them peacefully.

"Milo, you got a lawyer?" Bates asked. Scroggins merely shook his head no. They would have a public defender assigned as soon as possible. They led Scroggins to the car and loaded him in, with Sheriff Bates beside him in the back seat. Scroggins was silent, resigned, and hang-dog. He sat staring out the window. When they arrived at the jail and parked next to Phipps' patrol car, Scroggins was escorted into the jail, walking between Bates and Reed.

Deputy Melvin Phipps jumped to his feet as the jail door opened. He had a look of consternation and surprise written in capital letters over his face. "What's up, Sheriff?" he asked, trying to look innocent. "Why we got ol' Milo?"

"We, or rather I, have arrested him on suspicion of kidnapping and murder," Bates said.

"Who'd he snatch and kill?"

"Ben and I think he grabbed the Martin boy and strung him up in the oak grove." Bates ushered Scroggins into one of his two cells and locked the door securely behind him. Then he sat down in the chair behind his desk, which the deputy had just vacated.

"When did this all happen?" Phipps asked.

The sheriff was very patient with his deputy, filling him in on their suspicions. He felt a little guilty not having kept Phipps better briefed on their investigation. But not much. When he finished, Bates picked up the telephone to call the courthouse and ask for a public defender to be assigned to Scroggins. That done, he turned to Ben to ask if he thought there was anything more they could do until an attorney was appointed.

"I don't think so, just now. When the court assigns a lawyer for Scroggins, then we'll want to put him under the lights and sweat the truth out of him if we can and if the public defender will allow us to hard-question Scroggins. In the meantime, I wouldn't leave him alone. By that I mean I would always have two or more people in here from now on, in case Scroggins decides to spill. If he does, and I have known it to happen, it would be advisable to have witnesses present, someone other than you or your deputy."

"Good idea. I'll call on a couple of my standby deputies who only work part time during parades, fairs, and special events when we need extra hands. I'll call Sal, too, and order meals to be sent in for Milo. We can't starve him, although frankly, I'd like to."

"Maybe you can get someone in to give him a bath, Sheriff." Ben laughed as he saluted mockingly and left the jail. It was mid-afternoon on a bright, sunny Georgia Monday in the spring. Things were looking up. There was no doubt Milo Scroggins knew more than he was telling them, but eventually he would come around. Most of his wimpy type usually did.

Workmen, who were repairing the damage to Carol's house after the fire, were making remarkable progress. The installers were banging away, setting cabinets in place. The kitchen was beginning to look like new. Once the cabinets were done, possibly later that afternoon or for sure before noon Tuesday, her appliances could be slid into place and she would have her kitchen back in working order. Quick work. Money talked, and the workmen heard it loud and clear.

Ben returned to his room at the IdaHO Motel and packed his clothes into his backpack. Seemed like a year ago, but in reality, it was only a week ago tomorrow since he had arrived in Flint City. Impossible but true. He loaded his belongings into the trunk of his car, double checked to make sure his Beretta was still in its hiding place, and slammed the trunk lid.

Just then Pug came out of Room 6 with his mop, buckets, soiled towels, and a vacuum sweeper. He nodded at Ben then asked, "You leavin'? I seen you put your bags in the car trunk."

"Yep. I'm checking out."

Pug's grin gave him away. "Well, have a good trip, Mr. Reed."

"What makes you think I'm going on a trip, Pug?"

"People don't usually check out unless they're headed down the road to someplace else."

Ben could sense that Pug was hopeful. *A little bit too eager,* Reed thought.

Leaning against the front fender of his car, Ben slowly extracted a cigarette, his second of the day, from a pack, lit up, and dropped the still burning match on the gravel, which he covered with his brogan. He merely smiled at Pug and waited for him to say something else. He wasn't disappointed. Pug was usually talkative—sometimes to his detriment.

"The only thing in Room 3 is an office," Pug volunteered out of the blue, glancing sheepishly toward Ida's office.

"I thought you didn't know what was in there. You don't even have a key."

"Did I say that? Must have been someone else, not me."

"It was you right enough, Pug."

"No, no. If anybody should ask you, Mr. Reed, what's in that office, you didn't find out from me. Get my meaning?"

"Yes, and I thank you." Ben reached out and shook Pug's still wet hand. "Don't worry. I won't give you away." When Pug withdrew his hand, there was a fifty dollar bill folded up in it. He smiled broadly at Ben, showing his yellow teeth, then headed into Room 10—Ben's now vacated room—to tidy up.

"Have a safe trip, Mr. Reed, and come back real soon, ya hear?"

Ben shook his head, smiled, and snuffed out his half-smoked cigarette butt on the parking lot gravel, and walked to the motel office. Ida was in her usual place, slumped at her desk behind the counter, slurping ice cream from a bowl and reading the newspaper. Ben wondered if that was all she ever did. Read the paper and eat. From her size, he could tell she probably gobbled up everything she could get her hands on and her mouth around.

"I'm checking out, Mrs. Wainright." He decided to be formal and to use her last name to see if he got a response. He did. She belched loudly and looked up at him.

"Okay. You're paid up for the week, so ya don't owe me nothin'. No refund for checkin' out a night early. We don't charge for phone calls here. Nice gesture for our tenants, don't you agree?" Slurp. Belch.

"Very generous, indeed. See you around, then."

As he left, Ida asked, "Ya leavin' town, Mr. Reed?" Second time he had been asked that question in the last few minutes. A habit of the Wainrights? They certainly were anxious to see him out of town for some reason. *Why would Pug claim that Room 3 was an office?* Ben wondered. *And why would a rundown second-rate abode like the IdaHO Motel need more than one office anyway?*

Curious.

"Haven't made up my mind, yet," Ben replied. Although he was moving into Carol's house, he wasn't going to be the one to tell Ida. Chances were she would no doubt find out where he was soon enough. Then what? "Bye." No response, except another, deeper belch followed by a loud sniff and slobber. Ida returned to her paper, but Ben knew she was stewing under all that flab and watching his every move.

Curious and more curious.

Back at Carol's, Ben opened the car trunk, slipped his automatic pistol into a pocket, slammed the lid, and carried his backpack and bedroll inside. He knew Carol slept in the back bedroom off the kitchen, so he deposited his kit in her front bedroom. The few clothes he carried fit nicely into two dresser drawers. He had to travel light, riding the rails like he did. He carried a second pair of khakis, black jeans, some long and short-sleeved shirts, underwear, a shaving kit, and socks. Those were about all the duds he had, and they were travel weary. Before too much longer, he would need a new wardrobe. He hung his heavy coat in a closet and put his backpack and bedroll on the floor.

Ben drove to the appliance store to settle that account. With both obligations satisfied, the funeral home and appliance store, he returned to Carol's house. She got home from work a little after five-thirty. He heard her car door slam out front. He looked out and saw that she was tired and drawn—wearier than Ben had ever seen her. He met her in the living room, where they hugged briefly and kissed. She was shy about kissing in front of other people, especially workmen who were putting up their tools for the day before heading home.

"Tough day?" Ben asked, knowing the answer.

"Enough. I didn't sleep well last night, either. I got up already tired this morning, and it was a struggle to get ready and go to work."

"Well, you relax, and I'll run downtown and pick us up a pizza, some ice, and a big jug of cola, what do you say to that?"

"Anything is okay at this point, Ben." She headed into the bathroom that connected the front and back bedrooms and shut both doors. As Ben started out the front door to his car, he heard the shower come on.

He was back in forty-five minutes, packing soft drinks, a large pepperoni and cheese pizza, drink cups, paper plates, napkins, and ice. Miraculously refreshed from her shower, Carol was standing in the kitchen door, studying the remodeling. She was dressed in tight blue jeans, a loose-fitting blue blouse, with her wet hair tied up in a white sling. She was barefooted and appetizing, certainly more so than the pizza, Ben observed.

"Ben, it's really looking nice," she said, as they walked into the kitchen and looked around. "Think we'll be back in by tomorrow?"

"Sure. I was promised completion by the cabinet installers by noon tomorrow. The appliances will be delivered and set in place shortly thereafter. So we can probably cook dinner right here in your own kitchen tomorrow evening."

"Mrs. Laramie has offered to come over and begin washing my dishes and pots and pans as soon as the cabinet people clear out."

They returned to the living room, weaving between and around boxes full of dishes and other kitchen utensils, and sat close together on the sofa. Ben opened the pizza while Carol set paper plates, cups and napkins on the coffee table. They each dropped a handful of ice in their paper cups, then Carol did the honors and poured out the soda.

"Another picnic, Carol." They ate in silence. Night was donning its pajamas of pink and gray.

Carol looked at Ben and asked, "Are you moving in today?"

"Already did."

"Where are your clothes—your belongings?"

"In the dresser and closet in the front bedroom."

Carol smiled demurely, took both of his hands in hers and whispered, "You can put your things in my bedroom if you'd like." She lifted her lips to be kissed. The pizza forgotten, she led him by the hand into her darkened bedroom, where she began to unbutton his shirt. Ben tugged at his shirttail and opened the last two bottom buttons with trembling fingers.

He placed his shirt over the back of a chair. When he turned back around, Carol had unbuttoned her blouse. She wasn't wearing a bra, and her still firm, full breasts were alert in anticipation. Ben slid her blouse back off her shoulders and drew her fullness to his chest. They kissed again, passionately, their tongues explored the depths. Ben felt a rising swell from deep within that he had not experienced for over two years—since before Mary was killed.

Carol unzipped her jeans and let them fall to the floor around her ankles. She had nothing on underneath. Her slim, tantalizing body beckoned Ben, who by then had risen to the occasion.

They eased down onto the bed together, Carol on her back and Ben close beside her. She took his head in both of her hands and guided his lips to her swelled nipples. As he rose to kiss her lips again, this time with abandon, he sensed her passionate invitation. At first gently, timidly and then with more abandon, he probed the depths of her most secret, sensitive recesses. As his almost forgotten skills of lovemaking slowly returned, life's natural rhythm commandeered his muscles. Carol squirmed, accepting him fully. Completely. Her eyes rolled back, eyelids fluttering involuntarily as she tried to stifle cries of delight by biting down on the knuckle of her index finger to keep from broadcasting her pleasure to the whole neighborhood.

From deep below in Ben's reserves, a surge rose up and up until the overwhelming pressure exploded in a fountain of sparks, skyrockets, and Roman candles! Relaxing, he leaned to kiss her again, then collapsed fully exhausted by her side. They cuddled. Their breathing slowly became normal as they returned to the present.

"Ben, you were wonderful!" she panted. Then, after a few moments, "I don't know what I'll do when you leave here."

"Would you consider going with me?" He was tired of running away. From life, from happiness, from love.

"You mean go along with you to Florida?"

"Precisely. I know we've only been acquainted for a short time, barely a week, but I find I want you in my life from now on," he whispered.

"Oh, yes, Ben." She kissed him, nuzzled closer, and kissed him again tenderly. "I've never wanted anything more in my life. I just want to be with you wherever, whenever, and however."

"Then it's settled. When we solve this case, and the sheriff and I have a very solid lead now, we'll see about driving down to Titusville and to our new life there."

18

CAROL DID NOT WANT TO WAKE BEN up, so in spite of his insistence on taking her, she dressed and slipped out on her own and drove to the mill. Workmen woke Ben soon after her departure by slamming doors on their pickup trucks as they arrived to finish remodeling Carol's kitchen.

He lolled in her bed for a while, letting his senses absorb the remnants of her perfume still on the sheets and whiffs of hair spray on the pillowcase. Ben thought about the day ahead. A day for grilling Milo Scroggins again. This time the public defender would be present as they pried truth out of him about Sherman Getts. Scroggins knew more than he was telling. Also, Carol's appliances were due to be delivered and installed, which would take up part of his day.

Showered and shaved, Ben reached for his shirt, which he had thrown over the chair the night before during their foreplay. Tucked into the pocket was a brief note written on a slip of paper. He opened it and read, *Ben you were*—were was scratched out—*are great! I think I am falling in love with you.* It was signed simply with a capital "C." The word "think" bothered him for a moment, but he credited her use of the word to her timidity in saying she loved him outright. She was that kind of person. Shy in some ways but not in bed.

On the way to the jail, he stopped off at Sal's Café for a dozen donuts and three large takeout cups of coffee. He parked beside the sheriff's car in the lot and entered Bates' office while juggling the box of donuts and tray of cups full of hot coffee.

"Morning, Ben," the sheriff greeted him.

"Howdy, Sheriff." Ben put the donuts and coffee on one corner of the sheriff's desk.

"How come three cups, Ben?"

"Figured your guest might want a cup of java if Sal's waitress hasn't brought his breakfast in yet."

"She hasn't." Bates leaned back in his chair, hands locked behind his head. He gave the appearance of presiding over another ho-hum day, nothing special to do, when in fact on the agenda was perhaps the most important suspect interrogation of his career.

"Scroggins hasn't caused a ruckus now, has he?" Ben asked.

"Nope. He's been a lamb so far. My two part-time deputies said he slept most of the night. Funny, he kept trying to confess something to them in his sleep, but they refused to pay any attention to his ramblings without his mouthpiece being here. First thing when I relieved the second shift this morning, Milo started to tell me about wanting to clear things up. I told him to just hold on until you and his public defender got here."

The sheriff swivelled his desk chair around and banged on the bars of Scroggins' cell with his night stick. Whack! Whack! Whack!

"Wake up in there, Milo! Reed brought you some donuts and coffee. You hungry?"

Slowly, Scroggins sat up on the edge of his steel bunk and stared blankly at the wall only six feet in front of him. He looked like he had been shot at and missed, crapped at and hit. Bates unlocked his cell door, slid back the bolt, and placed a cup of coffee in Scroggins' shaking hand. He opened the box of donuts and held it while the inmate took one in his not-too-clean other hand and began to gnaw the side out of it.

"Your court-appointed attorney should be here any minute, and then you can tell us all about the Martin boy's hanging and how old Sherm bought the farm," Bates told him. He sat back down in his chair and swiveled back to his desk without bothering to lock the cell door. After all, where was Scroggins going to go with both Bates and Ben between him and the door? Scroggins was not going to run. He seemed anxious to spill his story.

The public defender came down the back steps of the courthouse and entered the jail. He knew the sheriff and introduced himself as Raymond Thomas to Ben. He said he was there to make sure none of Scroggins rights were abused and what the charges were. Bates told him that he was booked on suspicion of kidnapping, murder one, and accessory to murder. The attorney took a donut out of the box and washed it down with Ben's coffee.

Ben did not really care because he had half a cup at Sal's earlier while waiting to have the donuts boxed up.

Bates told Scroggins to come out of his cell and sit on one of the folding chairs. The sheriff made sure the chair Scroggins was assigned was blocked in by his desk and the chairs that Ben and the public defender occupied. Scroggins did as he was told, still sipping dregs from the bottom of his coffee cup. The attorney made sure Scroggins understood the charges against him, and Milo confirmed that he did.

"What questions do you have for him?" Thomas asked the sheriff.

"We just want him to tell us what happened to the Martin boy and to Getts, that's all," Sheriff Bates answered, knowing full well that was a tall order.

"I'll tell ya the whole story! But what do I get in return?" Scroggins sputtered.

"Milo, if you turn state's evidence—that is if you help us apprehend and convict the real perpetrators—those who committed these two murders, then I'll do everything I can to help you when you come to trial. That's a promise," Bates said.

"Is that straight?" Scroggins asked the lawyer.

"No one can promise you that you won't be convicted of the charges against you or that you will not do time for your alleged role in these crimes or that you won't face the death penalty. But if you come clean and help prosecute those who did the killings, then the judge might go easier on you and you could escape with a lighter sentence, or no time at all if you are found innocent," the defender assured him.

"I ain't sure what all that means, but iffin it means I mightn't hang, well then I'll tell you all I know about that night down at the railroad yard and how I found poor old Sherm shot through the head," Scroggins wheezed.

"Everybody, just hold on a minute here until I can get my recorder and get it plugged in," the sheriff said. "I want this story down so Milo can't dispute later what he says now. Is that all right with you, Mr. PD?" The public defender said it was fine, but the sheriff better not begin to trample on Scroggins civil rights or he would have to jerk the plug out of the wall. "Agreed," Bates said. He titled the recording with the date, time, and the names of those persons present in the jail.

Milo told his story. "Out of the blue I got a phone call from this here Big Man askin' me iffin I wanted to pull an easy job for him. Said it paid a cool thousand smackers."

"Who was this man and how did he know to contact you?" Ben asked.

"I don't rightly know, and that's the truth. He never said his name, and I didn't ask. He said I'd need a helper, and he'd pay him a thousand, too. I said I thought I could handle the job, and I knew just the feller to help me."

"That fellow would be Sherman Getts?" Bates asked.

"Right. Old Sherm was game for anythin', 'specially if it paid well."

"Go on."

"So this Big Man said for me to stand by for a few days. The job he wanted done was a boxcar right here in Flint City, so it didn't involve runnin' around or any long drives. He said all we'd need is a crowbar, tin snips, a wheeler, tarp, and a pickup truck big enough to haul some heavy wooden crates for a few miles. I had the truck and necessary tools, so me and Sherm, we were all set to replace the seal we planned to snap off the boxcar."

"When did this so-called Big Man phone you with a job offer that involved stealing a shipment of crates out of the boxcar?" Sheriff Bates asked.

"If I recollect right, it was a couple of weeks ago. We was supposed to pull the job late on Sunday night just after the northbound train spotted the cars on a siding," Scroggins answered.

"Then later you got the call about exactly when to knock over the boxcar?" Ben asked.

"Yep. Mr. Big called again a week ago this past Saturday and told me to look for a certain L&N boxcar with a number on it that I don't remember now. Started with eight, I think. He told me where and on which siding at the railroad yard the boxcar would be sitting. He said that Sunday night would be the time to hit it. We were told we'd have plenty of time without any interruptions because no one else would be comin' 'round to pick up anythin' special at that time of night. He warned us to be careful and to make sure the yardmaster wasn't anywhere around. The yardmaster would be our only danger, he said. We were to break open the car, load up the crates, and hide 'em here in town until he called back again to tell us where to take 'em."

"So, you and Getts drove your pickup to the yard a week ago last Sunday night to snatch the crates. Did you know what was supposed to be in them?" Ben asked.

"Nope. We were only told they were some kind of heavy and measured about four foot square. And heavy they was, but we managed to load 'em into my truck."

"Go on."

Scroggins told how he and Getts reached the yard and parked in a secluded spot where they could see the yardmaster's shanty, how they waited for him to leave, and made sure the coast was clear. "We drove down the dark side of the string of boxcars away from downtown. When we found the right car, I parked alongside of it. I snapped the lock, then cut the seal, and we got the crates out. The other long crates in the car weren't our concern. Getts climbed into the car, what with me bein' a little too large for that, and he rolled 'em to the door on my two-wheeler. After we got 'em loaded in my truck, which weren't all that easy, we shut the boxcar door and put a different seal on the latch."

"Was the seal the same one that was pounded down thinking no one would be able to read all of the numbers and trace where it came from?" Ben asked.

"You know about that? Well, Sherm got it from his cousin who works for Florida East Coast Railroad. I had hammered down some of the numbers on the seal so they couldn't be read too easy. Mr. Big Man figured if we didn't replace the seal, that someone along the line between here and Florida might notice it was missin' and raise all kinds of hell. We were tryin' to buy a little time. We knowed it would be discovered when the car reached its final destination."

"What about the lock. You didn't replace it?" Bates asked.

"It's in the Flint River along with the first seal. When we were told where and when to deliver them boxes, we kept 'em until we crossed the old bridge out on Lawrenceville Road. I stopped the truck, and Sherm tossed both of 'em as far up river as he could."

"So, after you got the crates loaded into your pickup, what did you do?"

"Well, then I turned on headlights to drive away, and that's when we saw the Martin kid spyin' on us."

"To keep the record straight, this would be Jeremy Martin, son of Mrs. Carol Martin of Flint City?" Ben asked.

"Yep. It was the Martin kid, as I said. I told Sherm we had to catch him. He'd tell on us for sure if we didn't. So we ran him down, pinned him to the ground on his belly. I wanted to throw some scare into his brain."

"Who hit the boy in the head?" Bates asked.

"Now, hold on you two," public defender Thomas interceded. "How do you know Mr. Scroggins or Mr. Getts hit him on the head? I think you are leading Mr. Scroggins in his statement."

"But I want to tell 'em!" Scroggins pleaded. Then without waiting for the attorney to protest, he blurted out, "The youngun' was cryin' and carryin' on somethin' awful, so Sherm hit him a smart whack over his left ear with a big crescent wrench to shut him up until we decided what to do with him," Scroggins said, wide-eyed now and shaking again.

"Go on then," the public defender said, resigned.

"We tied him up with a rope, kinda in a roll, with his arms pinned to his sides. We stuffed a gag into his mouth in case he woke up before we got shet of him. We covered everythin' with my tarp and headed into town."

"Jeremy Martin included?"

"Yep. He was out cold, so nobody would know he was under our tarp, now would they?"

"Suppose not," Sheriff Bates agreed.

"We didn't know what to do next. The man who hired us didn't say nothin' about killin' anybody, so me and Sherm figured we weren't gettin' paid to throttle the little snoop. We was as scared as the kid."

"So what did you do?" Ben asked.

"Well, we talked about leavin' him in his momma's front yard or on her porch, but that didn't seem like a good idea. We drove up and down Mrs. Martin's street a couple of times while we was decidin' what ta do."

"Then what?"

"Well, The Man told me ahead of time, if we ran into anythin' unexpected like we were to report to Mrs. Wainright."

Bates and Reed looked at each other, astonishment written on both of their faces. Barely able to contain his surprise at this new piece of the puzzle, the sheriff asked, "Milo, do you mean the same Mrs. Wainright—Ida Wainright—who owns the IdaHO Motel?"

"Yep."

"So you took Jeremy Martin to the motel? Then what?"

"She told us to leave the kid tied up and to put him and them two wood crates in Room 3 until she decided what to do with them."

"Was he still alive at the time?" This from Ben.

"Well, I reckon he was. He didn't make no sounds while we was unloading him in the room, but that don't mean he was dead."

"Did you check? Did you even try to see if he was still breathing?" Bates inquired.

"No. Listen. Me and Sherm just wanted to clear out as soon as we could," Scroggins replied, a little testy. "Like I done told ya, Ida told us to unload the crates and put them in Room 3 with the kid, so we did. Afterward, we drove on to my house. Sherm had left his Chevy there, so he cranked it up and left, and I went to bed."

"What time was this, approximately?" Ben asked.

"Around midnight or maybe a little after, I guess. We was both tired and plenty scared after that run-in with the Martin kid, and we didn't even think about what time it was."

"I see. Then what?" Ben asked.

"The phone woke me up real early Monday morning. The Man asked me if I got the boxes, and I told him we had 'em and that they was stashed in a safe place. He didn't ask where they was, and I didn't bother to tell him. He did ask if we had any trouble, and I told him no and didn't bother to mention the Martin boy. He said I was to take the crates out to this old barn on Blackshear Road, and we could pick up our money there. When he started to give me directions, I realized where it was. I had been there a time or two before."

"We will deal with the location of the barn in a minute. Let's go on with your story," Bates urged. "After the phone call, did you go fetch Getts to help you pick up the boxes at the IdaHO Motel and take them to this barn?"

"Yep. Only when I got there, Getts was already dead. Layin' in bed, he was. At first I didn't notice he was dead. He had his pillow coverin' up his head. I thought he was asleep, so I tried to wake him up. I picked up the pillow, and that's when I seen blood in his right ear, and I knowed right then that he was a goner."

"Milo, what time did you find Getts dead in his bed?" Bates asked.

"It was just after sunup. Around seven or so. I remember lookin' at the clock while I was talkin' to the Big Man about where to take the boxes, and it was six-thirty then. I had to dress before goin' to fetch Sherm, so it must have been around seven when I got to his house."

"You didn't try to call him ahead? To alert him that you were coming?"

"Naw. I reckoned I'd just bang on his back screen door and wake him up that way. That's what I done, but when he didn't come to the door, I went in to shake him out of bed."

"Were the screen door and back door both unlocked?"

"Yep."

"Was there anyone else around? A neighbor or another vehicle parked in Getts' yard?"

"No, but Sherm's old hound was fussing, growlin', and howlin'. That old dog must have knowed Sherm was in trouble or dead. Dogs have a way of sensin' things like that, you know," Scroggins stated.

"The dog wasn't around when we arrived," Bates said. "Now, Milo, tell us where you took the two crates and about the barn and what happened when you got there."

"I took off from Sherm's as fast as I could clear out! I went directly to the motel, and Ida called a couple of fellers I didn't know to come help load them crates."

"Was Jeremy Martin still in Room 3 at the motel when you loaded the boxes?"

"No, he weren't there. I found out later that afternoon that you, Sheriff, found him hung in a tree down at the oak grove. Anyway, after we loaded them boxes, I drove out to Blackshear Road, as I said, and followed The Man's directions to the delivery place. It turned out to be the old barn I figured it was, set back in the trees off the road. The Man said the turn-off was a mile beyond the Turkey Creek bridge where an old oak tree had fell near the fence. I found the turn-in and drove down the track until I came to the barn."

"Was there anyone around when you arrived?" Ben asked. "Did you see any other vehicles, like pickups, cars, or the like around the barn?"

"Nope. Not at first. But when I pulled up, this feller came out from behind the barn and asked me who I was and what I wanted. He was carrying a double-barreled shotgun. Them barrels looked as big as two cannons to me, right enough. Asked me where my helper was. I told him he overslept, which wasn't far from the truth now, was it?"

"Did you know him? What did he look like?" Ben asked.

"Never laid eyes on him in my life. He was a big man, much taller than me. He wore a ball cap, blue jeans, and cowboy boots. I noticed his boots 'specially. They had them silver toe points on 'em—bright and shiny, they was."

"What about his face?"

"Well, he had dangerous, threatenin' eyes. Deep-set, dark, and scary. He was wearin' a full beard, so I could only really see his eyes showin' under the bill of his cap, on accounta the rest of his face was bushy like."

"Would you recognize him if you saw him again?"

"Yep. Not likely to forget them eyes."

"Then what happened?"

"He said for me to stay in my truck. After a bit, two other guys came around from behind the barn with a rubber-tired wagon, one of them big ones like they use for baggage at train depots. They uncovered the crates and slid them onto this here wagon of theirs."

"What did they look like?" Bates asked.

"Can't rightly remember. Didn't get a good look at 'em, only through the rear view mirror in my truck. They was big, though. I remember that."

"Go on."

"Soon as they got them crates off, the man with the shotgun handed me an envelope. Told me to check it out, which I did. There was twenty one hundred dollar bills inside. Two thousand on the nose. With Getts dead, I figured it was all mine now. He couldn't spend it nohow, now could he?"

"So, you hightailed it out of there? Where did you go?"

"Got out of there as quick as I could, mindful of the narrow track and road I had to drive on. I went back home. Recounted my money," Scroggins admitted.

"Why are you telling us all of this now, Milo? You clammed up yesterday when we arrested you, but now you're a blabbermouth," Bates said, smiling.

"Thought it over durin' the night. Didn't sleep much for thinkin' you was gonna try to pin Sherm's murder on me. I know someone real smart done him in 'cause there weren't no gun layin' around on the floor or in Sherm's bed. I didn't see one, anyway."

"You stayed in his bedroom long enough to look around, Milo?"

"Naw. After I looked under Sherm's pillow, I took off quick like."

"You sure you and Getts didn't hang the Martin boy upside down in that grove of oaks to make sure he wouldn't or couldn't rat on you?" Bates asked, his smile gone now.

"Sheriff, you're leading my client again," Thomas interrupted.

"That's okay, Mr. Lawyer," Scroggins said. "I swear, we didn't do the kid in, Sheriff. I don't know nothin' about how the kid got hisself hanged. Musta been someone picked him up after we left him on the floor at the motel and strung him up good and proper by his heels."

"Is that your full story, your complete deposition?" Ben asked. Milo nodded. "You don't have anything to add? Anything you can think of right now like who may have murdered Jeremy Martin?"

"No, I got no idea who throttled the kid. Your guess is as good as mine, Sheriff. Maybe it was the guy at the barn who was packin' the shotgun," Scroggins ventured.

"If your lawyer will permit me asking, what do you know about a rattlesnake?" Ben asked. The attorney didn't object.

"Well, I know ol' Pug got hisself bit by a snake, that's all."

"Again with your lawyer's permission," Ben hesitated, then asked, "did you torch Mrs. Martin's house?"

"Now, what would I be doin' that for? I ain't got nothin' against her," Scroggins replied indignantly. "She's a nice lady, and I feel bad about what happened to her boy, too."

Sheriff Bates smiled again at Scroggins. "Have you been back out to that old barn since making your delivery?"

"Hell no. I'm staying well away from that place. Didn't like the looks of any one of them bastards. They is capable of killin', though, I'd say," Scroggins wheezed.

Sheriff Bates turned off the recorder and put it on rewind. "Well, I'm holding you for burglary, Milo. It remains to be seen what happens to the charges of kidnapping and murder first. If, and I say *if*, we find out you weren't involved in the Martin boy's hanging or in shooting Getts, then we may ask the court to consider leniency," Bates said.

The public defender said he wanted a copy of the recording as soon as the sheriff could get one made. Bates said he would send one up to his office that afternoon.

"While you're here," Bates said to the lawyer, "did you see any time when we interfered with Milo's statement? Just want to make sure nothing comes up later that might jeopardize our charges against him."

"Once or twice I thought you were leading Scroggins, but he wanted to answer so I didn't stop the proceedings," Raymond Thomas responded.

The men shook hands with each other and with Scroggins and thanked him for his statement, which cleared up a lot of questions and confirmed some suspicions. After the sheriff locked the cell door, Scroggins lay back down on his bunk, wheezing noticeably.

Thomas returned to his office. Reed and Bates withdrew to the side of the sheriff's office where Scroggins couldn't overhear them and reviewed what they had just heard.

"This bit about Ida puts a new wrinkle and sheds a whole different light on our investigation," Bates observed. "We'll have to confront her with what Milo said, but I think first we need to check out that old barn later tonight after it gets dark. Might just give us all the answers. Have to be damn careful, particularly if the guy with the double-barreled shotgun is still around." He shuddered at the thought of having to face up to a shotgun, especially one with two barrels. The sheriff knew in the right hands that "scatter guns" could punch holes in a man from quite a distance, and even if a few pellets struck sensitive spots, the victim would be done for.

"What say about midnight?" Ben asked. He had other plans, but he did not want to share them with the sheriff just yet. His plans didn't include Bates, or his deputy for that matter.

"Fine. I'll meet you here about midnight. One of my part-time deputies will be here to babysit Milo, so you, Mel, and I can check out that old barn," Bates agreed.

Ben didn't really want Deputy Phipps along on the stakeout, but how could he object? He had an uneasy feeling about the surly deputy, who sure seemed to be scarce around the jail most of the time. Wouldn't matter anyway. Ben planned to reconnoiter the barn by himself and be back at the jail in plenty of time for their midnight meeting.

19

IT WAS AFTER NOON WHEN BEN AND Sheriff Bates completed their questions. Scroggins was asleep again on his cell bunk when Ben left the sheriff's office and stopped by Sal's Café to grab a light lunch. The restaurant was filling up with hungry locals, but he found his usual booth empty. He plopped down. Tired already, and the day was only half over. At his age and considering the frolic the night before with Carol, no wonder he felt a little frayed around the edges.

Penny brought him water with a lemon slice hung on the rim of the glass. She smiled and handed him the luncheon menu. Ben ordered a ham on rye, with potato salad on the side and iced tea to drink. Sal brought his order when it was ready and plunked herself down opposite him in the booth.

"Hey, Ben. How's tricks?"

"Nothing new, I'm afraid." He did not mention that Sheriff Bates had arrested Milo Scroggins and charged him with burglary of the railroad boxcar. Nor did he tell her about how their interview went or that Scroggins had confirmed most of what they already surmised, and he had implicated Ida Wainright.

"Heard Sandy arrested that scoundrel Milo," she said.

Ben tried to hide his surprise. "And tell me, Sal, how in hell did you find that out? I haven't been five minutes getting here for lunch, and you already know about Scroggins' arrest. You're amazing!"

"I already told you that I have my sources. Did he level with you?"

"Now, Sal, you know I can't talk about what he told the sheriff and me. It's all confidential until he comes to trial. Let me correct that—*if* he comes to trial."

"Did he tell you there are some odd gorillas roaming around Flint City?"

"What kind of monkeys would that be?" Ben asked, trying not to show surprise and consternation. Frankly, he was getting a little annoyed about how Sal was always one or two steps ahead of their investigation.

"The other day, Saturday I think it was, a big, ugly guy came in here and asked me if we served borscht soup takeout. I told him we didn't. I suggested he go down Bond Street to Delivikov's. He'd find all kinds of Russian dishes on his menu."

Curious. "And?" Perhaps he shouldn't be so upset with Sal after all. This piece of the puzzle might just fit in somewhere. Maybe. Hopefully.

"He left. Didn't even say thank you. Real mean looking, you know, like he was ready and able to break somebody's neck."

"Can you describe him better than that?"

"Had bushy eyebrows that shaded burning eyes, puffy red cheeks, hairy arms hanging down almost to his knees, and a full, scraggly beard. He was wearing a short-sleeved dark blue shirt, dirty jeans, and cowboy boots with bright silver tips on the toes. Wore a baseball cap. Plain, nothing printed on it," she said as a matter-of-fact.

Kabang! Steel balls ricocheted off the walls inside Ben's head! *Big man, bushy eyebrows, full beard, wearing a blue shirt, jeans, boots with steel-capped toes, and a baseball cap. Wasn't that the way Scroggins had described the man with a shotgun who met him at the barn when he delivered the two wooden crates? Yes, the same!* Ben tipped his head down and stuffed half of his ham on rye into his mouth to keep Sal from detecting his delight at this piece of news. *Keep calm. Try to distract her,* he thought.

"Well, if that's the best you can do," he said, almost choking on his sandwich.

The spark was lit. "I'm sorry, I didn't think to ask his name, address, telephone number, boot size, or how many glasses of vodka he drank every day!" Sal spit out haughtily. His ploy worked. She slid across the bench, about to leave the booth in a huff, when Ben reached across the table and grasped her wrist.

"Ah, now come on, Sal. Please don't be mad at me," Ben apologized. "You did just fine remembering what he looked like. Couldn't expect more. I have other means of finding out who he is and what he's up to. Don't worry your gorgeous head about that."

"I forgive you this time. But don't be so presumptuous of our short friendship in the future, hear?" She had calmed down. Relaxed somewhat.

"I won't, never fear."

"To show you I don't hold a grudge, your lunch today is on me. I'll tell Penny."

"You don't have to do that, but if you insist, how can I turn down your charm and hospitality?" Ben gave her is biggest, warmest smile. Teeth showing. He hoped no bread was sticking to his upper teeth.

Sal smiled back, patted the back of his hand, and left to attend to other customers. Ben finished drinking his iced tea, waved at Sal and Penny, and left the café. He walked down Bond Street to Delivikov's restaurant, where he asked the owner about the man who came in for borscht takeout. The Russian owner was unable to give Ben a better description than the one Sal had. But he did say the same man had returned a time or two to buy more cold beet soup.

Curious? Indeed.

"How much did he buy each time?" Ben asked.

"A carton this size each time," he answered, pointing to a single-serving sample takeout box sitting on his counter. He could not remember exactly how many setups of napkins and plastic utensils the man asked for, but he wanted more each time he came in.

Ben thanked him. He walked back to his Ford, which was parked near Sal's Café, turned the ignition key, and drove to the appliance store to ask when Carol's order might be delivered. The store manager told him the appliances were already at her house and may even be installed already.

When he arrived at Carol's house, the installation was almost complete. The cabinets were in, the sink was mounted and hooked up, and the fridge was in place and cooling. Only the stove remained to be installed. He relaxed in the living room and wrote Sal's comments in his notebook. He reviewed the notes he had jotted down while Milo Scroggins was "confessing." Amazingly, most of what Scroggins had told them was what he and the sheriff thought had taken place. Now, all that remained was to check out Ida Wainright and the barn—if he could find it.

The workmen were through. It was almost five o'clock and time for Carol to come home from work. When she did, she would find a brand new sparkling and efficient kitchen, thanks to Ben. He would pay the carpenters and painters, who had left him their bill on the dining room table, at the first opportunity, but no later than tomorrow.

Carol arrived home a little after six. Ben had begun to pace the floor, looking out the front living room window every little bit. He was relieved when her car turned into the driveway. He opened the door for her. She smiled sweetly, kissed him warmly, and apologized for keeping him on pins and needles. She said there had been a small problem with one of the looms at the mill, and she had to stay late to help solve it. Her apology was accepted, of course.

He asked Carol to close her eyes, then led her by the hand to the dining room door where she could see into the kitchen.

"Open your eyes now."

"Oh, Ben!" She walked into the kitchen still grasping and squeezing his hand. "It's lovely! So pretty! How can I ever thank you?"

"None asked for nor needed. I'm happy 'cause you're happy, Carol." For the first time since Mary's death, he began to feel deep contentment. Like he was alive again, and the loneliness he had endured over the past two years was finally draining away. He had someone to cling to—someone to cling to him. Someone to love.

"Are we eating in tonight?" she asked.

"I had hoped to, but we don't have any food. Anyway, Mrs. Laramie hasn't been able to wash up the dishes yet. The workmen just finished installing everything only an hour or so ago. We'll eat out one more time, if that's okay."

Carol showered and changed into white slacks, a green blouse, and white shoes. He thought she looked delicious in anything she decided to wear.

On the way to Granny's, that's where Carol wanted to eat, he told her a little about Milo Scroggins' statement at the jail. He didn't go into great detail. Just enough so she would know the sheriff and Ben probably were getting close to solving Jeremy's tragic death. At least they had some solid leads. More than before Scroggins was arrested, anyway. He didn't mention Ida Wainright's possible involvement.

At Granny's Diner they sat in a back booth. They both ordered chicken fried steak, which was the special of the day, with iced tea. Ice cream cones, dripping and sweet, were dessert. On the way back to Carol's, Ben explained about the mysterious barn where Scroggins said he had taken the two wooden crates. How Milo's description of the man who held the shotgun matched the one both Sal and Delivikov had given him. Then he told her about his plan. "I've got to check out that barn tonight." He didn't tell her he was going soon after dark, rather than waiting to go back again at midnight with Sheriff Bates and Deputy Phipps. "I just hope I can find it in the dark."

Carol asked where Scroggins said the barn was located. Ben told her.

"I know exactly where that old barn is. I used to buy fresh fruits and vegetables from the elderly gentleman who lived there. I'm surprised the barn is still standing," she said.

"According to Scroggins, it's still there. He didn't see inside, so no telling what shape the interior is in. I guess I'll find out, somehow. I need to know what's so special and secretive about that old place."

Then Carol surprised him. "Ben, take me with you!"

"Carol, I can't do that." He almost said it may be too dangerous, but he didn't want to worry her. "You mean too much to me now to place you in harm's way," he confessed.

"You're so sweet to say that. But you see, you mean everything to me, too, Ben. Did you read the note I left in your shirt pocket this morning? You are my life, my heart, my reason for being." Her eyes welled up with tears. "I'd be heartsick if something happened to you and I wasn't there to—to maybe help you." After a pause, she added, "Remember, Jeremy was my son, and I need closure on his murder. If the barn is a key, then I think I deserve to be in on finding out what that key unlocks. Don't you?"

"Well, I can't argue with that. The only way I will take you, though, is if—and that's a big if—you promise me you'll stay in the car with the motor running when we reach the turn-in to the lane that leads to the barn. Otherwise, I can't let you go."

"Agreed. I'll be your moll, and I'll be ready for a quick getaway if it comes to that," she chided. Her face brightened.

"But you didn't promise."

"I agreed, and that's the same thing, isn't it?"

Ben let it go at that. He could tell there wasn't any way he could keep her from tagging along. Anyway, maybe it was a good idea to have his car nearby with the engine running and ready to speed away should the man with the shotgun show up.

20

IT GETS DARK EARLY IN SOUTH GEORGIA in springtime. That particular night, when Ben and Carol planned to find out what mysteries the old barn on Blackshear Road held, was no exception. The moon was just a dim, curved sliver playing tag with the southwestern horizon. Perfect darkness prevailed for the chancy business of slipping up on someone's blind side. At least they hoped the people in the old barn would not be on the alert.

They both dressed in dark clothing. Ben in blue jeans, with a blue turtle-neck sweatshirt, and dark blue stocking cap covering his already graying hair. He felt fully dressed after he stuck his Beretta inside the belt of his jeans and his pen and small notepad in one pocket. Carol glanced at his gun, but said nothing. Silently, she was praying there wouldn't be any gun play. Not now. Not after she had given herself totally to Ben.

Carol donned a black sweat suit and covered her head with one of Jeremy's black baseball caps, with her hair dangling out the back in a ponytail. She did not own a firearm or know much about how to handle a gun, or she would have secreted one away for double security.

Ben decided to take Carol's car. It would likely be less well known in the event prying eyes were watching them approach the barn or if somebody passed by on the road while Carol was waiting in her parked car. That's all they would need to blow the operation.

Carol navigated as Ben drove east along the highway. She warned him well ahead of time about the turnoff onto Blackshear Road. The country road wasn't paved, but it had been graded recently so some of the potholes were not quite tooth-rattling.

They slowed to cross the narrow wooden bridge across Turkey Creek. Ben glanced at his odometer to calculate when they had gone another mile. He slowed as he reached the three-fourths mile mark, turned off the headlights, and coasted quietly to a stop along the roadside where the old pine tree had fallen and was laying by the fence.

"This must be the trail leading up to the barn," Ben observed. "Remember, you promised to stay in the car until I get back. All I plan to do is get close enough to the barn to see in it or at least hear what's going on inside. If there are any cars or trucks parked there, I'll copy down their license plates, and Sheriff Bates can run them down in a jiffy."

"Ben, I think I should go up at least partway to the barn with you, just in case."

"Just in case what? No way, honey. You stay put," Ben ordered, all business and serious now. He asked her to cover the dome light in the car while he opened the door to get out. "If someone is looking this way, that light will glow like a lighthouse."

Carol did as she was told, even though she didn't like it. Resigned, she covered the light with her hand as Ben planted a peck on her cheek. He left the engine running and slipped out of the driver's side door, closing it quietly behind him. With a wave that was more like a salute, he disappeared down the track toward the barn.

Trees formed a canopy over his head, making the trail to the barn even darker and spookier. All of Ben's senses were on high alert as he walked slowly and warily down the narrow track. He noticed it was well traveled, as if cars or trucks had been going in and out frequently. Only the center of the trail was grassed, with the track on each side worn bare by passing vehicle tires.

About fifty yards along, Ben saw the barn through an opening at the end of the trail. He squatted down to minimize his profile and crouched in the tall weeds that grew around the trees bordering both sides of the trail. He stopped to reconnoiter. *Was someone watching the approach to the barn?* he wondered. Apparently not. Relief. But not much because he was still a good distance from the barn, and the last few yards were as wide open as a football field.

Ben paused again at the very edge of the protecting weeds and trees and surveyed the ground that lay ahead of him. Two pickup trucks were parked in front of the barn doors; one was headed in, and the other was backed in. So far so good. The vehicles would provide some cover for him as he approached the barn. He could see a sliver of light coming out of a crack between the barn doors where he planned to peek in. Two windows, one on either side of the doors, were painted over with white paint. No luck trying to see anything through the windows.

The brightly lighted interior shone through the painted windows. He guessed some activity must be going on inside, even though it was quiet. Otherwise, why all of the bright lights? And what were the two trucks doing parked at the barn?

Just as Ben was about ready to make a dash across the open approach to the barn, he heard a car turn onto the narrow trail, headed in his direction. Two steps backward into the undergrowth hid him completely from view. Nevertheless, he squatted down again and pulled the Berretta out of his waistband. He eased the safety off so it was ready to fire.

Then Ben realized he would not shoot at the car coming down the trail. It was Carol's! *What the hell had happened? Was she driving down the lane toward the barn, ignoring his instructions?* These thoughts raced through Ben's mind as he watched the car move slowly down the track, with only the parking lights on.

As he was about to jump out of hiding to confront her, he saw Carol was in the passenger seat, and someone else was driving. He watched, horrified, as her car slowly passed him, heading toward the barn. Carol was seated stiffly in the front seat. Head erect. Not looking left or right. More questions flooded his mind. *Did the driver know Ben was somewhere nearby? Did this big guy, and he was big, find her car and commandeer it with her still a passenger and leave his car back on the main road?*

While he mulled over these perplexing questions, the driver stopped beside one of the pickups parked in front of the barn. He got out and pulled Carol head first across the seat under the steering wheel and out the driver's door. None too gently, either! As big as the man was, Ben had a notion to tackle him on the spot. Or shoot him, but he might hit Carol. *Patience! The time will come,* he said to himself.

Carol regained her feet and, with the big guy half dragging her, entered the barn though a small door to the left of the big doors, which Ben hadn't noticed earlier because it was blocked from his view by one of the pickups. Ben realized he had been chewing his lips, and blood trickled down onto his chin. He wiped the blood away with the back of his hand as he edged cautiously and slowly toward the parked pickups. Squatting low. It would not help Carol or him to be caught out in the open.

He reached the side of the nearest pickup, which was parked with its front bumper almost up against one of the big barn doors. The truck was wearing Florida license plates. He copied the number down in his notebook. As he was about to slip around the first pickup to check on the license plate on the second vehicle, he glimpsed a car backed partially into the shelter of some trees off to one side of the barn.

The vehicle was a white and green sheriff's patrol car! On the side was a shield reading "Nagle County Sheriff." *What in hell was a sheriff's car doing parked alongside the barn? Was Bates here already? Why didn't he wait until the appointed hour? Or was the car the one assigned to Deputy Phipps?* More questions rattled around in his brain. Curious. More than that, curious as all hell!

Ben squatted back down on his haunches to ponder this new development. He decided, before doing anything rash, he had better peek into the barn to find out what was going on inside. That's what he did. Luckily!

Through the crack between the big barn doors he could see part of one wooden crate. The crack between the doors was not wide enough for a full view of the interior, but it was enough for Ben to see the big man had seated Carol in a straight-back chair and had tied her hands behind her back. Two other men were hovering around her. Watching and smiling.

One of the men, who had wadded up a rag to make a gag for Carol's mouth, was none other than Nagle County Deputy Sheriff Melvin Phipps!

At that moment, things began to fall into place for Ben. Whatever was going on inside the barn, Deputy Phipps was right in the middle of it. No wonder Phipps was watching his room at the motel, and no wonder he seemed disinterested in the investigations of two murders or in the rattlesnake attack or the fire at Carol's house. Ben would bet his inheritance that Phipps was fully involved, and maybe he was the Big Man that Milo Scroggins said telephoned him about robbing the train.

The corner of one wooden crate he could see fit the description Scroggins had given the sheriff and Ben. Scroggins had been on the level when he told the two investigators about the boxes and where he had delivered them. *Why were the boxes still in the barn? Are they about to be moved somewhere? And if so, where and when? How much time did he and Bates have to forestall movement of the crates and to corral these men?*

Good for Carol! Apparently, her captors were so confident in using an isolated barn for meeting they didn't think anyone was around, or they would have posted guards outside, armed with shotguns, who would be patrolling the woods around the barn. He did not know what excuse she had given them for being parked alone on a country road, but whatever it was, it had worked.

Ben knew he could not by himself take on the Big Man, Deputy Phipps, two workers, and no telling how many others he hadn't seen. He needed help. He could not risk cranking up Carol's car, even if the keys were left in the ignition. Keys or no keys, he could not spare the time necessary to drive back into town to summon Sheriff Bates. But there was a way.

Ben sneaked over to Deputy Phipps' patrol car, which was parked a ways from the barn. The windows were down, which told him the doors were unlocked, too. Quietly, he opened one door, risking the dome light's glare. He slid into the front seat lying on his back and let the door close enough so the dome light went out.

Phipps had left his keys in the ignition, which Ben turned on without starting the engine. He switched on the two-way radio and lifted the mike from its cradle, then whispered a quiet transmission to Sheriff Bates. "Sheriff, this is Ben Reed. Do you copy?" *Please let him be in his office with the base station on or in his patrol car so he will hear,* Ben silently pleaded.

After what seemed like an eternity, a response came from the sheriff. "This is Sandy, Ben. Go ahead."

"Sheriff, I'm at the barn. Mel Phipps is here, too, inside with several more men. They're holding Carol hostage. Can you come out here and bring your two part-time deputies with you?"

"What in hell are you two doing at the barn? I thought we decided to go out there together at midnight!"

"Never mind. I'll explain later. You know where the barn is, right?"

"Ten-four! I know. I'm just relieving one of the assistant deputies now, so I'll bring him. I'll stop by the other one's house and bring him too, if he's home."

"You better bring some firepower, too. I have a feeling these guys are well armed and ready for anything. Come quiet, though, no lights or sirens."

"Gotcha! I'm on my way. We'll figure out how to get in the barn once I'm on site."

So far, so good, Ben thought. Now, if he could just stay out of sight for a little while longer until reinforcements arrived, the four of them could storm the bastion and release Carol before the gang inside knew the cavalry was anywhere around. If—a big capital IF.

At what seemed to Ben to be two hours later, but was only about thirty minutes, three dark figures approached slowly on foot down the lane toward the barn. Sheriff Bates, Calvin Jenkins, and Vernon Parker had arrived. What a relief and none too soon! Ben was becoming antsy. All three men were carrying 12-gauge pump shotguns and had revolvers in holsters strapped around their waists. The sheriff had an extra shotgun for Ben, which was fully loaded.

Ben stepped from behind Deputy Phipps' patrol car and waived to attract their attention. Together now, the four of them huddled beside the patrol car and held a whispered briefing. The devised plan of attack was to send part-time Deputy Jenkins around behind the barn to secure any back doors. Deputy Parker was assigned to patrol along the track to the road and to apprehend anyone who might come down the lane from that direction. Ben and Sheriff Bates planned to crash in through the small door, with each one covering half of the room inside. The pickups were parked too close to the big doors, so they couldn't be swung open.

"Listen," Ben whispered. "Carol Martin is in there. They have her tied to a chair, but fortunately, she's sitting on the left-hand side of the room near the north wall. Last time I peeked in, no one was near her, so they feel pretty sure she can't escape to summon help."

"That may be a break for us," Bates observed.

"Don't shoot in her direction with these scatter guns! If there happens to be someone near her, I'll take care of him with my handgun. That's my first priority—to cover and protect Carol," Ben said quietly.

The sheriff said, "Ben and I will each shoot into the ceiling as soon as we step inside the door. If anyone tries anything, we'll shoot him, too. You," pointing at Parker, who was assigned to watch the track to the house, "when you hear our shots, keep watching the lane. If you're needed inside, I'll holler and you come running, understand?" Parker nodded that he did.

Then to Cal Jenkins, "When you hear Reed and me yell like banshees, you crash in through the back door, if there is one and its unlocked. When you gain entry, shoot at the ceiling, then yell like hell, too. If the door is locked, blow hell out of the latch! If you have to blast it two or three times, do it! You two got that?" The deputies nodded and smiled. "Okay. You two take your places. We'll give you two or three minutes, and then we go. Take off!"

They did.

Two minutes went by. Both Ben Reed and Sheriff Sandy Bates were breathing hard. Anticipation written plainly on their faces. Grim. Determined.

"They've had enough time to get on their posts. Are you ready?" Bates asked.

"As I'll ever be. Good luck."

Ben didn't hear the sheriff's reply, only the sound of him pumping a shell into his 12-gauge shotgun. Ben did likewise as he murmured a short prayer for Carol's safety.

The two men slipped across the open space to the barn. Bates kicked in the door and screamed at the top of his lungs as he crashed into the room and fired a round into the air. *Boom!* Right on his heels, Ben yelled and fired upwards as he burst through the doorway. *Boom!*

Not counting Carol, there were six people inside: a huge man, a fat woman, a well-dressed European-looking man, two other men, and Deputy Phipps, all of whom were startled into immobility. They froze in place and could only manage to stare in disbelief at the two noisy, shooting, menacing-looking intruders. Before any of them could recover, or think about bolting through the back door, Deputy Calvin Jenkins shot away the lock and hasp that secured the single back door, and squealing like a Kamikaze, he leaped inside and fired off the other shotgun shell into the ceiling. *Boom!*

As Ben had hoped and prayed, none of the suspects were worried about Carol or were even near where she sat gagged, bound hand and foot to a chair. In three strides, Ben was at her side, threatening with his shotgun anyone who came near. No one challenged him.

"Freeze! Get those hands in the air!" Bates yelled. "Now!" He, Ben, and Deputy Jenkins covered the miscreants with their double-barreled scatter guns. "You, too, Mel, you bastard! Get 'em up!" Bates yelled at his deputy, who was not dressed in uniform. Out of desperation, Phipps did a stupid thing. He tried to pull his gun out of the waistband of his jeans. Before he had it halfway out, Bates was on him and slammed the barrel of his shotgun down on the back of Phipps' wrist. *Crack!* It broke. Ben heard the bones shatter, even with the hubbub going on around him. Phipps yelped and sagged to his knees in pain. "One down," Bates yelled. He was counting! In one quick move, he kicked the deputy's gun across the barn floor toward Reed and out of reach of the other people.

Ben removed the gag from Carol's mouth, then cut the ropes binding her arms and feet to the chair. "Ben, oh, Ben, I was so afraid."

"I know, Carol. But you're safe now. It's all over," Ben assured her, as he cradled her in his arms. "We'll be out of here as soon as we can corral these guys and haul them into jail. You just rest easy now, okay?"

With Phipps writhing in pain on the floor, Sheriff Bates turned his attention to the suspect he thought was the Big Man and who he expected might be the next threat. The big fellow merely stood still, unable to comprehend what had just befallen their operation. He was unknown to the sheriff, who asked him who he was. The man growled, "Kunkle. And that's all you'll get out of me until I see my lawyer."

"We'll see about that," Bates snarled back.

The fat woman stood to one side, a smirk on her face, with her hands on her hips.

"Hello, Ida," Bates greeted her, as he backed her up against one of the wooden crates with the barrel of his shotgun. "I didn't expect to find you here." The overweight woman was indeed Ida Wainright, owner and manager of the IdaHO Motel.

"You bastard!" Ida managed to spit out. "Another day, and this would have been a done deal. Now you and that . . . that . . . that damn Florida hobo show up and spoil everything!"

Meanwhile, the fancy-dressed European-appearing man sat perched on the end of a sawhorse and looked dumbfounded. The two wooden shipping crates that Scroggins and Getts had stolen from the boxcar and delivered to the barn sat in the middle of the room with the tops removed.

"Ida, you, Kunkle, and these three other guys and Mel are all under arrest. I am charging each of you on suspicion of burglary of railroad property, a federal crime, two murders, arson, and kidnapping."

"You can't charge us with kidnapping, you bastard," Ida snarled. "This man," pointing at the European type, "is from Russia, and he ain't under your jurisdiction. He's here on his own volition. Nobody kidnapped him!"

"No matter. I'm not charging you with kidnapping *him* anyway. We'll sort out later who's who and who has jurisdiction. You are all under arrest for kidnapping and hanging Jeremy Martin, for the murder of one Sherman Getts, and for torching Carol Martin's house. Either of these charges is enough to hold the lot of you in custody for now," Bates shot back.

Just then, Pug stepped through the doorway Bates had kicked in earlier, with Deputy Vernon Parker close behind, covering him with his shotgun. "When you all fired and yelled, this one came running down the track. You can see I got him, though," Parker said proudly.

"Pug, are you in on this, too?" Ben asked. He could not believe what a good actor Pug had been all along. He had acted like he was innocent and diverted suspicion away from himself and Ida. Pug grinned, shuffled his feet, and looked at the floor. "So's you'll know, I didn't put that rattler in your room, Mr. Reed. That was Mel done that. He wanted to scare you out of town. Iffin I had done it, I sure as hell wouldn't have got bit, now would I?"

"Shut your damn mouth, you idiot!" Ida screamed. She made a move toward Pug, but Bates interceded by continuing to hold her at bay with the barrel of his shotgun pressed up against her abundant belly.

Sheriff Bates arrested Pug and the rest of them, including the Russian. He wasn't sure if it applied to the Soviet, but better to be safe than sorry. Bates sent Vernon Parker back down the lane to bring up his patrol car. When he returned, the gang of seven were cuffed and divided up for their ride to jail. Ida and two men who turned out to be her cousins sat in the back of the sheriff's car, with the harmless Pug in the front seat next to Bates. The Russian, Phipps, and the Big Man Kunkle rode in the back seat of Deputy Phipps' patrol car, driven by Deputy Parker. Part-time Deputy Cal Jenkins stayed at the barn throughout the night to guard the crates and the two locked pickups. Ben drove Pug's car to the jail, where he met Carol who had followed behind in her own car.

Fitting the seven suspects into two small jail cells with Scroggins already in residence presented a problem. Sheriff Bates telephoned a colleague in Albany, who said he had cell space open and could accommodate five or six prisoners if it was only for overnight. Bates assured him the prisoners would soon be on their way to Atlanta, where they would be held awaiting more formal state and federal charges and eventual trial. The sheriff unfolded a roll-away bed for Ida and put Pug on the bed now vacated by Scroggins. On the telephone again, Bates woke up a third part-time Nagel County deputy, Dale "Boon" Rogers, apologized for the late hour, and asked him to come to the jail to transport some of his prisoners to Albany that night. Deputy Parker would follow behind with the rest of the detainees.

Even though it was already midnight, Sheriff Bates telephoned Williams at his home number to tell him those responsible for the train robbery, along with the two crates with their contents intact, were in his custody. He reported that he didn't know what condition the contents of the crates were in because they were wrapped in plastic and partially covered with packing material.

"What's important is you got them back before they were shipped abroad somewhere," FBI agent Doug Williams assured Bates. "I'll have some of our agents with a truck down there first thing in the morning to load and transport them on to the Cape."

"Can't do that, Doug. We'll have to keep them here awhile for evidence. Can't you send a team to Flint City from the Cape or from Atlanta to check them out?" Bates asked. "See what harm, if any, has been done to the contents. We can secure them here at the courthouse until these characters are formally charged and tried," Bates offered.

"I disagree, Sheriff, this is a federal matter. You can take photographs of the outsides of the crates from all angles. My men will do the same. We can't have the contents held up or exposed to public scrutiny. Photographic evidence should hold up in court. I'll take full responsibility."

"Okay, it's on your head." The sheriff said he planned to send four of the prisoners to Albany and then to Atlanta, but he was going to hang onto Pug, Ida Wainright, and his deputy until he decided what to do with them. Bates had a good idea about what to do with Phipps, but shooting him like the coyote he was would only land the sheriff behind bars. He added, "Oh, by the way, you might also want to contact the State Department. One of the gang we picked up is apparently a Russian. He's been hollering for his ambassador."

"Oh, damn! Well, that complicates matters. You said you are sending them to Albany and Atlanta, which is acceptable for now. Send the Russian along, too. We'll sort him out up there with his Soviet consul-in-residence. The Americans may be tried in federal court in Georgia. If the charges stick, we may be able to arrange for a change of venue to Florida and submit both the photographs and the empty crates to the court as evidence. The Russian probably will be deported unless we can find a substantial and unbreakable reason for detaining him."`

"Well, be that as it may, I'll check with a judge here in Flint City first thing in the morning about what court orders I might need to send these people I'm detaining temporarily at the jail in Albany on up to Atlanta." He rang off with a promise to keep Doug Williams and the FBI fully informed.

Ben offered to split the guard duty at the jail with the sheriff, but Bates said he thought Ben needed to be with Carol after what she had gone through. It was going to be another all-nighter at the jail guarding Scroggins, Phipps, Bertram "Pug" Wainright, and his wife Ida, but for Sheriff Bates, long overnight duty was nothing new; he had pulled quite a few twenty-four-hour shifts during his career.

Ben drove Carol's car back to her house. It was well after midnight when they arrived, so they changed into their pajamas and went straight to bed. They kissed goodnight, too tired to do much more. Neither one felt like a repeat of the night before, not after the exhausting experience at the barn.

21

EARLY NEXT MORNING, WHILE CAROL WAS cooking breakfast in her newly refurbished kitchen, Ben dialed his daughter in Titusville. He knew she would not have left her apartment for work this early in the morning.

"Hello," Lynn answered with sleep overriding her voice.

"Lynn. It's me, Dad," Ben said, his voice filled with emotion.

"Daddy, where are you? Are you still in Georgia?"

"Yes, but we'll be coming home soon now, baby. We've pretty well cleared up the case I was working on here in Flint City. From the evidence, it looks like we've nabbed the guilty parties, anyway. Locked them up in jail last night—well, actually, it was early this morning."

"You said we? Is Carol coming with you, then?"

"Yes, Lynn. She'll be with me. We plan to be married before too long there in Titusville."

"Daddy, do you suppose she would want me to be a bridesmaid?"

"I'm sure she would, Lynn. I'm sure she would."

Epilogue

Before Carol and Ben left Flint City, she contracted with a realtor to handle the listing and sale of her house. Although she was reluctant to give up her brand new kitchen, her reluctance was overshadowed by her passion to become Ben's wife. Her house was sold furnished within thirty days.

Six months later, Carol and Ben were married in Titusville. Carol wore a pale pink floor-length dress with dark rose-colored shoes and carried a bouquet of pink and white spring flowers. Ben's daughter Lynn, wearing a matching gown, served as bridesmaid.

Ben was dressed in a traditional tuxedo. The white handkerchief in his jacket pocket was the same one he had used to wipe away Carol's tears when they sat on her couch in her house following Jeremy's funeral. The gold wedding band that Ben slipped onto Carol's finger was the same one he had removed almost three years before from his wife Mary's limp hand and that he had worn every day since her tragic death, suspended on a chain around his neck. At the instant they exchanged solemn wedding vows, Ben's bitterness, grief, and loneliness totally vanished.

The Methodist Church in Titusville was packed with Ben's friends and former colleagues. His ailing mother was able to attend their wedding, and she sat proudly in her wheelchair in the center aisle beside the first row of pews.

When gifts were opened at the reception following their wedding, a small square wooden box patterned after the crates robbed from the railroad boxcar was handed to the couple. The top of the box had already been opened by Ben's best man, Titusville Chief of Police Brad Timmons, to whom the gift had been mailed a week earlier. Inside, packed in tissue paper, was a sizeable solid silver chalice. Etched on one side were the words: *To Benjamin Alford*

Reed For His Friendship and Good Services / From the Grateful Citizens of Flint City, Georgia. Tucked into the top of the chalice was a card from Nagel County Sheriff William C. Bates on which he had written: *With every good wish to you and Mrs. Carol Martin Reed, Sandy.*

Nearly two years after Ben and Carol were married, he received through the mail the very best delayed wedding present of all. Stuffed in a fat manila envelope was a copy of the final official report from Sheriff Bates containing the disposition of the crimes they had worked on together in Flint City. The full report filled ten single-spaced typewritten pages. Ben read and reread the complete document and smiled as he did so. He also shared parts of the report with Carol. The gist of the contents read:

Mrs. Ida Wainright, owner of the now closed IdaHO Motel in Flint City, Georgia, along with former Nagel County Deputy Sheriff Melvin Phipps and one Stanley Kunkle—who Milo Scroggins had referred to as the "Big Man" in his deposition and court testimony—were convicted in Federal Court in Atlanta on five counts, including one count of kidnapping; two counts of murder in the first degree of Jeremy Martin and Sherman Getts; and conspiracy to commit espionage by stealing and attempting to sell property belonging to the Government of the United States to agents of a foreign power. Their jury recommended that Phipps and Kunkle be given the death penalty. Ida was spared and sentenced to life in prison without parole.

During his testimony, Pug Wainright stated under oath that he, Stanley Kunkle, his wife Ida, and Deputy Melvin Phipps had parked in Phipps' patrol car at the railroad yard, nearby but out of sight, to watch when Milo Scroggins and Sherman Getts robbed the L&N boxcar. Pug also testified that they saw the two men catch and carry off Jeremy Martin in their pickup truck. Scroggins, Getts, and the four who had been watching the theft met later at the IdaHO Motel to store the stolen crates in Room 3. When Room 3 at the motel was searched and found empty, it was because Deputy Phipps had read the note about obtaining a search warrant for the motel on Sheriff Bates' notepad and tipped off Ida Wainright. Phipps and Getts insisted they hang Jeremy Martin. Pug and Ida both objected, but Phipps and Getts were adamant and eventually prevailed. It came out in trial testimony that Phipps and Getts insisted on hanging the Martin boy because his mother Carol Martin had more than once snubbed their romantic advances, and they felt justified in taking revenge. Also by hanging her son upside down they believed they had humiliated her and paid her the "ultimate insult." "After all," Phipps was quoted as saying, "his mom deserves it, and the kid's probably dead already so what's the harm?" Unconcerned whether or not Jeremy was dead or alive, Stanley Kunkle, Getts, and Ida Wainright's two cousins hanged the Martin boy by his heels in the tree next to the railroad yard. Phipps did not participate in the hanging because he said he was too well known around Nagel County and was afraid someone might recognize him.

Ida Wainright's two cousins were found guilty as accessories to Martin's murder and guilty of arson in setting fire to Carol Martin's house. They were also found guilty of being conspirators during the attempted sale of United States Government secrets to a foreign nation. For these crimes, they both received life sentences in a federal penitentiary.

Bertram "Pug" Wainright and Milo Scroggins were convicted for conspiracy to sell United States Government property to a foreign country and were sentenced to forty-five years in federal prison. Additionally, Scroggins was found guilty in the kidnapping and death of Jeremy Martin, and he was given a life sentence in a federal penitentiary.

The only conspirator to escape completely was the Soviet, who planned to purchase the missile guidance systems. His consul general in Atlanta agreed to his deportation, and the Russian was more than satisfied that the United States Immigration Service only cancelled his visa to reenter this country. Although their scheme was convoluted and risky, the attempt to sell missile components nearly worked. There were two reasons why the crates were still in the barn near Flint City when raided by Ben Reed and Sheriff Bates, accompanied by his deputies: The Russian buyer's transatlantic flight had been delayed several days, and he was waiting for approval of his price negotiations from authorities in the Soviet Union, which he was in the process of carrying out when Ben, Sheriff Bates, and his deputies crashed into the barn. The scheme probably would have succeeded had Ben not returned to Flint City to help the sheriff solve Jeremy Martin's hanging.

Armed with a search warrant for the IdaHO Motel, Sheriff Bates had found a .22 caliber revolver with one missing round among the junk, newspapers, and butt-filled ashtray on Ida Wainright's desk in the office. During ballistics examination in Atlanta, sufficient traces were found to prove the gun was the one Stanley Kunkle had used to kill Sherman Getts. In further testimony, Pug Wainright stated that he knew Kunkle had killed Getts with Ida's revolver and that Milo Scroggins was next on the hit list, but Pug had not said anything before their trial because he was afraid he might become number three on the hit list.

The two hired hulks wielding shotguns who were at the barn when Scroggins delivered the two crates were apprehended a month after the raid and found guilty of conspiracy to steal federal government secrets. They both received fifty-year prison sentences. The last man to be tried was Getts' cousin, who had provided Scroggins and Getts with the railroad seal. He was found guilty of tampering with railroad property and received a ten-year sentence in the Autry State Prison in South Georgia.

A personal note signed "Sandy" was penned at the bottom of the last page of the report. It read: "Ben, I earnestly hope you will pass this way again and you will stop by to see us. The criminals all got what they deserved, and I like to think of their convictions as hobo justice."

Author Bio

Larry Benson has been a freelance writer for over thirty years and has been fascinated by trains since he was a youngster growing up in Oklahoma a block from the main line of the Rock Island Railroad. He stood beside the tracks and waved at the engineers driving steam locomotives as they roared past. His passion for all things railroad and his proclivity for writing led him to contribute ninety articles for publication in the local train club journal.

While writing these and other various articles, a railroad mystery began to evolve. Ten years in the making, *Hobo Justice* is his first novel.

He and his wife have two daughters and five granddaughters and currently live in Tallahassee, Florida.

CPSIA information can be obtained at www.ICGtesting.com
Printed in the USA
235637LV00005B/2/P

9 781935 083351